Call it Home

Catherine Cloud

Catherine Cloud
c/o easy-shop
Kathrin Mothes
Schloßstraße 20
06869 Coswig (Anhalt)
Germany

ISBN-13: 9798335010832

1

This is, without any doubt whatsoever, the worst day of Ryan's life.

The worst-est. That's not a word. But that doesn't really matter because he's about to die in a ditch. Unfortunately, that's not some sort of exaggeration. He's in a ditch. Well, he's in a car, but the car is in a ditch with him in it. So, yeah, very much literally in a ditch.

Ryan deserves to be in this ditch.

He deserves whatever comes next.

Lil Nas X is playing quietly as Ryan assesses just how fucked he is. Do his limbs work? He wiggles his toes. Yeah, okay. Toes. Still there, still working. That's something. You can't feel your toes when you're dead, so it's reasonable to assume that he's still alive since his toes work as they should.

There's still the ditch issue, though.

Ryan probably won't be able to get his car out of here without some help. He's not entirely sure his car is still in one piece. The airbags went off, so he can't get a good look at the damage. His car is fucked to hell, isn't it? He totally deserves pain and suffering, but his poor car does not. This car deserved to survive him, but unfortunately, *nothing* survives him.

Everyone has a purpose in life. Ryan's purpose, apparently, is to destroy good things.

He stares down at his hands. Wiggles his fingers. Those work, too. Maybe he's not about to die, which would be great because dying was not on the agenda. Winning back his boyfriend was on the agenda. Technically ex-boyfriend because Kaden did break up with him over text two hours ago. Ryan drank a beer about it and decided that *sorry I don't think I wanna do this anymore* wasn't good enough for him.

So he hopped in his car.

He did think about staying home because the snow was getting pretty bad, but who breaks up over text? Kaden could have at least called him. They could have talked it out, whatever the problem even was—Ryan wouldn't know, though, cause it's not like Kaden told him.

Fuck, honestly, trying to win him back was a terrible idea in the first place. Ryan should have some self-respect; he shouldn't even want to win back a guy who dumped him over text. Only assholes do that. Right? Or maybe that's just how things are done now and Ryan is being old-fashioned when he wants to be broken up with in person.

Yeah, he changed his mind. He doesn't want to be broken up with in person, he wants to tell Kaden to go fuck himself in person.

He can't, though.

Because of the ditch he's in.

Does he need to call the police? Someone has to pull his car out of here. He looks around for his phone. It was in the cupholder before he started sliding, but it's now on the passenger side, down on the rubber mat and out of reach.

"Shitting fuck shit," Ryan says and fumbles for the seatbelt buckle. Since both his fingers and toes are working, it's probably okay to move.

Hazard lights come on behind him and a moment later a woman with big eyes and a pink hat appears by the window and pulls open the door. "Are you all right?"

"I think so," Ryan says. Apart from the obvious ditch situation.

The woman nods. "I called 911. Don't move, just wait until they get here."

"I'm not hurt. I wasn't even going that fast," Ryan says. He doesn't move, just to be safe. And he doesn't want to put this nice lady through any more distress. She was going somewhere. Home? Grocery shopping? To a boyfriend who loves her and didn't just dump her ass? Either way, this absolutely wasn't how she expected her day to go.

She eyes him, like she's trying to figure out if he's lying, or maybe like she's wondering why he looks familiar. Everyone in Toronto watches hockey. Everyone and their pets and their potted plants. She may have seen him on the posters or on TV.

She doesn't say anything else because an ambulance arrives with the police in tow. Snow swirls into Ryan's car when she steps aside to make room for a paramedic. A scruffy, tall-dark-and-handsome snack of a man. Ryan cannot call this guy a snack—he's supposed to be straight. Straight people don't call other men snacks.

Unless that straight person is called Davis Carrolton. If your name is Davis Carrolton, you're so deeply rooted in straightness that you can say the gayest shit in the world without anyone batting an eye. Sometimes, Ryan wishes he was more like Carrot.

Aw crap, he's going to have to tell Carrot that he drove into a ditch. Ryan will never hear the end of this.

"What's your name?" the hottest man alive asks.

"Ryan." Does he have to mention his last name? People know him. This will end up on the internet somehow. Fuck, he shouldn't have had that beer. No way is he over the legal limit, he's not drunk, his car just slid into a ditch because it's the snowpocalypse out here. Fuck. Whatever. "Ryan Harris."

The paramedic doesn't react to that at all. He just keeps asking his questions. "Do you know what year it is?"

"Twenty-uhhh…" Ryan knows what year it is. "2022."

"Are you allergic to any medication?"

"I'm okay," Ryan says. "I just… the car started sliding."

They insist on taking him to the hospital, even though there's nothing wrong with him. Ryan doesn't kick up a fuss because that would also end up on Twitter somehow. Slaw slipped on a patch of ice outside a bar a few weeks ago and it was *everywhere*. Sometimes the guys still call him Slippin' Slaw.

Ryan has been through concussion protocol. He plays hockey. Going through concussion protocol is some fucked-up rite of passage, just like getting hit with the puck somewhere unfortunate and playing through an injury during the playoffs.

He does not have a concussion. Just a cut on his forehead from the airbag that's easy enough for them to patch up.

The doctor knows who Ryan is.

She says, "Good game yesterday" while she's disinfecting the cut.

Ryan stares at the writing on her coat—her name is Dr. Watson.

Ryan does not ask her where Sherlock is. "Thanks," Ryan grits out instead. He's a big baby when it comes to injuries. He hates blood. Being a hockey player, blood is kind of part of his job, because he's constantly banged up in some way or other. Ryan should have thought of that before he picked hockey over everything else. It's not that he'll faint or anything, it's just gross. The hospital smells like a hospital. Also gross.

"Don't even need stitches," the doctor says. "Guess you've had worse."

"Yeah, the broken clavicle last season really sucked," Ryan says. He liked that one better, though. No blood.

"You're alive," someone says. Carrot. He's frowning at Ryan with his arms folded across his chest. Not happy to be here, then.

Ryan didn't call him; he asked one of the nurses to do it. He's like a dog who broke into the pantry, tipped over a potted plant and dragged a roll of toilet paper across the house. He knows what he did. Ryan deserves to be stabbed by all the daggers Carrot is glaring at him right now just as much as he deserved being in that ditch. Carrot did tell him not to go out into the snow.

He came to pick him up anyway. Ryan's car is… maybe not in a ditch anymore, but probably not in any condition to be driven anywhere. Ryan didn't get a good look at the front before they whisked him away. He assumes it resembles a crumpled bag of chips.

"Very much alive," Dr. Watson confirms.

Ryan gives a weak thumbs-up.

"Nothing's broken?" Carrot asks. "No internal bleeding? No concussion?"

"You're making it sound like I was in a pile-up or something."

"You drove your car into a ditch."

"The car drove itself into a ditch," Ryan says. He didn't do it. The car just had a mind of its own all of a sudden.

"Told you to stay the fuck at home, but you had to…" Carrot trails off into a sigh, because Carrot is a good bro who'd never tell Dr. Watson that Ryan just had to drive to Kaden's place to convince him that they could still work as a couple. Because as soon as Ryan steps out of their apartment, he's straight. Maybe he should hit on Dr. Watson like a real straight dude.

Shit, what is wrong with him, of course he shouldn't.

Maybe he does have a concussion.

"I'm sorry," Ryan says.

He really is sorry. He's glad nobody got hurt, other than his car. All he wants right now is to go home and crawl into bed and forget about all of this.

Since Ryan plays hockey in Toronto, he doesn't get to forget about it.

Articles about his accident start floating around before he even gets home. Within the following days, some asshat finds out that Ryan was— he wasn't drunk. But the asshat who gets to write whatever he wants as long as it generates clicks makes it sound like he was totally wasted.

Obviously, no one gives a shit that Ryan had *one* beer. He still has his license and there was barely any alcohol in his blood. But now he's the guy who drunkenly drove into a snowstorm for no good reason.

And, obviously, he refused to tell people where he was going. When the police asked, Ryan said he was going to a friend's house. They thought he was a Pennsylvania dumbass who doesn't know how to drive in the snow. They do get snow in Pennsylvania, but obviously not as much as Toronto.

Either way, the media gleefully pounces on his mistake. Ryan has to apologize over and over; has to hang his head in shame for the cameras. And he really is a little bit ashamed of himself, but what the team PR expects of him is absolute clownery and Ryan is fucking tired.

"I'm fucking tired," he tells Carrot three days after the accident.

"Give it time, they'll find someone else to shit on," Carrot says.

He is, of course, correct.

They *always* find someone else to shit on.

Ryan would prefer it if they found someone else to shit on right now though.

They have a game that night, but Ryan isn't playing. Officially, they want to rest him after his car accident. It feels like a punishment. It *is* a punishment. The media will most certainly frame it like a punishment.

In the room, some of the guys aren't as talkative around him as they used to be. He's become a distraction—he's become one of those guys. Like it wasn't bad enough that they're having a terrible season, now he went and threw a scandal into the mix. Although Slaw, at least, thanked him for his service because they've stopped writing about whether or not Timothy Cole deserves to wear an A for the team because of his abysmal performance this season. In all honesty, Slaw's performance is fine. It's completely fine. Maybe he's not a hundred percent all day every day, but it's not like he's dragging the team down or whatever it was that the media ghouls were saying about him.

Ryan should have known that getting torn to shreds on every possible platform and sitting out a few games wouldn't be the entirety of his punishment. When it comes to hockey, Toronto doesn't do things halfway.

Since Ryan has been here for his entire career, ever since he got drafted five years ago, he should be waiting for the other shoe to drop.

It does drop somewhat unexpectedly. About a week after the Ditch Incident, their GM decides that Ryan's not worth the trouble and sends him packing. Ryan deserves that, too.

"Where?" Ryan asks when they pull him off the ice during morning skate. He's so proud of himself that his voice doesn't crack. He'll cry at some point today, but he has no idea if it'll be in the showers or at home when he packs his most important stuff or on the plane he'll undoubtedly have to get on in a few hours or in some hotel room that his new team will stick him in for the time being.

"Cardinals," is the answer he gets.

Ryan almost laughs. Of course. The team that's known for taking in strays that nobody else wants.

Ryan isn't a budding star player anymore. He's a stray now.

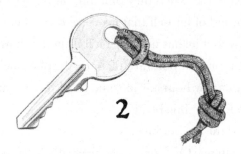

2

This is the best day of Louie's life. So far. He won't get ahead of himself.

He's made that mistake before.

Louie watched the Cardinals game last night. He saw Petrov go down in the first. He didn't come back for the second or the third period. Coach Beaulieu wouldn't comment on Petrov's status after the game, which usually means it's bad. So Louie was expecting that one of them would get called up.

The first thing the Cards announced this morning, though, was that they're sending Virtanen back to their farm team in Springfield.

"Do you think Santana's ready to come back?" one of the guys asks as they're getting ready for practice.

Louie doesn't look up. "Don't think so," he says. Santana, one of the Cardinals' best defensemen, has been out with an injury since December and it sounded like he may not come back before the end of the regular season.

Clearly, the Cardinals made a move this morning. Got themselves a new d-man, someone who can actually replace Santana. Virtanen is good, no doubt about it, so whoever they got must be better. They'll find out who it is soon enough.

Maybe the team also traded for a forward while they were at it. The trade deadline is looming and the Cards were actually doing pretty well before they got rattled by all those injuries. Loads of guys have gotten called up during the past few weeks. It was mostly day-to-day stuff, so they came back to Springfield quickly.

Louie wasn't one of them. He stayed on the farm team, worked hard, scored his goals. Hat trick last week, and he's on a seven-game point streak. He's the AHL Player of the Week. So, when their coach comes into the room that morning and zeros in on Louie, he knows it's his lucky day.

"Hathaway, they want you in Hartford," he says.

The Cards want Louie in Hartford. If he's extra lucky, they'll want him in Hartford until Petrov comes back.

Of course, there's a chance that he'll join the Cards and will sit on the bench the entire time. That's what he did last November. He was only there for two games and didn't get to play. But if Petrov is out for weeks instead of days, Louie may get more than one opportunity to prove himself this time around.

"Nice," Mortensen says and gives Louie a pat on the back.

Louie pulls off his pads.

Looks like he's not joining the guys for practice.

At this point, Louie knows the drill. He's been called up a few times. He'll grab a suitcase full of clothes and his gear, then he'll drive down to Hartford.

Well, Silver Lakes. That's where the Cards have their practice rink. Same difference.

So far, he's always stayed with one of his teammates. Back in November, Liam Hellström let Louie sleep in his guest room. He checks his phone, but no one from the Cardinals has reached out yet. He'll just hope they'll have a place for him to stay.

Louie heads back to the house he shares with two of his teammates. He'd rather live alone, but he couldn't find an apartment he liked. This was supposed to be temporary.

Actually, all of this was supposed to be temporary.

He thought he'd have a roster spot on the Cardinals by now. His brother, who was drafted two years after him, is playing in the NHL. He's made it. And Louie is still waiting for his turn.

This time, he has to make sure he won't spend his entire time in Hartford on the bench. Louie has seen guys leave for the big league and never come back to the farm team. The Cardinals just decided to keep them. Like Lampinen, who got called up last season. He's still with the Cards. He has an NHL contract now.

That's what Louie wants.

He wants to stay. He wants this constant back-and-forth to end.

Back at the house, Louie is rooting through his closet, looking for clean clothes, when his phone starts to ring. He almost doesn't answer, in a hurry to get to Hartford, except he's been putting off doing the laundry, so he barely has anything to throw into his suitcase. He'll have to go out and buy some underwear because he only has three clean pairs.

He chucks them into his mostly empty suitcase before he grabs his phone. Liam Hellström is calling. So he does have somewhere to go.

"Hey," Louie says.

"Lou," Liam replies. "I hear you're coming back."

"I am. Packing right now."

"Listen, I'm about to hit the ice, so I gotta be quick… I'd let you have my guest room, you know I would, but it's already occupied. Kid from Toronto got traded half an hour ago and I said he could stay with me before they told me you were coming, too."

"Hey, it's fine, don't worry about it," Louie says. Internally, he sighs. It's not Liam's fault, but Louie already hates the kid from Toronto, whoever he is. "I'm sure they'll find me a hotel to stay at."

"Do not worry at all, Lou, I've found you a place to stay."

What a rollercoaster. "You have?"

"Yeah, you can stay with Santa. David Santana. You're driving down, are you? Because he's not at the rink every day, so he can't give you a ride to practices and stuff. Actually, he may ask you to give him a ride every now and then instead. That okay? You can also have a hotel room. I'll find out where they want to put you."

"No, I'll stay with Santa," Louie says. "Thanks, Lee."

"Of course. I'll text you Santa's address. It's not in Silver Lakes but close. Next to an apple farm."

"Sounds… idyllic."

"Hope you like apples," Liam says and Louie can't tell if he means it or if he's making fun of where David Santana built his house. "And you'll come over for dinner this week."

"Uh, yeah?"

"Yeah," Liam says. "You're not allowed to say no."

Someone on Liam's end of the line laughs.

Then, "Can I also come over for dinner?"

"No," Liam says. "Just Lou." He huffs. "Waldo wants free dinner, but he's old enough to cook for himself."

"I just love your wife's meatballs," says Waldo presumably.

"Ah. Fine. You can come. They're good meatballs."

They're the best meatballs, and Louie likes Liam and staying at Liam's house, and the Swedish meatballs his wife makes are a big part of that. Liam has two kids and the older one, Ida, used to help Louie with his workouts. She made him give her piggyback rides all over the house.

Two minutes after Louie hangs up the phone, a text from Liam comes through with an address for Santa's house, although at this point Louie may as well drive to the Cards' practice rink in Silver Lakes. If they're only just hitting the ice, they'll probably still be around by the time he gets there.

Louie grabs the shirts and hoodies the Cards gave him last November, his ancient iPod, and the sneakers he goes on runs with nearly every morning. He used to go on runs in Liam's neighborhood; he's not sure he'll be able to do the same wherever Santana lives.

Before Louie leaves, he pulls out his phone to check the trade tracker.

Louie can't help but laugh.

Ryan Harris to the Cardinals in exchange for a third-round pick.

Obviously, Louie didn't miss the latest Toronto drama. Ryan Harris got drunk and drove his car into a ditch during a snowstorm. Although there were some debates about whether or not Harris was *actually* drunk. He seems to still have his license, so either he has connections or money was exchanged or the media made it up because they needed a fresh scandal.

Harris is a d-man, so at least Louie won't be competing for a spot with him. Clearly, he's a cheap replacement for Santana. Maybe cheap isn't the right word. Harris is good, he just came cheap because his team presumably wanted to get rid of him.

He likely won't arrive until later and it's not a game day, so they won't cross paths until morning skate tomorrow.

On the drive to Silver Lakes, Louie's phone keeps buzzing. Texts, not calls. At this point, the Cardinals must have announced that they've called up Louie and his always-online brother and his connections-everywhere father must have seen.

He parks in the lot outside the rink in Silver Lakes, both sheets of ice reserved for the Cardinals this morning. It's a nice, modern rink, only built some ten years ago, and the facilities are definitely better than the ones in Springfield.

There was some construction on the way down, so most of the guys aren't on the ice anymore, but the locker room is teeming with people. The Cardinals' captain, Josh Roy, is talking to the media.

"Louie, hello," a girl says. She's one of the social media folks. Louie cannot, for the life of him, remember her name.

"You got here so fast," she goes on and holds up her phone. It has one of those extra shatterproof cases and a pop socket with the Cardinals logo on it. "May I?"

"Uh… sure?" Louie says. She wants to take a picture of him standing in a hallway? Sometimes Louie doesn't understand social media.

Looking at Instagram regularly drives him into a fit of rage.

"Liam, come here for a second please?" she calls into the room.

"I can't!"

"Just for a second!"

"I have to… do push-ups," Liam shouts. "A lot of them!"

Some of the guys laugh.

"Louie Hathaway is here."

"Oh, Louuuuu!" Liam, still with his pads on, appears in the hallway and gives Louie a squeeze for the camera. "Good to see you, kid." He follows that up with a pat on the back. "Exciting day."

Louie nods, although he won't be excited until he knows whether or not Coach Beaulieu is planning on putting him in the lineup tomorrow.

Coach himself appears just after Liam has waddled back into the locker room to get out of his gear. Or to do push-ups. Who knows.

"Hathaway, good to have you back," Coach says in passing.

Is it good to have him back? Coach benched him the last time he was here, so Louie clearly didn't make a big impression.

It's Beaulieu's first season with the Cards and his first season with an NHL team. Louie was in Silver Lakes for training camp last fall and fought for a roster spot, but Beaulieu sent him to Springfield after the third preseason game. Said he wasn't ready. That's what Coach Trenton said, too, the season before. And the season before that one.

Louie ends up just nodding at Beaulieu as he passes. He nods a lot when he's here because he doesn't want to say the wrong thing to someone important. Someone who decides who comes and goes, who gets to dress for a game, and who sits in the press box.

He talks to some of the guys, gets a workout in, and snags some food. When everyone else heads home, he gets into his car and looks up David Santana's address on his phone. His house is only six minutes from the rink, but it's not in town.

Liam wasn't kidding. It's right next to an apple orchard. A small store by the road is advertising their new spring decorations on an intricately decorated chalkboard, even though patches of snow are still dotting the parking lot out front.

Santa has a weirdly long driveway that ends by several garages and a house with a decorated porch. A snowman with a welcome sign greets Louie by the door. The Santanas probably get their decorations from the orchard next door. A dog barks when Louie rings the doorbell.

Oh. He probably should have asked Liam if Santana had dogs.

Louie takes a deep breath. Steels himself.

The door opens, revealing a tall woman with shoulder-length black hair. She smiles brightly. "Hi, you must be Louie, come on in," she says. "I'm Bianca, but please call me Bee." She looks over her shoulder. "Dave, Louie is here!"

"Hey, hey," Santa says as he comes shuffling into the hallway. He's still hobbling a bit. Definitely not close to coming back. "Sorry, I had to put the kid in timeout."

"You guys have a kid?" Louie asks. He did not know that. Although he really prefers kids over dogs.

"The kid is a Labrador puppy," Bee says, rolling her eyes.

"Oh," Louie says.

She narrows her eyes at him. "Are you allergic?"

"No, just..." Louie shrugs. "I've met some dogs that weren't, uh..." Another shrug. His great-aunt from Montreal had this wiener dog that wouldn't stop barking at him and chasing him when he was four or five, so his mom had to lift him off the top of the couch, where he was hiding from the little demon, and carry him to the car when they left.

"He's *very* sweet," Bee says. "But if this is a problem, we can—"

"No, no, it's fine," Louie says quickly. He's not *scared* or anything. Just not a huge fan. He can deal with it; this is still better than a hotel room.

3

Ryan's phone buzzes just as he pulls his suitcase off the conveyor belt at Bradley International.

That's either his mom, who has been texting him all day, or Kaden, who has also been texting him all day. Ryan's mom is worried about him, so those texts basically just make him feel worse. But Kaden's texts. Those piss Ryan off. He hasn't talked to him since he broke up with him.

So their conversation literally went from last week's *sorry I don't think I wanna do this anymore* to today's *just saw, u ok?*

Ryan did not answer his question. He also didn't reply to any of his other thirteen texts. Ryan counted when he was bored on the plane. Before he goes looking for Liam Hellström, he does check his phone.

From: World's Greatest Asshole

Ryan what the fuck?? stop ignoring me

Ryan locks his phone. He will not stop ignoring him. In fact, Kaden deserves to be ignored for the rest of eternity.

Maybe Ryan should get a new number. Since he's not in Canada anymore. He did get a plan that works here and there because they do travel a lot, so it's not an immediate concern, but—fuck, he has to change his address on everything. Actually, some of his paperwork has his parents' address in Pennsylvania on it.

His mom is planning on coming by soon, she told him earlier. Maybe she'll bring Dad. As much as getting traded fucking sucks, Ryan doesn't mind being a little closer to home.

Piling all his bags onto a cart, Ryan looks around for Liam.

He isn't hard to spot. He's tall, blonde and Swedish. And he's holding the hand of a little girl, who's waving at him with a sign that says RYAN HARRIS in big glitter letters.

"Hey," Ryan says, holding out his hand to shake Liam's. "I'm Ryan."

"Liam or Lee or Hellie, or, if you must, Satan," Liam says, keeping a straight face the entire time. "Good to meet you."

Well, they've met, technically. Twice this season already. But it's not like they talked—they were just on the same sheet of ice for a little while.

Ryan crouches down next to the kid, who is just as blonde as Liam. "And what's your name?"

"I'm Ida Hellström," she says.

"It's so nice to meet you, Ida Hellström," Ryan says and hopes he doesn't butcher the last name to hell and back. Heh. Hell. "I'm Ryan Harris. Thanks so much for picking me up."

"She insisted on coming," Liam says, smirking down at the kid.

Ida bounces on the balls of her feet. "I'm the welcome committee," she says proudly and holds the sign out to Ryan. "You can keep this."

"Thank you, that's really nice," Ryan says. He doesn't know why he suddenly feels like crying. Today has been an absolute shitshow, so maybe that's it. Or maybe it's that at least two people are happy to see him.

Ryan made the mistake of looking at the Cardinals' trade announcement on Instagram. Nobody in the comments was happy that they traded for him. Someone said the Cardinals may as well be adding a trash can to the lineup. So. Yeah.

"Why don't you carry it to the car for him, hmm?" Liam suggests, giving Ida's head a gentle tap. "He's got enough stuff to carry already."

"Of *course*," Ida says and reaches out to take Ryan's hand. "Come on, let's go."

Okay, Ryan is definitely going to cry.

He's glad that Liam starts leading the way to the car and pushing Ryan's cart because Ida was not happy about the prospect of letting go of Ryan's hand. Clearly, Liam has taken in trades and call-ups before. He rattles off a perfectly rehearsed list on the way—when he usually leaves for practice ("I can give you a ride"), when his wife goes to the grocery store ("She'll buy you whatever you want"), tidbits about the rest of the team ("If you need anything, just ask Yoshi. He knows everyone and everything and people will do whatever he wants, no questions asked. Don't talk to Jordie early in the morning. He's great to talk to otherwise, though. Oh, and Waldo will eventually knit you a hat. You will like it and you will smile and say thank you, understood?")

Ryan isn't sure anyone wants to give him anything, but he still nods along.

Ida tugs at his hand. "Ryan, you have the day off on Saturday—"

Liam huffs at her. "Ida."

"I have a hockey game and Papa is coming and can you come, too? Please?"

"Uh, yeah, if we have the day off," Ryan says. He was about to go on a roadie to Seattle and Vancouver and now he suddenly isn't. The Cardinals have a completely different schedule (duh) and that probably should have occurred to him much earlier.

"You do." Ida nods excitedly. "I'm going to ask Lou if he's coming, too. He came to one of my games last year."

Ryan has no idea who in the absolute fuck Lou is. He did think he knew the Cardinals' roster, though. He looked it up on the plane. Maybe Lou is a weird nickname?

"She's talking about Louie Hathaway," Liam says, coming to his rescue. "He just got called up this morning and he usually stays with us."

"Oh," Ryan says. Did he steal some guy's room? Great. One of his teammates probably already hates him and he hasn't even met him yet.

"Lou is staying with Dave Santana," Liam says. "He'll like it better there because Ida won't be waking him up in the morning to ask if he wants to play with her, even though we told her that she's not supposed to do that."

"I thought it was way later," Ida says. "I was worried he was dead."

Ryan snorts.

"He wasn't," Ida adds helpfully.

She falls asleep on the drive back to Liam's house. Liam fills Ryan in on the Cardinals' season so far—not bad in the beginning, but lots of injuries getting in the way, and now they're trying to still make the playoffs. They're only a few points out of a wild card spot, so it's not impossible.

"Santa isn't coming back before the playoffs," Liam says. "I guess you'll give us a chance at least."

No pressure. Ryan only makes a vague noise to hide just how much all of this makes him want to throw up all over Liam's car. Honestly, in all honesty, straight up looking at the facts, Ryan has no idea why the Cardinals wanted him. He's a PR nightmare on legs. His last few games weren't even that great. He does score a lot for a defenseman, but he hasn't contributed much goal-wise recently. He must have been a last resort.

"What are you worried about?" Liam asks, eyes firmly fixed on the road. "That everyone will hate you?"

"Well…"

"This isn't Toronto. Nobody here hates anyone."

"I mean, people didn't hate me in Toronto either," Ryan says. "At least not until last week."

"Look. You know Lucky? Luc Girard?"

"Yeah," Ryan says. Everyone knows Luc Girard. Drafted by Nashville, first round, a new hope for the franchise, a chance to finally rebuild, all that jazz. Girard made the NHL team in his first season, went on to sign a five-year contract and three years in, he got tripped into the boards during a game. One of his own teammates, who just happened to be in the wrong place at the wrong time. It took him ages to come back from that concussion. Nashville didn't re-sign him. Then Hartford came along and said, "Let's take a chance on this guy."

They do that a lot.

Case in point. Ryan is here.

"Nobody thought Lucky would work out for us," Liam says. "When Nick Rivera got traded here? Everyone said he was such a problem in the locker room. You know who plays hockey on the floor with my kid when she's at the rink? Nick Rivera."

"Really?" Ryan asks. He cannot see a guy like Nick Rivera on the floor. Nick Rivera is the second-best paid guy on this team. He lives and breathes hockey. He is a god on skates.

"See?" Liam says. "You fell for it, too. It doesn't matter so much what other people say about you. Half of it isn't true anyway." He glances at Ryan. "I'm guessing you weren't blackout drunk when you wrecked your car."

"I didn't *wreck* my car," Ryan says with a sigh. "It just slid into the ditch. And I'd had a beer, like, two hours before I drove."

"Yeah, so they're just saying stuff. It doesn't matter. The team matters. And nobody on this team hates anyone. It's not what we do." Liam takes the highway exit for Silver Lakes and Cedar Mills. "You don't get to hate anyone either, by the way. And if you do, you keep that shit to yourself."

"I don't really want anyone to hate me *quietly*, though," Ryan says. "I don't want anyone to hate me."

Liam laughs.

"What?"

"There's always someone out there who hates you, even if it's just some douchebag with a stupid username somewhere on social media."

"True," Ryan says.

He also hates himself a little for fucking up this badly. He could still be in Toronto. Because one thing's for sure: they wouldn't have traded him if it hadn't been for all those rumors. They didn't care what the truth was—at least Liam asked. The team even put out this press release where they were all like, *we're aware of the allegations, we take them very seriously, blah blah*.

Well, Ryan will definitely make a point of not falling in love with some dick who'll break up with him over text in Hartford. That's his promise to himself and he's sure as shit going to keep this one.

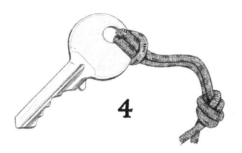

4

Ryan Harris seems to think that Louie has to be his best friend simply because they joined the team at the same time.

Since Louie isn't a dick, he lets Ryan be nervous in his general vicinity and gently tells him that it'll all be fine. His general vicinity means the stall next to his because apparently someone in the Cardinals organization also thought they have to be best friends.

"—don't know why this feels so weird," Ryan is saying, fumbling with his practice jersey. It got caught on his pads somewhere. He's about an inch taller than Louie, his mousy brown hair cut in a kind of mullet-and-undercut-marriage that shouldn't work but somehow does. And he talks. A lot. "I guess it's because I've never played on another team before. Like, in the NHL at least. I've played on other teams, but it's been a while. It's like… I don't know any of these guys."

"You know me," Liam says. He's on Louie's other side. "Don't be dramatic. It'll all be fine."

"I'm not being dramatic," Ryan says and unsuccessfully tugs at his jersey.

No, he's not being dramatic. He's scared. Louie has been there. When he got called up for the first time, he was terrified. Terrified of doing everything wrong, terrified of being put in the lineup and fucking up, terrified of not being put in the lineup and returning to Springfield without even stepping on NHL ice.

By now, he's not lying awake at night anymore, wondering if he'll score his very first NHL goal tomorrow. He's done that and he's been called up a few more times between then and now. Louie isn't new to this. Sometimes he wishes he was.

Not being new at this just means that he's failed too many times.

He reaches out to pull Ryan's jersey into place.

"Thank you," Ryan mutters.

Liam shoots Louie a smile, then he waddles away to get on the ice. Louie wanted to be out there five minutes ago, but listening to Ryan's laments distracted him.

"One of the PR people… she said she wanted me to talk to the media after practice and—" Ryan groans. "What if they ask me—"

"Listen," Louie says, because he knows the media dance and he's talked to those guys before, "you're happy you're getting a fresh start. You love Hartford. You're closer to home now. You loved hitting the ice with these guys for the first time. You can't wait for the game tonight. Your mom is coming. She's so happy. You're looking forward to helping this team win some hockey games."

Ryan frowns at him. "How did you know my mom is coming?"

"I didn't," Louie says. He shrugs. "I just figured she was coming when you said you were from Pennsylvania. Somewhere close to Philadelphia, right? It's not *that* far."

"Are your folks coming?" Ryan asks. "I mean, your dad—"

"No, I don't think so," Louie interrupts. "It's not like it's my first game. Honestly, we don't even know if I'm making the lineup."

"Eh, you will," Ryan says and gently punches Louie's upper arm.

Louie… doesn't know what to do with that. Ryan doesn't know him and probably hasn't seen him play because Louie spends most of his time on AHL ice. Their paths have never crossed. "You don't know that," Louie says. He doesn't like hopeful platitudes that are in no way rooted in reality.

"Dude," Ryan says.

"What?"

Ryan, going red-faced in real time, waves him off. "Nothing."

"No. What?"

"You tried to make me feel better and now you're being a shit about me doing the same thing?" Ryan shakes his head. "You will make the lineup."

"Fine," Louie says, resigned. "I will."

When Ryan talks to the media after morning skate, he tells them exactly what Louie told him to say. Ryan's face is flaming red the entire time, but he makes it through.

Afterwards he turns to Louie. "Dude."

That seems to be his favorite word. "Yeah?"

"Can you do that every day?" Ryan says, pulling off the rest of his gear. "Tell me what to say to them? You seriously saved my ass."

"It's not hard," Louie says. "Just don't tell them anything real."

Nick Rivera, who is in the stall next to Ryan, was apparently listening in because he snorts. Nick practically invented never telling the media anything real. Watching his interviews was where Louie learned how to make it out on the other side of a media scrum without making a total fool of himself.

"Well, my mom *is* coming," Ryan says with a shrug.

"Yeah. But did you really want a fresh start? Are you actually happy to be here?"

Ryan shrugs again. "I'm trying."

That startles a laugh out of Louie. "Good for you."

"It was just kind of sudden," Ryan says.

Nick looks away. He clearly doesn't think it was sudden. Louie doesn't think it was sudden either. Some teams will forgive a slip-up, some teams will forgive way more than a slip-up, depending on who you are and how good you are at hockey, but Ryan may have not been a priority in the first place. Maybe they'd already been thinking about trading him. Hard to tell now.

Louie won't say any of that to Ryan's face.

"Not much you can do about it now," is what he does say. It feels kinder but too harsh at the same time.

Ryan nods, pulling a face. Before Louie actually met him, he would have sworn that Ryan is one of those perpetually sunshiny people. And maybe he is. Life just shoved a cloud in front of him and flicked on the rain switch.

Louie almost wants to give him a hug, except he's not a hugger and Ryan Harris won't change that.

Nick shoots them another look, then he wanders away toward the showers.

"I don't think he likes me," Ryan says.

"You've been here for two minutes," Louie says. "Calm down."

"You calm down." Ryan sticks out his bottom lip. "I just…"

"What?" Louie says. He hates it when people don't finish their sentences.

Ryan shrugs.

So Louie leaves him be. Like he said, Ryan got here what may as well be two minutes ago. He needs some time to get to know everyone and learn what the guys' quirks are. Nick, he doesn't say much. Liam says a lot. Yoshi is everyone's dad, which isn't necessarily a captain thing, he just has four kids and he probably doesn't bother switching off Dad Mode anymore.

Santa is more like a mom. He told Louie to put on a hat when he left for the rink this morning. Santa's wife Bee chirped him into next week for it while Santa grumbled about below-freezing temperatures and having promised Liam that he'd take good care of Louie.

When Louie gets back from practice, unlocking the door to Santa's house, his phone buzzes with a text.

From: Dad

Are you playing tonight?

Louie sighs. He is very much not playing tonight. Coach pulled him aside after the game, said, "Hathaway, you'll get your chance, but not tonight," and that was that.

That's why he doesn't hope. He shows up, does his best during practice, and then it's up to Coach. Today, he clearly didn't do enough.

Louie takes a deep breath before he replies.

To: Dad

not tonight no

From: Dad

That's too bad. Your mom wanted to come watch you play.

Oh, great. Like he wasn't feeling shitty enough already. Mom wanted to come watch him play. They would have driven down here from Boston.

To: Dad

next time? i'll probably be here for a bit

Then Louie locks his phone.

"Hey, you're back!" Santa comes shuffling into the hallway. "How was your first— oh. What's with the face?"

Louie holds up his phone to answer that question. He'll let Santa draw his own conclusions because he doesn't like talking about his dad. People know Martie Hathaway. Born in Boston, drafted to Atlanta, traded to Ottawa, where he met Louie's mom, who'd just left Montreal for a job there. His dad decided to leave after ten years—Louie barely remembers living in Montreal—to play for his hometown team. Boston is where

Louie grew up. If anyone asks, that's where he's from.

"Look," Santa says, "I would suggest holding the puppy to get rid of the look on your face, but—"

"Dave, don't bug him about the puppy. He doesn't like dogs," Bee shouts from her office.

"I don't not like dogs," Louie says, palms up. "I'm willing to say hi."

Five minutes later, Louie is on the couch with a Labrador puppy sleeping on his chest. Way better than that villainous wiener dog. It doesn't keep his dad out of his head, though.

Louie's glad he's not coming. He would have loved to see his mom, but when his dad watches his games, Louie always gets an itemized list of things he could have done better afterwards. Sometimes he wants to ask Bastien if he gets the same treatment, but Louie's afraid he won't like the answer.

Bastien doesn't do a lot of things wrong. Bastien was drafted by the Bears two years ago and made the NHL roster this season. Bastien scored a hat trick in his third game. Bastien will probably be a Calder nominee.

When you look at the pictures from Louie's and Bastien's draft days, Dad's smile is way bigger in Bastien's. Because Bastien was drafted eleventh overall. Louie was the very first pick in the second round. The Cardinals traded for that pick. They really wanted him.

But he's still a second-rounder and Bastien is—well, he's Bastien.

Louie isn't even playing in the NHL.

He's watching NHL games from the press box with the injured players and the other healthy scratches.

During the first intermission—they're losing, even though Ryan Harris went and got his first assist five minutes into the game—Louie takes a look at the upcoming games. He just talked to Petrov and he's clearly week-to-week, so if Coach Beaulieu doesn't decide that he hates Louie personally, he'll be here for a while.

They have tomorrow off. Louie knew that because he's been invited to attend Ida Hellström's hockey game in the afternoon and to have dinner with Liam's family in the evening. Practice on Sunday, game on Monday, then they leave town on Tuesday for two road games.

Those are followed by three home games. The third one is against the Minnesota Bears. Great. So Louie will either be playing against Bastien, or he'll watch him play from up here.

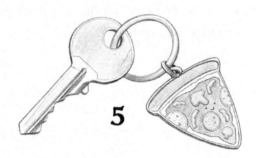

5

Ryan can't tell if Louie likes him.

He definitely tolerates him. Gives him the smallest of smiles when he sits down next to him to watch Ida Hellström and the Little Vikings play. There's something very polite about it that threatens to rub Ryan the wrong way.

It almost feels like Louie is making fun of him somehow.

He chooses to ignore it.

"Okay," Liam says, "I'm getting food. What do you want? Nachos, popcorn, hot dog?"

"Um," Louie says.

Louie is definitely one of those guys who doesn't eat nachos or popcorn or hot dogs. Kale all the way.

"Water?" Louie goes on.

"Listen, Dad says it's okay to have a treat," Liam says and turns to his wife. "Babe, what do you want?"

"Popcorn chicken for me, please," Ella says.

"Lee, you didn't mention the popcorn chicken," Ryan says. He's definitely not saying no to popcorn chicken.

"Louie?"

"I… yeah… popcorn chicken." There's some resignation to Louie's voice, like the popcorn chicken was forced upon him. Peer pressure.

"I'll be back," Liam says and is immediately stopped halfway up the stands by two teenagers in Cardinals hats who must have recognized him.

"Boys," Ella says to Ryan and Louie, "will you take Maja for a second? I need to run to the bathroom and I have a feeling that Liam will need some help carrying all that chicken."

"I would love to," Ryan says and reaches for little Maja, who beams when she is handed over. He spent all morning entertaining her with stuffed animals. Ida got involved as well and told Ryan he could borrow her humongous stuffed IKEA bear when she found out that he hadn't brought any stuffed animals from Toronto.

Ryan doesn't own a single stuffed animal, but he didn't have the heart to tell Ida that. He obviously took the bear to his room. His name is Gustav and Ryan kind of loves him.

He starts bouncing his leg, so Maja won't get bored with him and start crying. That's where his expertise ends. When kids cry, Ryan likes to hand them back to their parents or someone who is better equipped at dealing with tears.

Maja points at Louie.

Louie smiles at her and it looks so much more genuine than the smile he greeted Ryan with. "Hi," he says.

"Look, she totally knows how to…" Ryan gives her another bounce. "Maja, can you say Louie? Loouuu–iiieee."

"Luu," Maja says.

"Wow, so good," Ryan says. "Amazing."

Maja laughs.

"Now say Ryan," Louie says and leans closer.

Ryan snorts. "Oh, I tried that this morning, she won't do Ryan." He tried hard. He bribed her with the big stuffed bear, but it didn't work.

"Aw, come on," Louie says and gives Maja a gentle poke. "Say Ryan."

"Rah," is what they get.

"Ryan."

"Rah-rah."

"Close enough," Ryan says and gives the bobble on top of Maja's little hat a boop.

Ryan never did stuff like this back in Toronto. He mostly hung out with Carrot and Slaw, they played video games, and sometimes Ryan went to see Kaden. Not that they saw each other a lot. Kaden was—is—on the farm team, so most of the time, one of them was out of town.

At least Kaden has finally given up on texting him. He even tried to message Ryan on Instagram, so Ryan blocked him. Maybe he should block his number, too. Although he somehow can't bring himself to do it.

"Maja," Louie says, voice soft, "say Rah-rah."

"Rah-rah," Maja parrots.

"Good job!"

Maja claps. She's wearing humongous gloves that are way too big for her tiny hands. It's stupidly cute.

A group of women, all in those long parkas and hats with big fluffy bobbles, all of them holding Starbucks to-go cups, shuffle into the row in front of them. They all smile their bright toothpaste ad smiles and one of them waves at Maja, who at the very least attempts to wave back. The woman clutches her heart. "Your daughter is so cute."

"And she has two very handsome dads," one of her friends adds.

Ryan is—is he having a stroke? Are these very blonde ladies insinuating that Ryan and Louie are Maja's dads? Like that's just a thing? Two dads coming to a kids' hockey game with their daughter.

He should correct her. Right? He can't let her believe that he and Louie are—what? Married? With one or possibly multiple children?

"Oh, we're not her dads," Louie says nonchalantly. Like he corrects people on not being a gay dad every fucking day.

"Yeah, we're just entertaining her until her parents get back," Ryan adds when he remembers how to speak.

The women laugh. "Aw, that's so sweet. Looks like you're great babysitters."

They thankfully move along, further down, where they join four more women in identical outfits and with identical Starbucks cups.

Louie shakes his head. "Do I really look old enough to be a dad?"

"There are dads who are way younger than you," Ryan says.

Louie, for some reason, doesn't seem to like that. He sighs and stares out at the ice, his expression stony.

Ryan shoots him a look. So, Louie was upset because the hockey moms thought he was old enough to be a dad. Not because they thought he might be gay. Not that he is. It's still—nice? Yeah. Nice. Refreshing. Because things are not terrible in most locker rooms these days, or at least they weren't terrible in the locker rooms Ryan has been in, but most guys still don't want to appear gay.

Ryan also doesn't want to appear gay. Even though he is super-duper gay.

Maja makes a displeased noise.

"Hey," Ryan says, dismayed because he's totally failing as a babysitter, "don't do that. We were happy two seconds ago, what happened?"

Telling her not to do that, of course, only makes her more displeased. If she was one of Ryan's nieces and nephews, Ryan would hand her to someone else right about now.

He turns to Louie. "Here, take her."

"Why?" Louie asks, eyes wide. "I don't know what to do."

"Maybe she just wants a change of scenery," Ryan says, waggling his eyebrows at Louie.

"Right, because things are so different over here." Louie presses his lips together and considers Maja. "That's not gonna help."

"What, are you scared of little kids?" Ryan asks.

"Babies don't like me. They like me better as they get older."

"Good thing she's not a baby. She can practically say my name.

Babies can't talk."

Louie takes Maja like she's a bomb that's about to go off, carefully sitting her down on his lap. "Okay, fine," he says. "But if she starts crying, it's your fault."

"She looks so happy, though," Ryan says and gives Maja's chubby cheek a poke.

She giggles.

Yeah, handing her to Louie was a great idea. Ryan goes in for a round of peekaboo to keep her happy. And to make Louie look less freaked out about having to hold a child. It's kind of funny. He's doing just fine.

"We're great at this," Ryan says and holds up his phone. "Smile."

Maja beams at him, but Louie frowns. "You're not posting that on Instagram, right?"

"Why not?"

"Because… you have to ask Lee first," Louie says.

"Good point." Ryan is so used to posting stuff on Instagram, he kind of didn't consider that. Carrot and Slaw never cared. He shows his phone to Louie. "Look, so cute, though."

Louie's lips twitch the tiniest bit.

It kind of feels like an in.

"Hey," Ryan says and pulls up one of the five thousand tabs he has open on his phone, "I've been looking at apartments. And houses. Mostly houses, because the apartments around here aren't that great. I found one that's above a pub in Silver Lakes, but… do I want to live above a pub?" He shows Louie the page with the pub-adjacent apartment. It has really nice exposed brick walls. High ceilings. Loud people just outside every night.

"Probably not," Louie says.

He is correct.

"So, I also found this one," Ryan says and pulls up another option. "It's pretty close to the arena, but most of the guys live out here, right?"

"I think so, yeah," Louie replies. He's gone back to sounding very polite.

Ryan doesn't know what to do with that. He shows him another option. A house in Cedar Mills, not in town but close by. "What do you think about this one?" He holds out his phone and swipes through the pictures. "It has a red door."

Louie's eyebrows twitch, like he's saying, really, that's what matters to you? The color of the door?

"It also has really nice floors. And it comes with furniture, which is great because I don't have *any* furniture." Ryan moves on to the pictures of the kitchen. "New appliances. And that black backsplash looks really cool."

Louie doesn't comment until Ryan gets to the photos of the living room. "Does it come with the piano?"

"I think so," Ryan says.

"Do you play?"

Ryan shakes his head. "No, but it looks cool."

"Hm," Louie says and it has a slightly judgmental undertone.

"I like it," Ryan says and it ends up sounding a bit like a question. It's not that he needs Louie's approval to rent a house. They barely even know each other—he's also asked Carrot and Slaw what they think. Ryan just doesn't like making big decisions all by himself.

"But?" Louie prompts.

"It's kinda big," Ryan says. He nudges Louie. "Are you gonna look for a place?"

Louie frowns.

Maja frowns along with him and makes another fussy noise.

"Nooo, do you think it's a bad house?" Ryan asks.

"That's—" Louie lets out a sigh of relief when Liam and Ella return with several trays.

Liam takes Maja, who looks a lot happier all of a sudden. "Papa," she says and smacks him in the face.

"Yeah," Liam says with a laugh. "Is that what these guys have been teaching you? How to hit people?"

"We would never," Ryan says. "But she knows how to say my name now."

"Oh, does she?" Liam says, like he doesn't believe him. "Maja, can you say Ryan?"

"Rah-rah," she says, even more delighted than before.

Ryan claps for her and she claps along with him.

Maybe being a dad isn't so bad.

He obviously changes his mind about that when Maja stars crying a few minutes later and Liam has to abandon his chicken to take her up the stands and change her diaper.

Ryan doesn't want to have anything to do with diapers.

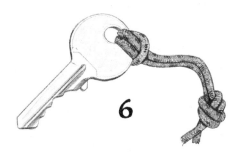

6

"Hey."

Louie just wants to leave this rink. He wants to leave this rink and take a nap and think about what he has to do right at morning skate tomorrow so Coach will put him in the lineup.

He does not want Ryan to sidle up to him after practice and say *hey*.

"Hey," Louie says. "What's up?"

"I'm gonna go look at that house," Ryan says. "The one with the red door. You wanna come?"

How does Louie tell him, gently, that he really needs a nap?

How does he tell him, also gently, that he doesn't want to?

"Uh," Louie says.

"I was thinking," Ryan goes on, "because it has a second bedroom, you could take it? If you want?"

But Louie already has a bedroom. At Santa's house. Although—Louie likes Santa and Bee and he also likes their puppy, even though it chews on everything, but he feels like a guest at their house. He was also a guest a Liam's house last fall, but it *felt* different.

Ryan definitely has the same energy as Santa's puppy, but he won't chew on Louie's shoelaces. Probably.

"You don't have to," Ryan says with a shrug. "I just thought...

35

because you're probably sticking around for a bit… maybe even until the end of the season…"

Ryan's optimism is apparently endless. But he was already wrong once when he said Louie would make the lineup when he'd only just arrived. He could be wrong again. Coach could bench Louie another time tomorrow, and could decide that calling Louie up was a mistake and get someone else from Springfield. In a few days, Louie could be back on the farm team.

Louie almost asks Ryan why he even wants to live with him, since they barely know each other, but he's got this one figured out. It's just because they got here at the same time and Ryan decided that he was the easiest to latch onto. It's a smart move.

Admittedly, Louie is a little bit charmed by that red door. He's a little bit charmed by the black backsplash in the kitchen and the piano in the living room.

"You're going right now?" Louie asks.

"Right now," Ryan confirms. "Have a look. It's fine if you hate it."

Louie has a feeling that it will not be fine at all if he hates it, but the second he steps into the house, he knows it's impossible to hate. It's cozy in all the right places with a big couch and shelves that have some knickknacks on them, with a soft blanket draped strategically over an armchair, but it also has a big TV, a huge fridge, and a shower with different showerheads.

When he looks around the living room, he gives one of the piano keys a tap.

Ryan turns to grin at him like that means Louie approves of this place.

The guy from the management company has so, so many great things to say about the house. At this point he could casually throw in that someone was murdered violently in the main bedroom and Ryan would still go for it. He's walking around with a huge smile on his face, peering into rooms, pointing things out to Louie. "Did you see the size of that bathtub?" and "That porch in the back is so nice—we could have dinner out there when it gets warmer" and "The door. Fucking love that door."

He signs the lease. It's month-to-month, which helps when you're not a superstar with a no-trade clause in your contract. Louie would know. His career so far has mostly been about coming and going. Over and over again.

Louie doesn't get to stay.

He won't kid himself: this is just another guest room, but it won't be one until he leaves. For now, for a little while, this could be *his* room.

"So?" Ryan asks when he finds Louie outside the door.

The building manager has just left with a bounce in his step as he headed to his car.

Ryan's smile is so bright, it's impossible to look away from. It draws you in. *There's happiness here*, it says. *Stick around.*

Ryan shoots Louie a probing glance. "Before you say anything…"

"Yeah?"

"You should know that I can't cook," Ryan says. "Like, at all. Except for grilled cheese."

"What about pasta?" Louie asks. Because everyone can make pasta. Right?

"With varying success, yeah."

"How do you ruin pasta?" Louie isn't a master chef either, but he at the very least knows the basics. Not that anyone at home ever bothered to teach him. It was his billet mom who insisted that he couldn't leave her house without learning a few things. Louie misses her—she died three years ago and he couldn't even go to the funeral.

"I'm very good at ruining things," Ryan says with a shrug. "I just figured I'd mention it."

"I wasn't expecting you to cook for me," Louie replies.

"Okay." Ryan bounces on the balls of his feet. He looks like he's about to confess that he robbed a bank. "There's something else."

"What, do you like to scream for no reason at two in the morning?" Louie asks.

Ryan frowns. "That would be a weird fucking thing to do." He smirks. "Oh, oh, Louie, I think that was just your roommates having sex."

"I wasn't even—" Louie was not being serious. "Never mind."

Ryan cackles and pokes him in the side. Right. He obviously got that Louie wasn't being serious. "Dude."

"So, what is it, then?" Louie asks. Can't be worse than him ruining pasta.

Ryan clears his throat. Shuffles his feet a little more. "I'll just say it, huh? I, uh... I'm very gay. I guess you should know that."

"Oh," Louie says. Not nearly as bad as ruining pasta. "My brother is gay."

"Your... brother?"

Crap. Louie was so excited that he wasn't going to mess this up. He wasn't thinking. Obviously, Ryan, being a hockey player, would think of Bastien first. "Not that brother," Louie says. "My older brother. Dominic."

Ryan frowns. "I didn't know you had an older brother."

Most people don't. Dominic is very much okay with that. Their dad very much isn't. Neither with Dominic quitting hockey nor with him being gay. "He's a pediatrician. Or, like, on his way to becoming one."

"Wow," Ryan says. "He really said fuck the family business, huh?"

"Sure did," Louie says. "Although my mom never played hockey either."

"Your Olympic medal-winning speed skating mom?"

"Okay, yeah..." Louie shrugs. "Maybe Dominic is adopted." Or maybe Dominic was smart enough to get out while he still could. Maybe he realized it was impossible for all three of Martie Hathaway's sons to live up to his sky-high standards and took himself out of the equation.

Louie had a chance to do the same, but he wanted to live up to those standards. He wanted to be exactly like his dad. That was before Bastien turned out to be the golden boy who would keep the Hathaway name alive in hockey.

"So, your maybe-adopted brother is gay," Ryan says, "and by telling me that, you were also trying to tell me that you're okay with me being gay?"

"Yeah," Louie says. "I'm absolutely okay with it."

Ryan tilts his head and considers him. "What did you say to your brother when he came out?"

"That I love him," Louie says. "Didn't seem appropriate right now."

"Hm." Ryan nods slowly. "Yeah. Okay. I think we'll file this away as a success?"

Now it's Louie turn to consider Ryan. Dominic sat Louie down years ago when Louie was still in high school. He'd met someone at college. A guy. They're not together anymore, but Dominic told him later that the guy in question—Louie never met him—was a hockey player. Now Dominic is engaged to an elementary school teacher. When Dominic spilled the beans about his college boyfriend, he was sweating. Wringing his hands. He wouldn't even look Louie in the eyes.

None of that with Ryan.

"You're... I'm not the first person you've told," Louie guesses.

Ryan laughs. "No, dude, you're really not." He bites his lip. "I just... took a long look at you and figured you'd be cool with it."

Louie laughs. "You took a long look at me?"

"Not a gay look." Ryan raises his palms. "No homo, et cetera, et cetera."

"You don't have to do that with me," Louie says, even though it was probably just a joke. Maybe it was ninety percent joke and the remaining ten percent was some kind of insurance. Just in case.

Dominic does it, too. Tones himself down. And Dominic isn't even playing a sport that is still homophobic enough to keep every single gay NHL player in the closet. Louie has no doubts that they exist. One of them is standing right here with him and he can't be the only one.

Ryan nods. "Room's all yours, then."

All his. At least for a little while.

7

Ryan wouldn't say he *knows* Louie, but since he didn't die on the spot when Ryan came out to him, he's fairly confident things will work out. They can't move into the house until Ryan's deposit check clears, so they go their separate ways on Sunday.

Louie makes the lineup on Monday and it's the first time Ryan sees a real smile on his face.

He plays a good game but doesn't score. Gets an assist on Ryan's goal. Because Ryan does score. He practically sweeps Louie off his feet when he barrels into him to hug him. Ryan thanks him after, but Louie shrugs it off, like it doesn't mean anything.

He catches Louie checking on the Minnesota Bears' game in the app after the game, lingering over one of the goals. Scored by Bastien Hathaway.

That entire family is ridiculous. Minus the gay pediatrician brother, who is apparently just some (really smart) guy. But the Hathaways are known for hockey. Not just Louie's dad and younger brother, but also his uncle, and his cousin who just got drafted this year. Third round.

Hockey is a foreign concept to Ryan's family. His people aren't athletes—they're musicians and writers and painters and photographers. Ryan only got into hockey because the kids on his street—Adrian and

Benji and Spencer—were playing hockey and Ryan didn't want to be left out, so he asked his mom if she could sign him up, too.

It was just for fun at first. Ryan didn't dream of playing on NHL ice when he was four. They picked Ryan's number for him, said "You're playing defense", and then it turned out that he was actually pretty good at this whole hockey thing. *Then* Ryan started dreaming of playing on NHL ice.

He made it there in the most basic way possible. He got drafted, second round, played for the farm team, got called up before the playoffs during his third season and never left.

Until last week.

Louie's journey is looking a little rockier. He's been called up and sent back down many, many times during the past few years. Louie is a year younger than him, so he definitely has time. For him it's not a matter of wanting it. He wants it so much. He's leaving it all on the ice. Ryan doesn't think he's not ready yet either. That's the case with some of the guys: they're just not there yet. They need to be a little patient and work on themselves a little more.

Louie just needs to be given a chance and needs to play more than two games before he gets sent down again. The Cardinals are pretty stacked, so it's hard to make the lineup. Well, it's hard when they're not injury-riddled and falling apart at the seams like they are right now.

When they get on the plane—they end up sitting together because everyone else already has a plane buddy—Ryan and Louie talk. About hockey. Only hockey. Ryan loves hockey, but sometimes he also needs a break from it. He needs to play some Minecraft and watch dog videos and buy funny socks on the Internet.

"Look at this," Louie says and holds out his phone. It's Vincent Nyberg scoring an absolutely filthy goal.

"Whoa," Ryan says.

"He's so good and he's only twenty. Just imagine what he'll play like in five years. In ten years."

"Kinda glad he's in LA and we're all the way over here," Ryan quips.

"It's like he can read everyone's mind," Louie goes on, awe in his voice. "He knows exactly where they're going, and not just his teammates."

Ryan fucking wishes he could read minds, at least selectively. Not just because it would be really helpful during a game. He wants to know how other people see him. Do they think he's a good guy? Do they hate his hair? Do they actually want to hang out with him or do they just tolerate him?

Louie was definitely reluctant to move into the house with Ryan. And Ryan is trying not to take that personally. Louie's right, he's not staying indefinitely, but Ryan still thought that it may be better than a guest room at Santa's. And Louie did say yes eventually.

Ryan was clearly right about Louie—he's not one of those homophobic shitbags who are scared that A Gay will look at them the wrong way. So, yeah, he's glad he asked, even though Louie talks about hockey all the time. He talks about hockey when they go out for dinner with the team and he talks about hockey when they have breakfast in the morning. Ryan's pretty sure that Louie's coffee is cold by the time he's done waxing poetically about Ravens captain Elliot Cowell's soft mitts.

When they have a day off before their game in Tampa Bay, Ryan and Louie get Froyo with Mikko Lampinen, who used to play with Louie in Springfield, and his fellow Finn, the Cards' backup goalie Sami Peltola. Sami has a humongous and fluffy shelter dog that Ryan just has to meet as soon as they're back home.

"Maybe you should have stayed with Santa," Louie says to Ryan. "He just got a puppy."

"No way." Ryan gasps. "Why are you saying that like it's a problem?"

"I'm just not..." Louie shrugs.

"Louie is scared of dogs," Mikko says offhandedly.

"I'm not scared," Louie says. "I just don't trust every dog I come across."

"Smart," Sami says.

"Okay, but most dogs are..." Ryan trails off when Louie's phone starts buzzing.

"One second," Louie says and picks up. "Hey, Dad."

"Oh, it's *Dad*," Mikko whispers. He must have met Dad Hathaway back in Springfield.

Louie glowers at Mikko. "Yeah," he says, answering a question that none of them heard.

Honestly, Ryan hopes he gets to meet Dad Hathaway at some point. He's in Boston most of the time, so he's bound to come watch his kid play, right? Martie Hathaway has his own hockey academy and their summer camps are legendary. Ryan tried to get in a few times. No dice.

Louie probably got to go every summer.

"I don't know," Louie is saying. "I get two. I'll see if I can have more, but I can't—"

His dad clearly cuts him off and says something else.

"Yeah," Louie says. A beat. "Yeah. Ask Bastien. Away teams—yeah."

The face he's making is, uh—Ryan made that face when he tried to drink spoiled milk a few weeks ago. He doesn't make that face when his dad calls. His parents call him once a week, at least when he's not traveling, and Dad tells him about whatever he's working on in the garage. His mom tells him about the weddings she's been photographing. Then they ask him about hockey and if he has a boyfriend and which podcasts he's been listening to.

They talk for an hour. Maybe two.

Louie's done talking to his dad after two minutes, barely says anything, mostly listens, and stares at his frozen yoghurt as he talks.

When he hangs up after a curt and unenthusiastic, "See you next week," he picks up the cup and ignores that everyone is staring at him. At least for half a minute. Then he says, "What?"

"Your dad's coming?" Ryan asks. He's well aware that he just sounded like he's asking if Taylor Swift is coming.

"Yeah," Louie says and keeps eating his food.

Maybe having a famous hockey dad isn't that much fun when everyone's all over you and wants to meet him. Ryan won't ask. He won't. Seriously. He'll die if he doesn't get to meet Dad Hathaway, but he'll just have to deal.

Louie glances at Ryan. "You wanna meet him?"

"Um," Ryan says because he wasn't going to ask. Really.

"I'll introduce you, don't worry," Louie says, sounding dreadfully bored. "Although he'll probably want to see Bastien, so I don't know if he'll come to our room."

"I mean, he's gonna want to see both of you, right?" Ryan says. He didn't think it was a controversial statement, but Louie's face clouds over like they've got a major storm coming. Screen doors banging, patio furniture flying.

"Guess that depends on how the game goes," Louie mumbles and pokes at his food. He looks around. "Do any of you guys have leftover tickets for the game against the Bears? My dad wants to bring my grandma and my older brother."

"You can have mine," Ryan says.

"Thanks," Louie mutters.

It's like Louie knows that Ryan is dying to ask him about his dad. About his family. He's dying to know what it's like to grow up in a hockey family that actually understands the game. Not that his family didn't do their very, very best to learn the rules. Not that they didn't show up to his games. They did. They screamed the loudest. But they never *got* it.

So, since Louie seems to be sensing that Ryan is two seconds away from asking a crap-ton of personal questions, he talks about hockey even more.

Ryan won't ask. Really.

When they're back from their roadie, they move into the house, and Ryan attaches the pizza keychain Carrot gave him once upon a time to his new key. While they get sorted, Louie talks about two things: 1) if Ryan is okay with him rearranging the furniture in the guest room and 2) the Cardinals' struggling power play and how he'd fix it.

Ryan truly doesn't give a shit if Louie pushes the bed up against the wall. And Louie kind of has a point about the power play. Coach should try Louie on the power play instead of on the penalty kill, but Ryan definitely won't share those thoughts with anyone who has a say in anything. Coach Beaulieu wouldn't appreciate it.

It takes Ryan about fifteen minutes to put all his stuff away. When he looks around his room, and when he walks around the house, all he sees are the things he wasn't able to bring from Toronto. He'll have to go back in the summer and pack properly. Have it all sent down here. He hopes he won't have to do the same thing all over again next season when his contract runs out.

Ida Hellström was very sad to see Ryan go already and made him take Gustav, which Ryan did after getting the okay from Liam and Ella. Gustav makes his bedroom look like someone actually lives there. Ida also made Ryan promise to come over for dinner all the time, which won't be a problem in the slightest.

Ryan promised he'd be by soon, then he carried Gustav to his car, with Ida watching to make sure he'd buckle him in. He did not miss Liam's smirk as he piled Ryan's bags into his rental car. Ryan very much appreciates that Liam didn't make a joke about Ryan driving Gustav into a ditch.

"Did you steal that bear from a child?" Louie asks drily.

Ryan jumps. "Jesus fucking Christ." He takes a deep breath. "Anyway. No. I did not steal him. Ida gave him to me."

For some reason, Louie smirks. Ryan gives him a nudge and holds up his phone. "Here, let's take a selfie, I wanna send it to my mom."

Louie lets out a long-suffering sigh and tips his head a little closer to Ryan.

"Dude, can you try to look less like I'm torturing you?" Ryan says after he's taken five pictures. Louie has murder eyes in all of them.

"But you are torturing me," Louie says. "Selfies are a disease."

"You sound like my boomer uncle who doesn't know how to install apps on this phone."

"I'll smile once," Louie says. "And then I'm taking a nap."

Ryan puts his arm around him and Louie smiles, bright and delighted-to-be-here and so fake that Ryan almost regrets asking him to smile. Louie does put his arm around Ryan in turn, though, and that's not something Ryan made him do, so at least he didn't destroy this still very fresh friendship.

Ryan would really love to not ruin a good thing for once.

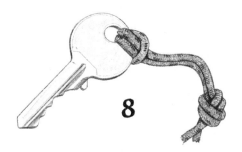

8

Louie doesn't sleep at all the night before the game against Minnesota.

Two scenarios are on repeat in his head: Coach tells him he's been doing a good job and puts him in the lineup and he'll play against Bastien for the very first time. And their parents will be watching. And one of them will lose. Or Coach tells him that he hasn't been working hard enough and that he'll sit this one out and Louie will watch Bastien play an NHL game in person for the very first time. And Bastien will win, or lose, and Louie will have no part in it.

He gets up at three in the morning and gets himself a glass of water, nearly bumping into Ryan in the hallway.

"What are you doing?" Louie whispers. He's not sure why; there's nobody left to wake up.

Ryan tugs his fingers through his brown hair. It looks messy most of the time, but at three in the morning it's a regular bird's nest. He's wearing long plaid pajama bottoms but no shirt. It looks like he's about to lose those pants. "I heard a noise."

"That was me. Sorry."

"No, it's fine." Ryan yawns. "Everything okay?"

"Just getting some water," Louie says. He hasn't slept a wink ever since he went to bed four hours ago. Essentially, he's a total mess, and he'd obviously never admit that to anyone, but for a second, in this dark hallway, at three in the morning, he considers telling Ryan that he's barely keeping it together.

Because Ryan is still looking at him, like he knows that Louie isn't telling him the truth, but he eventually just nods and shuffles back into his own room, leaving Louie and his glass of water to their own devices.

Louie takes a sip, puts the glass on his nightstand, and proceeds to stare at it in the darkness. The guest room definitely needs better curtains. Louie sticks a leg out from under the covers. Hmm. No. That's not it either.

He lies flat on his back and closes his eyes. Breathes in deeply. Ryan has probably gone right back to sleep. He doesn't seem like the kind of person who overthinks hockey. He goes out there and plays his game with a confidence that Louie lets himself admire. Ryan's not his competition, so he can admit that he's impressed.

He probably shouldn't be. Ryan was good in Toronto, and obviously he's also good in Hartford. He didn't get traded because he didn't play well. Just some bad luck. He hasn't asked Ryan what *actually* happened because chances are it's really boring and just got blown out of proportion by the media.

Louie has met several people who were allegedly creating problems for their teams. And, like magic, suddenly those guys weren't doing that anymore once they were on a different team. Almost like it wasn't the player who was the problem.

With a sigh, Louie grabs his phone. Checks the time. 3:36. Louie sighs again and turns over, grabbing his second pillow to hug.

The second pillow does nothing.

He checks the time again at 4:07.

At least he took a long nap in the afternoon. Bastien asked if he wanted to meet for dinner in Hartford. Louie almost said yes. Then he made up an excuse about how he had to drive up to Springfield to grab some more of his stuff and how he didn't have time. So sorry. He'll see Bastien at the game.

Since Louie doesn't like to lie, he actually did drive to Springfield to grab some stuff. Mostly dirty underwear that he threw into the washer as soon as he was back.

At 4:37 he glances at the clock again.

Then at 5:15.

The sun comes up. Louie finally falls asleep.

The Bears hit the ice for their morning skate at the arena in Hartford this morning. Knowing this helps Louie breathe on the way to the Cardinals' practice rink in Silver Lakes.

Ryan is driving.

Not having to focus on traffic also helps Louie breathe.

Ryan talks. He's been listening to some science podcast.

Not having to carry a conversation helps Louie breathe as well.

When they get to the rink, one of the social media admins pulls him aside to talk about the game. Because Louie is playing against his brother for the very first time and isn't that exciting?

Louie misses being able to breathe. He nods along to whatever she's saying because he knows there's no way around talking to the media and acting like he's looking forward to the game tonight. Like this isn't the worst torture he's had to endure in his career so far.

He can't fucking wait for this day to be over.

First, he gets on the ice and goes through practice on autopilot. Coach gives him a pat on the back and asks if he's excited to play against his brother tonight. So he's in the lineup.

Suddenly, he wishes he wasn't. Which is—Louie hates the person he becomes in Bastien's general vicinity. He hates that he doesn't want to play.

"Dude, you look pissed," Ryan, ever-observant, says as he peels off his gear after morning skate. He leans closer, his eyes wide and full of sincere worry. "Is Coach benching you?"

"No," Louie says.

"Then what—"

They're thankfully interrupted by the PR brigade that is coming to deliver him to the media room. Part of Louie actually appreciates that the Cardinals don't let the media into their locker room anymore and have a dedicated space for reporters to ask their questions. It can feel almost claustrophobic when they crowd around your stall.

Up on that little stage, behind the table, Louie has the upper hand. Or so he tells himself as he stares at them while they stare back at him. He doesn't know them well and doesn't often talk to them. He's on high alert while they ask their questions.

He tells them that he's excited for tonight.

Yes, of course it's special to play against his brother.

No, he's not nervous, it's just like any other game in the end.

Yes, his parents will be there.

Yes, he's learned a lot from his dad.

Yes, it's special for his family to watch them both play.

When Louie gets up, Ryan and Nick are waiting by the door. Their turn to spout a bunch of half-truths and rattle off meaningless phrases about getting pucks to the net and playing a full sixty minutes.

Ryan gives Louie a pat on the back on the way out, like he's saying *good job*, like he knows how exhausted Louie is already. And they're not even at the arena yet. Louie isn't religious by any means, but he still prays to whoever is listening that he'll be able to sleep this afternoon.

On the way home, Ryan stops to buy them smoothies. Louie doesn't have it in him to say no, so he sits in the car and watches messages pop up in the Hathaway family group chat. The Bears are clearly done with their skate because Bastien just posted a picture of himself in the arena's tunnel, next to a picture of this season's Cardinals—*can't find Louie*, he said.

Of freaking course he can't find Louie.

Louie didn't make the opening night roster.

Bastien knows that. Bastien is being a shit. And Louie would bet that everyone in the group chat thinks it's such a neat little chirp. Louie wants to kill him. Not actually. But something is burning hot in the pit of his stomach and he's doing everything in his power to stay in the passenger seat and not rip the door of this car open, get out and run through the streets of Silver Lakes screaming.

Ryan returns and hands over a red smoothie with a smile. It's pleasantly cold against Louie's fingers and that's what he decides to focus on.

Somehow, Ryan keeps doing things that help him breathe.

When they're back at the house, they go in through the garage door. Ryan makes some noises about having to go grocery shopping because they barely have any food. Tomorrow after practice maybe.

Louie makes some noncommittal noises back at him.

Ryan eventually trails off in the middle of a sentence that may have been about his lettuce preferences, although Louie can't be sure. "Everything okay?" Ryan asks, an echo from last night.

Louie looks at him for a long moment. Ryan must know the answer; he wouldn't be asking if he wasn't sensing that something's off with Louie. No, he's not okay. He didn't sleep. He's playing against Bastien tonight. Their dad will be in the crowd. He can't breathe. "I'm fine," Louie says. "Why?"

Ryan shrugs. Yawns. "I'm taking a nap."

Louie nods. He will, too. Hopefully. If he can bring himself to actually get into bed. He—"Ryan?"

Ryan stops in the door. "Yeah?"

"Do you mind if I nap on the couch?"

"All yours," Ryan says and wanders away to his room, humming a song under his breath that Louie doesn't recognize.

Louie lies down on the couch, grabs the soft chunky knit blanket that he wants to steal for his room and is asleep within a minute. Usually, his body knows when it's time to wake up from his pregame nap, but today his phone alarm, always set just to be safe, has him diving off the couch to turn it off.

Ryan drives them to the arena, no questions asked. He knows. Maybe he doesn't know what exactly Louie's problem is, maybe he just thinks he's nervous, but he's doing what he can. Louie wishes he could bring himself to say thank you.

He takes deep breaths in the passenger seat instead.

He's still taking deep breaths when they walk into the arena together, the social media folks snapping pictures.

The players always arrive two hours before puck drop, at least, but Louie likes to get there even earlier and Ryan doesn't seem to mind. He also didn't mind when Louie told him that he wants to get to practice early. He just took that information and ran with it, simply assuming that Louie likes to be early for everything.

Louie can work with that.

His pregame routine is simple. Run-of-the-mill. None of that superstitious nonsense. He doesn't care which skate he puts on first, which stick he plays with, where on the ice he stretches. He's the one who plays and if things don't go well, it's his fault and not because he missed a step in his routine.

Warm-ups somehow arrive faster than usual and before Louie knows it, he's on the ice and the Cardinals' and Bears' social media minions have banded together to get a picture of him and Bastien. Fine. Better to just get it over with. Louie holds out his fist for Bastien to bump; gives Bastien's helmet a little tap.

"Hey," Bastien says before he skates away again, "good luck."

He doesn't say *You'll need it.* Louie still hears it. He doesn't have a good reply at the ready and before he can convince himself to answer, Bastien is already out of earshot, bugging one of his teammates. He's smiling like this is the best day of his life. Every day is the best day of his life.

Louie can already see him winning the Calder.

He'll be happy for him when it happens. He'll be happy.

"Hey, Lou, stop staring at those guys, they're evil," Ryan says, coming to a stop next to him. He gives Louie's butt a slap with his stick. "Come on, shake it off, get your groove on."

"My groove," Louie repeats, deadpan.

Another slap. "Yeah, baby." Ryan cackles and skates away. Louie follows, finds a good place to stretch, and ducks his head.

Fans are crowded around the glass, many with posters, and most of them for Josh or Nick. Today, Louie doesn't look. His mom loves to watch warm-ups at the glass and if he doesn't find her, it means she chose Bastien. Louie doesn't want to know. This way he can pretend she was there and he just didn't see her.

During the game, he occasionally wonders when the broadcast is showing his parents in the crowd. When Bastien leaves the Cards in the dust on a breakaway but ultimately fails to get that puck past Sami? When Louie accidentally assists on Nick's first goal of the game just after a botched line change? When Bastien pulls a beautiful move and tries to pass the puck through his legs in front of the Cardinals' goal but has the puck stolen by Nick, who goes on to score his second of the game? When Louie nearly scores on the empty net but realizes a second too late that the pass is headed his way?

In the end, Louie gets off the ice with that one assist in his pocket. Bastien assisted on a goal as well but didn't score. Louie tries not to be smug about it and fails. He almost wants to hug Nick, who essentially brought home the win for them tonight. Louie was only on the ice with him for a few seconds, and was actually supposed to be on the bench, but something felt right that doesn't feel right when Louie plays with his line. That's probably just Nick being Nick. Guys like him, they click with everyone.

As he pulls off his gear, Louie briefly wonders what Nick's dad thinks of him and his career. He must be ridiculously proud of him.

Louie hits the showers and gets back into his suit. He promised Ryan he'd introduce him to his dad and he intends to keep that promise. Ryan doesn't know yet that he'll be the buffer Louie so desperately needs.

"Louie, your brother is waiting outside," he's told in passing.

His brother. So his parents went to say hi to Bastien. Louie predicted this but somehow still hoped that they'd come see him first.

With a sigh, he grabs Ryan. "Ready to meet my dad?"

9

Ryan is so not ready to meet the great Martie Hathaway.

He's back in his suit, but he can't find his tie and fuck knows what his hair looks like. Louie won't wait, though—he's got his fingers curled tightly around his biceps and is pushing him toward the locker room door.

Ryan, by now, knows many of the people who are milling about in the tunnels; one of them is Liam's wife with Maja. Ida is trading what looks like hockey cards with a girl her age—one of Yoshi's girls, going by her jersey. Although Ida is wearing Nick's jersey but is definitely not his kid, so Ryan can't be sure.

"Rah-rah!" Maja greets him, holding out her tiny arms, wanting to be picked up.

"Awww," Ryan says and tugs Louie with him. No sign of Martie Hathaway, so he can say hello real quick. He grabs Maja, Louie impatiently shifting his weight next to him, and clearing his throat when things are taking too long. Ryan hands Maja back to her mom and promises that he'll come by to play with her soon.

"Both of you," Ella says, shooting Louie a look. "I'll make the meatballs."

"Can't say no to the meatballs," Ryan says and elbows Louie in the side.

Louie only nods, distracted, looking at a tall guy in a Cardinals jersey who's grinning at them. He's handsome. Really nice eyes. *Kind* eyes. And once Ryan has said goodbye to the Hellströms, Louie is taking Ryan straight over there.

"There he is," the guy says and pulls Louie into a quick but tight hug.

Louie's smile is about as tight as that hug. "Ryan, this is my older brother Dominic." He nods at Ryan. "This is Ryan Harris, I—"

"Your roommate!" Dominic says and shakes Ryan's hand. "So nice to meet you."

Louie's older brother. The gay brother. The doctor. Or maybe not-yet-doctor. Ryan should have seen it. They have the same dark hair, the same greenish-brown eyes. "Hi," Ryan says, instantly embarrassed that he thought the guy is handsome. He is, but Ryan absolutely cannot think that about Louie's brother.

"Ryan wanted to meet Dad," Louie adds.

Dominic laughs. "Doesn't everyone?"

Ryan is starting to feel like he's majorly inconveniencing everyone around him. "Look, if you guys don't have time for that—"

"No, no, it's fine," Dominic says, still smiling. "We're used to it. Louie and Bastien in particular. I, uh, quit hockey before people got annoying about it." He gives Ryan's shoulder a pat. "Not to say you're annoying. It's honestly fine."

Ryan is fascinated by this guy. He would have never guessed that he's gay. Well, Ryan hopes he looks straight to other people, too, but knowing that Dominic is into men and not getting any vibes in that direction has Ryan looking at him a little harder than he maybe looks at most other people. At first glance, he's just your regular beer-drinking "shoot the puck"-shouting hockey fan.

"I have no idea when they'll get here, though," Dominic goes on. "They went to see Bastien because his team is flying out tonight."

Ryan shrugs. "I have to wait for Louie anyway. I'm his ride."

"Really nice of you to let him stay with you," Dominic says. "Louie said you just got here. Where'd you play before?"

Louie talked about him? But he didn't mention how Ryan ended up in Hartford? And Dominic doesn't seem to follow hockey coverage either. "Toronto," Ryan says with some delay.

"I hear they're big on hockey up there," Dominic says, lips twitching. Ryan rolls his eyes. "Yeah, you could say that."

"Better here?" Dominic asks.

"I haven't been here for very long," Ryan says. He misses his friends. He texts Carrot and Slaw pretty much every day, but it's not the same as having them around. He hasn't found his people on the Cardinals yet. Louie is his person, technically, but only because they live together. They haven't had time to get to know each other properly, at least not beyond hockey.

Ryan just shared his biggest secret with him. No biggie. Real talk, though, he wanted that out of the way. He didn't want any awkwardness and he didn't want Louie to find out by accident.

"Yeah, takes some time to get used to new places," Dominic says, sounding like a wise old man who knows everything about getting used to new places. He gives Louie a gentle nudge. "Remember when I first moved to Hartford and got lost on the way back from the grocery store? Being a little lost is like a rite of passage. If you weren't a little lost, did you really arrive?"

Weirdly, that makes Ryan feel a lot better about being traded here and not really fitting in. He doesn't have time to reply, though, because Louie becomes very still next to him. Unnaturally still. Like he's on a hike and about to be eaten by a bear.

"Here they come," Dominic says and nods at a group of people who have just come into view. An old lady with a Cardinals hat—it's one of the new ones they just started selling at the store—and a woman with long blonde hair and a Bears jersey, and behind them Martie Hathaway, also in a Bears jersey, this one in white, matching the team's away sweaters.

"Louie, my sweetheart," the old woman says and pulls Louie into a hug. He looks like he wants to die, but he obediently says hello. Must be his grandma.

"Mom, Dad," Louie says, not going in for a hug with either of them— Ryan's mom would never let him get away without a hug. "Glad you could make it."

It almost sounds like he means it. Ryan can't even put his finger on why he's not buying it. Something about the smile on Louie's face. Ryan has seen that smile before: when Ryan asked him to smile.

"Of course," Louie's mom says. "Wouldn't have missed seeing all my boys play." She smiles at Dominic. "Well, almost all my boys."

"Yeah, no one wants to see *me* play," Dominic says and laughs.

"Who knows, if you'd stuck with hockey, you could be playing with these guys," Martie Hathaway throws in.

Dominic shrugs. "Yeah, well…" He's definitely over the whole hockey thing and is absolutely not interested in what-ifs. "Can't eat a $20 burger while you're playing."

Martie Hathaway looks deeply offended by the burger comment.

"We had a good time, that's what matters," Mama Hathaway says. The words of someone who's been trying (any maybe failing) to keep the peace over the decades.

"And we would have had an even better time if Louie had kept his head up and scored, hmm?" Martie says and gives Louie a pat on the back. "Empty net was wide open, kid. Can't expect them to keep giving you chances when you don't convert on opportunities like that."

Okay, *harsh*.

Ryan feels slightly invisible and maybe no one will notice if he slowly backs away, but he can't just leave, right? Louie's face is ghostly white, his left hand balled into a fist. Yeah, Ryan is not going anywhere.

"Did you see Bastien's game against the Grizzlies?" Martie goes on, hand still on Louie's shoulder. "That was one beautiful goal."

"Most players don't score every game, Dad," Dominic says. Another peacekeeper. He reminds Ryan of his older sister Emery, who spent most of her teenage years keeping the peace between the twins.

"Our Louie is overdue for a goal, though," Martie says good-naturedly.

Louie's lips have become a thin line, like he's trying to keep something in. Words. Or maybe vomit.

He must have known. All day, he must have thought about what his dad would say to him tonight. He must have known it wouldn't be kind. That's why something seemed off about him.

So this is what it's like to have a dad who knows his way around hockey. Ryan will keep the carpenter dad who builds wacky furniture in the garage and paints it weird colors and tells him that he did a really good job, even if it was the worst game of Ryan's life.

"Don't make that face, Lori," Martie says to his wife. "Your son's a forward—he knows his job is to score and he's not doing that right now." He ruffles Louie's hair. "He just needs to work harder. And to get a haircut."

Louie works harder than most of the guys Ryan has played with. He would know because he always gives Louie a ride after practice and Louie likes to stay late. Ryan has started to stay on the ice with him and a few of the other guys because it's better than waiting around. Louie also makes sure he only eats food the team nutritionist approves of, he doesn't stay up too late to play Minecraft like Ryan, and in the mornings, he goes on runs. Yesterday, he even did push-ups.

Ryan will only do a push-up at gunpoint.

He desperately wants to say something, but he has a feeling that Louie wouldn't like it.

"Dad," Dominic says, "Louie's teammate wanted to meet you."

"Oh!" Martie Hathaway brightens and turns to Ryan like he only just noticed him standing there. "Ryan Harris, drafted 2017. Second round if I'm not wrong?"

"That is correct," Ryan says, shaking Martie's outstretched hand. That man could shake hands for a living and it'd make him as much money as hockey did.

"You've been playing a lot of minutes," Martie says. "Looks like these guys made a solid move."

So he does know how to say nice things. Well, he said nice things about his other kid, the goal he scored, so maybe, if he'd tried just a teensy bit, he could have found something nice to say about Louie's game as well.

This, all of this, seems like a big mistake.

"Thank you," Ryan says, once again telling himself that Louie wouldn't appreciate it if Ryan brought him into this. "It's so great to meet you."

"Want me to take a picture of you guys?" Louie asks.

Ryan hands him his phone and Louie snaps the picture, then the Cards' rookie sneaks up on them to ask for a picture as well and Ryan extracts Louie from that huddle. Dominic follows them.

"You didn't want to bring Cameron?" Louie asks Dominic. That must be the elementary school teacher fiancé.

Dominic laughs. "Right. Like I'd do *that* to him." He turns to Ryan. "It's not the hockey. Dad doesn't like Cameron."

"Why?" Ryan asks. "He's... Louie said he's an elementary school teacher?" How do you dislike an elementary school teacher? Shouldn't be possible.

"He is," Dominic says, his smile never faltering, "but he's also a guy."

"Oh," Ryan says. He already knows where this is going.

"Dad would never say that he has a problem with it out loud," Dominic says, "but we all know. And since I love Cameron, I'm not doing Dad to him."

Dad Hathaway barely exchanges another word with Louie and eventually he collects his people to take them to the hotel they booked for the night. Dominic is going back to his place. Before he goes, he tells

Louie to come by on a day off sometime.

Louie makes vague noises about it.

On the drive home, he doesn't say a word. Ryan doesn't try to strike up a conversation, just turns up the radio and takes them home through gentle snow flurries.

At the house, Louie immediately takes off down the hall.

"Hey," Ryan says. When Louie stops and turns around just outside his bedroom door, Ryan realizes that he doesn't even know what he was going to say. "You okay?" he finally asks, even though it's obvious that Louie isn't. At least he asked, at least he gave Louie a chance to tell him if he needs anything.

"Not really," Louie says. Then he disappears into his room.

Ryan does not know what to do with that. Is that a cry for help? Is it Louie telling him to leave him alone? Ryan takes off his suit, then he tries to find an answer in the mostly empty fridge. He grabs the cheese and eats a slice, then he takes the bread and the butter. A grilled cheese sandwich can't fix everything, but at least it's delicious.

And Ryan's exceptionally good at grilled cheese.

He also grabs a can of tomato soup, which Louie scoffed at when Ryan brought it home, but it's part of the experience. He heats up the soup while he makes the sandwiches. Two. One for himself, one for Louie. And if Louie doesn't want it, Ryan will just have a second one.

He scours the kitchen for a tray, finds a pale pink one with polka dots, and carefully arranges the bowl of soup and the absolutely perfect sandwich. Ryan will eat the one that's less perfect (he flipped it too late).

Careful not to drop the tray, which would be very Ryan of him, he walks down the hall and sets it down just outside Louie's door. He knocks and makes sure it's loud enough that Louie will actually hear it. "Um, so, I made grilled cheese and I made you one, too, and it's outside your door. You don't have to eat it if you don't want to, I'll just come back in five minutes and if it's still there, I'll eat it, so no worries. Uh. That's it."

He's about to leave, but he forgot some crucial information.

He knocks again. "Oh, and I should mention, I'm really good at grilled cheese. Like, this isn't normal grilled cheese. It's *my* grilled cheese and it's better than all the other grilled cheeses. But, again, if you don't want it, just leave it right where it is."

With that, he shuffles back to the kitchen and dunks his own sandwich right into the pot with the leftover tomato soup. He's so glad no one can see him right now. His mom would be appalled.

He does stop eating for a second when he hears a door click. No one says no to a Ryan Harris grilled cheese.

Ryan is cleaning up the kitchen—somehow there are tomato soup splatters everywhere—when Louie comes shuffling into the room in sweatpants and a shirt from his AHL team.

"You were right," Louie says, voice soft, as he sets the tray with the empty dishes down on the counter, "it was really good."

Ryan nods. Glances at him. Louie's eyes are a little red. "While other people were out partying, I studied the grilled cheese. And I made out with my hot neighbor. In that order."

Louie laughs and opens the dishwasher, putting away the bowl and the plate and grabbing Ryan's from the sink as well. "Thank you," he says.

"Well, you said you weren't okay…" Ryan shrugs. "And I know you don't eat chocolate."

"I sometimes eat chocolate," Louie whispers.

"Oh, so you're saying I could have just dropped a Hershey bar outside your door?"

"I eat *good* chocolate," Louie says.

Ryan snorts. "Blasphemy." He gives the counter a little pat. Spots more tomato soup. "I, uh… I'm sorry. Y'know, for asking you to introduce me to your dad."

"You didn't ask me," Louie says. "I offered. It's all right. Everyone wants to meet him and when he's busy meeting people, he says less about how I need to work harder."

"Hey, that's…" Ryan shakes his head. "You don't need to work harder."

"Maybe I do."

"No," Ryan says. He reaches out to pull Louie into a hug because he definitely needs one. "No, really, if you work any harder, you'll probably die."

Louie freezes and awkwardly pats Ryan's back. "I'm fine now, don't worry."

Ryan lets go of him after a short moment because hugging is clearly not Louie's thing. "I know you're not," Ryan whispers, "but I'll pretend that I believe you if that's what you want."

Louie stares at him like he's grown a second head. Then he says, "Thank you."

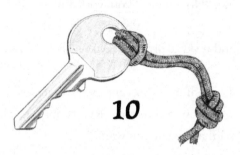

10

Louie isn't big on social media, but he does have a locked and mostly empty Instagram account that he uses to follow his teammates. He checks it about once a week. That's enough for him.

The day after the game against Minnesota, Louie finds a picture of his dad and Novie, the Cards' rookie, beaming at the camera. There isn't a single picture of Louie and his dad where either of them looks that happy. He checks Ryan's profile as well—he's one of those compulsive posters. *Look, it's my lunch, look, it's my new skates, look, it's me at the gym with my abs out.*

No picture from last night. No *look, I met the great Martie Hathaway.* He's posted a story. Maybe it's there. Louie taps on it, knowing full well that Ryan will know he peeked. It's the grilled cheese. A video of him pulling apart one of the sandwiches to show the cheese. "Beautiful," Ryan whispers in the background. That one is definitely a little on the burned side, so it wasn't the one he left outside Louie's door.

The next bit is a screenshot of a comment by *hockeycarrot*, one of Ryan's former teammates: *did you set that thing on fire.* Ryan has added a very simple *IT'S CRISPY AND DELICIOUS* in all caps.

It's not that burned. Louie would have eaten it. His dad would have told him not to put that crap into his body. So Louie savored every single bite.

He's never made a grilled cheese, but he assumes there was a lot of butter involved. It's a cheat meal kind of thing. Maybe he'll ask Ryan to make him another one after their next roadie. The tomato soup wasn't that bad, either, even though it came out of a can. Louie makes a point of not eating anything that comes out of a can. Except the cranberry sauce when the Hathaways gather at Grandma's for Thanksgiving dinner.

Louie's chest feels tight when he thinks about Ryan not posting that photo. He probably just forgot. He wasn't even thinking about Louie. Why would he?

Although Ryan is surprisingly thoughtful at times. He makes coffee in the mornings and always asks if Louie wants some. "I don't drink coffee," Louie tells him every day. "You can stop asking."

"Doesn't feel polite not to ask," Ryan always says.

So Louie doesn't tell him to stop asking anymore.

Their next game is a good one, but Louie once again doesn't contribute much. At least this time Coach puts him on the power play with Nick and Yoshi because Connie blew a tire and Coach needs someone out there. Louie snags an assist on Nick's goal again and Yoshi gives him an appreciative tap on the bucket when they get back to the bench.

Despite all of that, Louie is still surprised when Coach puts him on Nick's line during practice the next day.

"I saw something last night," Beaulieu says. "I want to check if I'm right."

Whatever he saw, whatever he wanted to check, Louie must have done something right because when the Cardinals go to New York for a game against the Ravens the next day, Louie is still on the second line.

"Look at you, moving up the ranks," Ryan says, ruffling Louie's hair in the locker room before the game.

Louie glares at him.

Ryan winks.

Louie still sits next to him on the way to the city. They end up getting stuck in traffic but arrive at the Garden with plenty of time to spare. Since they're playing in Philadelphia in two days, they're spending the night in the city and taking the train down tomorrow. Louie will never, ever tell anyone this, but he loves it when they take the train. One day, he'll fly to Europe in the summer and just hop on a ton of trains. So many trains.

Since Louie hasn't played a lot of road games with the Cardinals yet, their night at the Garden has his heart beating a little faster. It's an iconic venue and a bunch of their fans have made the trip, cheering for them when they hit the ice.

Louie gives himself a moment to look around. Take it in.

With a whoop, Ryan stops next to him, showering him with ice. "What's up, Lou?" He gives Louie's butt a tap with his hockey stick. This is starting to become a thing. "Pretty decent sheet of ice, isn't it?"

"Yeah," Louie says, "pretty decent."

The best part is that Martie Hathaway is not in this crowd. He's not even watching on TV because Bastien is playing against the Sailors tonight. Should be a good one. A mandatory watch for Dad. And Mom will watch with him, although she'll probably watch a recording of Louie's game tomorrow. Dad will glance at the highlights and send Louie his thoughts. Sometimes that just means that Louie will get a text that says: *Missed you in that game recap.*

Dad doesn't watch his AHL games. Or even just the highlights. Not the big league, not important enough, not worth his time. Louie suspects it's supposed to make him want to work even harder.

He scores twice against the Ravens. Doesn't help them win, but he scores twice. The second one is a redirect off a pass from Ryan, who barrels into him a millisecond later. Ryan's not tall enough to actually pick him up. Well, he's tall. But so is Louie. He's pretty sure Ryan kisses his helmet, though.

"Lou, Lou, Lou, we have to buy you drinks," Mikko shouts in the locker room after the game.

Which is how he ends up in a bar that's chockfull of Ravens players—Luc, who took them here, greets all of them like old friends, even though he's never played in or anywhere close to New York. At least not until he signed with the Cardinals.

Miraculously, they find a table. It's like they saved it for them. Or for Luc.

"How do you know all of them?" Louie asks him two drinks in.

"Oh, uh, when I was still ages away from getting back on the ice, I saw some specialists in New York and I went to a Ravens game because one of my former teammates was playing for them and they… took me here." Luc laughs, glancing at the Ravens captain and his alternates. "I didn't have a team back then, but for an evening, I was on their team, you know. I stayed in touch with a bunch of them."

"Oh," Louie says. "That's… that actually sounds a lot like them." He doesn't mean that in a negative way, and Luc clearly understands as much.

He smiles. Gives Louie a tap on the head. Then he leaves to hug a bunch of Ravens and is greeted like a king. Good for him.

Louie doesn't understand how he can get along that well with guys who are his competition. Obviously you look up to the really exceptional guys, the generational talents. But even on your own team, you have to keep an eye on who's around you and who may overtake you. Louie just moved onto the second line and it worked for them tonight, and he wants to stay where he is. That just means he has to work for it, at least as long as Petrov is out of the picture.

When Luc is gone, Ryan slides into the empty seat next to Louie. "Dude, you speak French," Ryan says. "Right? That was French just now?"

Louie narrows his eyes at him. "My mom's from Montreal."

Ryan shrugs. That shrug is tipsy. "You don't have an accent like

Lucky."

"Not everyone has an accent," Louie says. He can't help but laugh. "My name is literally Louie."

"Anyone can be named Louie. And your last name is Hathaway," Ryan says and really sounds it out and it actually sounds weirdly nice.

Because Louie is also a little tipsy and suddenly thinks it matters how someone pronounces his last name. He shakes his head when he realizes that he kept staring at Ryan's lips even when he was done talking. "Seriously, how did you not know this?"

"I thought your folks were from Boston." Ryan giggles and pats Louie's upper arm. "I'm so sorry, I'm a terrible friend." He sticks out his bottom lip and pulls out the most serious puppy dog eyes Louie has ever seen.

"It's fine," Louie says. His folks are from Boston, he is from Boston. It's where he grew up.

Ryan gives him a nudge. "Say something in French."

Louie rolls his eyes. "I just said several things in French."

"Please?"

Louie leans as close to Ryan as he can without it being weird and says, "Non."

Ryan just stares at him for a moment, his mouth hanging open the tiniest bit, then he starts giggling again. "Wow."

"It was French," Louie says and picks up his drink. "You're welcome."

"Well," Ryan knocks his drink against Louie's, "I actually took French in high school, so. Listen, listen… Quel est ton numbéro de téléphone?"

"It's numéro," Louie says gently.

"Close enough." Ryan grins. "Enough to get hot guys' phone numbers at—" His grin grows wider "—the Côte d'Azur."

Louie snorts. "Uh-huh."

"So many phone numbers, Louie," Ryan says. "It was raining numéros de téléphone, I'm telling you."

"Good for you," Louie says. He means that. It can be tough for guys like Ryan. Not just gay guys, but gay hockey players who are essentially stuck in the closet. Unless they want to be the very first NHL player to come out.

Luc passes their table and sets down a drink in front of Louie. "From the Ravens. I made sure they didn't poison it."

"Hm," Louie says, although he'll trust Luc on that. He didn't actually want another drink. He barely ever drinks. Only sometimes during the season, and a little more often in the summer. When Dominic invites him over and makes Long Island Iced Tea. He's never invited Bastien along—those two hang out on other occasions. Probably. Louie wouldn't know.

Three-drink-Louie is one hundred percent ready to go home. Nick and Liam are sitting with him now—Ryan went to the bathroom and afterwards disappeared into a gaggle of Ravens—and they're talking about how well the game went for their line today, all things considered. The Cards didn't win, but those two want to keep Louie.

They're not the ones who decide, but Nick at the very least has some pull and if he tells Coach he likes Louie on his wing, then Louie has more of a chance of keeping that spot. It makes Louie all light inside, although he doesn't have much to contribute to the conversation because his thoughts are too blurry.

So he wants to go home.

He finds Ryan, tugs him aside. Because when Ryan got traded here, he decided that they had to be best friends or whatever, and now he has to deal with the consequences of his actions. "I want to go home," Louie tells Ryan.

"Okay," Ryan says. "I'll take you back to the hotel."

"The Ravens got me a very strong drink," Louie says once they're out on the sidewalk. "I think they did that on purpose."

"They didn't," Ryan says and pulls at Louie's jacket. "We're turning right."

"Okay, but what if they did?"

"We already played against them," Ryan says, "and we're not playing tomorrow."

They're not even practicing tomorrow. Big thanks to the people who make the schedule. Louie really needs to sleep. Right now. He sways against Ryan, who catches him like a pro. "You should be a goalie."

"No, thanks," Ryan says. "My precious little heart couldn't take the mean chants. I'd legit cry. The first time they wrote mean things about me in Toronto, I actually did cry."

"Nooo," Louie says.

"Yeah, I totally did."

"No, I mean... that's... so mean." Louie frowns. "There are two *means*."

"Yeah, there are two of a lot of words," Ryan says. "Because the English language is fucked."

Ryan stops to flag down a cab, which he manages instantly. A wizard. He gives the driver the address for their hotel, which Louie didn't even know. He always knows. What's wrong with him today?

"I don't get drunk," he tells Ryan.

"Well," Ryan says.

"I don't," Louie insists. Then he falls asleep in the cab and Ryan pinches his nose to wake him up again, which was totally uncalled for.

They have a late curfew because they're not practicing in the morning, although they probably got back early compared to the other guys. Louie has lost all sense of time. It may as well be four in the morning.

Ryan takes him to his room, unlocks the door for him and ushers him inside.

"I'm not helping you take your clothes off," Ryan says. "Maybe your shoes. But that's it."

"Why, are you into feet?" Louie asks and promptly trips over his own feet. He lands on his bed.

"Jesus," Ryan says. "You should get drunk more often. You're actually fun."

"I'm not." Louie starts unbuttoning his dress shirt. "Can you get me a shirt?"

"Sure." Ryan pulls a shirt from Louie's bag and chucks it at him. "Need your, uh, beautiful polar bear pj pants?"

Louie shakes his head. "Don't make fun of those. They're cozy."

"But you don't want them? Even though they're cozy?"

"Go away," Louie says.

Ryan laughs. "So, you're good?"

"Ugh." Of course Louie is good. He's always good. "I'm always good."

"Maybe that's your problem," Ryan says. "Gotta let loose more often."

"I don't do that."

"Yeah, we've established that." Ryan looms over him, hair sticking up around his head and lit up like a halo. "Why not?"

"Because I have somewhere to get to and I'm not there yet," Louie says, the words coming out a little garbled and sloppy. "You're already there, you don't get it."

"You mean, like, an NHL team."

"What else could I possibly mean?"

"Louie," Ryan says. He huffs as Louie struggles to get his dress shirt off. "I'll help with this one thing and that's it. I don't want you going around saying your gay teammate hit on you."

Louie glares at him. "I'd never do that."

In the most satisfying way, that wipes the smile right off Ryan's face. "Okay. I'm sorry, I... I know some people are very cool with this, Carrot was, but I'm not expecting it and—"

"Just help," Louie snaps and waves his sleeve at Ryan, who undoes one button and there it goes. He pulls on the old t-shirt Ryan grabbed from his bag and pulls it on, then he wiggles out of his pants, snatching his phone before Ryan can take them away.

He's too drunk to even unlock his phone, but he manages on the third try—he still has a passcode because only he knows the passcode and his face is just… right there. He pulls up the scores from this evening and—he groans.

"What?" Ryan asks. "Don't throw up."

"I'm not throwing up," Louie grumbles.

"Then *what?*"

"I scored two goals," Louie says. "Two."

"And they were great."

"Yeah, well, Bastien scored his second career hat trick in Seattle tonight."

Ryan sits down on the bed and takes Louie's phone. "Hey, but the Sailors still won." He narrows his eyes at Louie. "Do you compare everything you do to your brother or—oh, shit, you do." He locks Louie's phone. "Don't."

"If I don't check, my dad will let the family group chat know tomorrow."

Ryan blinks at him.

"My dad cares a lot about that kind of thing," Louie says. "But Bastien just does more things, you know? He does *all* the things. And he does them better than me. That's what Dad cares about. That Bastien is doing all those amazing things. I wish he could stop being sooo amazing for just one second and give me a chance. Look at me, I can't even stay on an NHL roster."

He shouldn't have said that. None of that. Now he actually is going to throw up.

"Lou," Ryan says softly, "that's fucked up."

"No, I mean, he just wants me to work harder," Louie says. "And he's right. I'm not living up to my potential. I'm not—"

"You scored two goals tonight," Ryan says and starts pulling at the sheets. "Get in bed."

Louie obeys. It didn't sound like there was any room for an argument.

His thoughts are too messy to argue anyway.

"You did well," Ryan says. "Fuck your dad."

"You can't say that," Louie whispers.

"No, *you* can't say that." Ryan pulls up the sheets all the way. "I can."

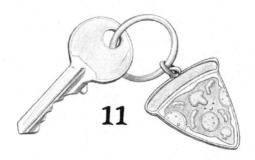

11

Louie is kind of fucked up. Ryan won't judge because everyone is kind of fucked up in their very own unique and beautiful way. He's sure people look at him and think, *Wow, Ryan Harris is kind of fucked up.*

And they're correct.

Ryan is mostly just a ball of anxiety.

Louie, on the other hand, is a ball of family issues. Not even just your regular run-of-the-mill daddy issues. It's a special kind. Sucks for him, truly.

Since Ryan is incapable of minding his business, he physically traps Louie and his nightly glass of water in the kitchen when they're back home from their road trip. Okay, he's not actually trapped. The kitchen has two doors, one to the hallway and one to the dining area that's sort of muddled in with the living room.

He could escape if he wanted to and he's choosing not to. He's standing in the middle of the kitchen with his glass of water, vaguely amused, staring at Ryan, who's leaning in the door to the hallway with one of his legs up so Louie can't get past him without kicking his leg.

"Wanna come home with me tomorrow?" Ryan asks.

"Huh?" Louie says.

"Tomorrow? When we have the day off?" Ryan won't put it past himself that he got their schedule wrong. Maybe they actually have an early as fuck practice that Ryan is in no way mentally prepared for. No. Liam definitely said he was hanging out with the kids all day so his wife could have some time to herself. No hockey tomorrow. So Ryan can safely bug Louie. "Do you want to come with me? To beautiful Pennsylvania?"

"Oh, uh... I don't know. I wanted to sleep in." Louie frowns at him. "Are you sure you want me there?"

"Why wouldn't I want you there? Let's do something fun, come on."

"Sure, but..." Louie shrugs. "Sure."

Ryan stares at him for a moment, wondering if he should ask, and just how deeply he'll offend Louie if he takes this the wrong way. "What do you do on your days off in Springfield?" is what he settles on. That's a normal question.

"I don't know. Depends."

"Do you..." Ryan clears his throat and stands up straight because his leg is starting to hurt. "Do you hang out with the guys?"

"Not that much, no."

"Why not?"

"I didn't realize I was supposed to," Louie says. He sets his water glass down on the counter, like he's tired of holding it. Or like he needs both hands to slap Ryan for being such a nosy shit.

Unfortunately, Ryan can't stop himself. "Do you have friends?" he asks. It's so fucking rude. Fuck. Why is he like this?

"Of course I have friends."

"Name one friend." Yes, of course he has to keep going now that he has started digging this hole.

"Liam is my friend," Louie says with a shrug. He's being weirdly chill about this line of questioning. Ryan would have slapped himself by now. Except maybe Louie knows that Ryan has seen right through him.

"Liam. Liam Hellström," Ryan says. "Really. He's your friend."

Louie sticks out his chin. Someone else is digging a hole in this kitchen.

They're in a hole-off.

Jesus, that sounded *so* wrong.

It is a competition. Louie loves a competition. "Yeah," he says.

"What's Lee's favorite color?" Ryan asks, taking a step closer.

Louie attempts to stare him down for a few seconds, then he rolls his eyes. "This is stupid."

"Yeah, it really is," Ryan says. "So. Tomorrow. Are you coming with me?"

Louie sighs. "Fine."

Ryan has never driven home from Connecticut, so he nearly gets them lost. Twice. But they make it and that's what matters.

Louie is an astoundingly pleasant passenger. He doesn't complain about the music, and doesn't complain when Ryan stops at a gas station to buy another coffee. He doesn't even complain when Ryan nearly gets them lost (twice). The way he just gets into Ryan's car without ever asking about what happened in Toronto makes Ryan feel some kind of way.

He has yet to figure out what kind of way.

They don't talk a lot and Ryan is usually very uncomfortable sitting in silence, but today it doesn't seem so bad. Louie occasionally comments on a car, or a driver, or something he spots at the side of the road—he enthusiastically alerts Ryan to the horses that are grazing on a field that belongs to the Johnson farm. Ryan's sisters used to be obsessed with those horses.

Almost home.

Ryan takes a left once they've passed the farm. He ticks off the sights one by one: the high school, the stretch of Main Street that still has stores left, the post office and—"Here we are."

"This is where your parents live?" Louie asks, clearly skeptical.

He should be.

Ryan just parked his car outside the fire station. "We're saying hi to a friend first."

"A friend," Louie says, "who works here?"

"Don't sound so surprised," Ryan says and climbs out of the car. "I have *very* cool friends."

"I've never been to a fire station," Louie says.

"Oh my God," Ryan says and nudges him toward the wide open door. "Do you want to sit in the truck? They'll let you."

"He would know, he wanted to sit in *every* truck last summer," someone says.

"AMI!" Ryan shouts and sweeps her into a hug.

In the depths of the firehouse, someone hollers. "Oooooh, is that Ami's hockey boyfriend?"

"Hey, hey, hockey boyfriend!"

Ryan ducks behind a fire truck because when hot men who save lives and put out fires and pull people out of car wrecks pay attention to him, he starts to sweat and blush and he'd rather not, honestly. The attention kills him. It's too much. They're too hot.

Ami laughs at him because she knows exactly how he feels about the buff men in uniforms. "You're ridiculous."

"I'm trying to be straight here," Ryan says, rolling his eyes. He does not look very straight when he's sweating about hot firefighters.

Ami flicks at his temple and lands a devastating hit before Ryan can duck out of the way. "So, are you going to introduce me to your friend?"

"You know him," Ryan says and turns around to grab Louie by his jacket sleeve and pull him forward. "If anything, I need to tell him who you are."

"Just be a polite little boy like your mom taught you," Ami says.

Ryan sighs. "Ami, this is my friend and roommate and teammate Louie Hathaway. Louie, this is my sun and stars, Ami Kuroda."

Ami lived one street over from Ryan when they were kids. They were backyard buddies essentially. When they were little, long before hockey, they always played together. She let Ryan use her Barbies and he let her borrow his dinosaurs. Sometimes the Barbies opened their very own Jurassic Park, and sometimes they got eaten by the T-Rex.

She was Ryan's very first kiss during a game of spin the bottle in middle school. She was the first person he told that he wasn't really feeling it. She wasn't exactly surprised. She still went to his junior prom with him, even though they didn't go to the same school anymore at that point.

They kind of lost track of each other for a little bit while Ami was dating Brody—the guy who convinced her that sometimes men are evil, actually. After they'd broken up, Ami came to one of Ryan's games and then they were back to texting all the time. Although Ryan has been neglecting their friendship a tiny bit ever since he got traded.

Ami is wise. Much wiser than Ryan will ever be. She told him to break up with Kaden when he stood Ryan up the first time.

He should have listened.

Anyway, he couldn't come home without seeing her. She *is* home, in a way. And Ryan likes firetrucks, okay? Who doesn't fucking love a firetruck? (Except some of them aren't trucks but engines, as Ami has very helpfully taught him.)

Louie shakes Ami's hand and says, "Nice to meet you."

"She pretends to be my girlfriend in the summer," Ryan adds, just in case Louie didn't understand the *my sun and stars* part.

"Voluntarily?" Louie asks.

Ami cackles. "I like him. He can sit in whichever vehicle he wants. Hell, I'll turn on the lights for him."

Ryan gasps. "You'll turn on the lights for him? But not for me? I'm breaking up with you."

"Oh no, whatever am I going to do?" Ami rolls her eyes. "Come on, you guys have to come meet Derek. He's from Danbury and he loves the Cardinals. I didn't tell him you were coming and I can't wait to see his face."

It's an unfairly handsome face.

Ryan is such a sucker for a handsome face, although Derek from Danbury has a girlfriend (who is from here and worships the Foxes), so Ryan will not be making out with him in Ami's backyard during the summer. Unfortunate. He has made out with Firefighter Alvarez behind a shed and Firefighter Alvarez promised he wouldn't tell anyone. Alvarez is Ami's work husband, so he knows that Ryan and Ami are not actually a thing.

Thankfully, Firefighter Alvarez isn't here. He has studied the art of turning Ryan into a puddle with one look.

Handsome Derek shares the cookies his girlfriend made for the station with them and when Louie, who is pretty quiet the entire time, takes a second one, Ryan feels like he did something right when he asked him to come along today.

Derek also gives them plastic firefighter hats to put on when they take a picture in front of the engine and the ladder truck. Handsome Derek turns the lights on for them and Louie gets to sit behind the wheel and Ryan snaps a bunch of pictures for him. When they leave to head to the Harris house, he has a huge smile on his face.

"Louie, it was so great to meet you," Ami says. "Can I borrow Ryan for just one second before you head out?"

"Of course," Louie says. "Thank you for…" He points at the engine. "Thank you."

Ryan hands him his car keys, then he turns to Ami. "Why do I have a feeling that you're about to use my full name and tell me off for something?"

Ami takes his hand. "Ryan Atticus Harris," she says and smiles, "I'm so sorry, but I met someone."

"What?" Ryan asks and gives her a shove. "Who is she? Why are you telling me this *now*, when I'm about to *leave*?"

"Because I've only known her for three weeks and it isn't anything yet, but I want you to be prepared…"

"Prepared for—oh." Ryan gets it now. This isn't just his friend telling

79

him about her crush. "You're breaking up with me."

Ami makes a face. "We can still be friends."

"Ugh, *fine*." Ryan pulls her into a quick hug. "Guess I'll be single and ready to mingle this summer. I'll always have Firefighter Alvarez."

Ami bites her lip.

"Oh, hell. He's got a boyfriend now, too?"

"I'm sorry, babe," Ami says and gives Ryan's arm a gentle squeeze. "Promise we'll still hang out?"

"Obviously, you'll have to introduce me to your girl."

"What if it's a guy?"

Ryan narrows his eyes at her. After Brody, she said she was never dating a man again. She could have changed her mind because sometimes love just does its thing, but that's something she definitely would have had a crisis in Ryan's texts about. "Is it?"

"No, I'm just fucking with you," Ami says. She nods at Ryan's car. "What about your, uh—"

"My teammate, Ami," Ryan says, seeing right through where she is going with this. "My very straight teammate."

"Is he?" Ami asks.

"Yeah?"

"Okay," Ami says and gives him another hug. "Don't be a stranger. Text me. Invite me to a hockey game."

"I keep inviting you," Ryan complains.

"Well, invite me when I don't have to work." She winks at him. "All right. I have to get back in there. Thanks for dropping by and showing me you're still alive."

"Can't come home without seeing my sun and stars," Ryan says. He's about to turn away, then—"Wait, you think Louie isn't straight?"

Ami shrugs. "None of my business. Probably none of yours either."

She is one hundred percent correct about that, but Ryan will still quietly make it his business until he knows for sure. Because Ami knows these things. She knew Ryan was gay before Ryan did.

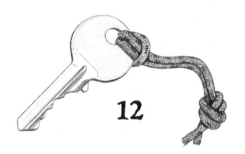

12

Ryan gets into the car with a deep sigh. "My fake girlfriend broke up with me."

"Oh," Louie says. "I'm sorry?"

"It's fine," Ryan says. "Although I kind of need people to stop breaking up with me."

Louie glances at him. He's kind of curious. He isn't usually. When his Springfield roommates talk about their girl drama, Louie zones out every time. But if Ryan was dating someone, it must have been a guy. He can't help but wonder how that works in hockey when you're in a closet that's inside of a closet.

"Anyway," Ryan goes on when Louie takes too long to say something, "I never asked. Do you have a girlfriend?"

"No," Louie says. "There was this girl last season, but..." But things fizzled out before they'd really started. Louie was out of town too much, he didn't make enough time to text her or call her, and he spent too much time at the rink when he was actually in town.

"But?" Ryan prompts. He could have just let that one go and didn't. Louie is so going to hold that against him.

Immediately.

He'll have his revenge immediately. "So, who else broke up with you?"

Ryan doesn't seem to have any issues sharing his relationship drama. "Ugh, fucking Kaden."

"What did fucking Kaden do?" Louie asks as Ryan pulls out of the fire station's parking lot.

"He broke up with me over text and when I went to his place to demand a break-up in person, my car decided that it'd rather be in a ditch."

"Oh," Louie says. "*Oh.*" So that's the story.

"What did the girl last season do?" Ryan asks.

"That was totally my fault," Louie says absentmindedly. Ryan is taking him down a small stretch of road with shops on either side and Louie eyes them with curiosity. He doesn't go to small towns a lot. It's kind of charming. Which is such a city person thing of him to think. Every teenager in this town is probably waiting to get out of here. "What was it like growing up here?"

"It was okay," Ryan says. "Lots of underage drinking. I didn't spend a lot of time here anymore when I started to get serious about hockey. I got a scholarship for a private school about fifteen minutes from here and I didn't live there but... eh, I kind of did." He glances at Louie. "You're a city kid all the way, aren't you? Have you ever seen a cow in real life?"

Louie... has not. "I know what a cow looks like."

"Uh-huh." Ryan cackles. "Hey, my parents are friends with a farmer at the edge of town. She has cows. You wanna stop there before we go home?"

Louie does not dignify that with a response.

"Oh," Ryan says when he pulls into a long gravel driveway. "I forgot... you don't like dogs, right?"

"I'm fine with dogs," Louie says. He's not a huge fan, but he'll live.

"What about cats?" Ryan asks. "Because there are cats."

There most certainly are cats. The house Ryan has pulled up to is a huge light blue Victorian with a wraparound porch. On the railing, two white-and-orange cats are watching them approach. "I like cats," Louie says and follows Ryan up to the house.

"Good," Ryan says. "My parents have a serious cat issue."

"As in… they have too—"

"Ryan, my love!" A tall woman with Ryan's nose has opened the front door. The two railing cats seize the opportunity and disappear into the house. "And you must be Louie! It's so lovely to meet you!"

"Thank you for having me," Louie says. He still feels like he's barging in on family time, although Ryan didn't seem to be lying when he said he really wanted Louie to come.

At least in part, Ryan must have invited him out of pity. Because Louis's family is— well.

He said too much when they were in New York. He said things he shouldn't have said. About his dad, and about Bastien. To Ryan's credit, he didn't mention it again. If Louie wasn't hellbent on never bringing his family up again, he'd thank Ryan for it.

"Of course," Ryan's mom says. "I'm Monica. It's so nice to meet you. Ryan's dad will be back soon, he's just finishing some things in the garage. Come on in. I hope you boys aren't starving."

"We had cookies at the fire station," Ryan says.

"Did you go see Ami?" Monica beams. "Good. I ran into her at the store the other day and she said you invited her to Hartford."

"Duh," Ryan says. "She had to work, though."

"She works so hard," Monica says. She squeezes Ryan's arm. "All of you kids work so hard."

Ryan takes his shoes off by the door, so Louie does the same. He's been taking them off at Ryan's place as well because Ryan always does. They have a huge pile of shoes by the door; Ryan owns way too many sneakers.

"Louie, do you want anything to drink? I made the raspberry lemonade Ryan likes, but aside from me, he's the only who likes it."

"That's because the girls don't have taste," Ryan says.

"I'll try it," Louie says because Ryan does know his way around food. He can only make grilled cheese, but whenever he orders food for them, he manages to pick something out-of-this-world delicious.

"Go have a seat. I'll be right there."

Louie follows Ryan into a spacious living room and—"Holy crap."

"Yeah," Ryan says. "It's a bit extra."

"It's amazing," Louie says. His mom would hate this house. One entire wall is just bookshelves, painted black, with the books organized by color. The couches are turquoise and the coffee table is made of wood but painted black with turquoise flowers to match. A piano across from the shelves has been decorated with the same flowers. A black cat is snoozing in a basket on top of the piano, and a calico is sitting by the window, tail swishing.

Louie stops by the piano. In black picture frames, the Harris family is beaming at him. In one of the photos, a maybe ten-year-old Ryan and four girls are dressed in green, all of them holding up candles so they look like a human Christmas tree. In another one, the entire family is making weird faces. The next one shows just the girls in overalls, all holding power tools. The tiniest one has a humongous chainsaw. Then: all the girls and their dad in tutus. Ryan, his dad, and six cats, all sitting on the stairs. The entire family in Ryan's jersey with Ryan in the middle.

They're fun photos. Not the stilted *everyone smile and look at the camera* stuff. Ryan mentioned something about his mom shooting weddings; she probably studied photography.

"I have a lot of sisters," Ryan says off-handedly. "Although I really only grew up with Ivy." He points at one of the girls, maybe two or three years older than him. "The twins were twelve when I was born. And my oldest sister was a sophomore in high school." Ryan's lips twitch. "I was, uh… an accident."

"A happy little accident," Monica says, marching into the room with a tray and three glasses of lemonade. She's put straws and actual raspberries in their drinks. "Here you go."

"Thank you," Louie says. "I love your piano."

"Oh, yeah, it's really something," Monica says. "Frankie will turn everything into a work of art. The piano, the kitchen cabinets, the basement door…" She laughs. "Frankie is Ryan's dad," she adds when Louie looks confused.

"Your dad?" Louie asks, eyes on Ryan.

"Yeah, selling painted furniture to rich New Yorkers is kind of his thing," Ryan says. "Well, I guess he's really branched out. Where did he ship that huge chest with the water lilies? Paris?"

"London," Monica says. "Yeah, he'll get an order from Europe every so often. But he's painting a shelf he wants to give to the kindergarten right now, and he's not taking any orders until he's done with it."

"I told you," Ryan says to Louie, "they're all really artsy. Be careful, Mom may whip out her camera."

Monica smiles. "You do have a very photogenic face, Louie," she says. "But I won't bug you. I took the day off." She nods at the piano. "Do you play?"

"Not well," Louie says.

Ryan shakes his head. "You play the piano? We have a piano at our house."

"You can't really call it *playing*," Louie says. He used to take lessons, but at some point, his dad sat him down and told him it was time to get serious about hockey and to forget about piano because piano wasn't going to make him any money. He still played every now and then, mostly when his dad wasn't home, and his mom was the only one who was listening, but he hasn't had access to a piano in a while.

He's thought about sitting down to play, but he didn't want to annoy Ryan.

"Huh," Ryan says and takes a lemonade. "Mom. Delicious. Thank you, for real."

"I made extra for you to take home," Monica says.

Louie sits down and takes a sip of his. He was never particularly passionate about lemonade, but he is now. It's sour and it's sweet and there's just enough raspberry coming through.

"So, Louie," Monica says, "tell me about yourself. Where are you from? Sounds a little like Boston."

It's funny that Louie is happy because for once someone doesn't already know everything about him. Or his family. "Yeah, I grew up in Boston."

"His mom's from Montreal, though," Ryan whispers. "He speaks *French*."

Monica smiles. "Maybe he can teach you some. Do you remember any of your high school German?"

"Nein, not really," Ryan says with a grin. "You'll just have to deal with your non-artsy son."

Monica's smile only gets brighter, then she turns back to Louie. "When Ryan started playing hockey, it was a whole new world for us. I've learned so many things."

"Although off-sides took a while," Ryan says.

"Only a season or so," Monica says with a laugh. "We do know what's going on now, though."

"Uh-huh," Ryan says. "You texted me *good game* when I caused the worst turnover in the history of turnovers."

"I am your mom. I think all your games are good." Monica tuts at him. "That's literally my job. Someone else can worry about your turnovers."

Louie would pay actual money for his dad to care less about turnovers. Or whatever else Louie did wrong. He would take a *good game*, even if it was a shit game.

A cat hops onto the couch next to Louie. Not one of the ones they saw outside but a huge gray tabby that climbs into Louie's lap.

"Chicken," Ryan and his mom say at the same time. "That's Ryan's cat Chicken," Monica adds. "He found him when he was... how old were you? Seventeen?"

"Yeah, something like that," Ryan says. "He followed me home. And we did try to figure out if he belonged to someone, we didn't steal him. Just to be clear."

Well, maybe Louie is going to steal him. He's purring like a lawnmower in his lap and he sticks up his chin when Louie scratches him. Louie wouldn't mind having him sit on the couch with them, watching their division rivals' games.

"I thought about bringing him to Toronto," Ryan says, like he was reading Louie's mind, "but I think he'd be sad without the others, and this place is—"

The front door opens and a tall man—is everyone in this family really tall?—in paint-splattered overalls comes striding into the living room. He has great hair. Kind of like Ryan, who will probably never go bald.

"Sorry for making you wait," Ryan's dad, presumably, says. "Hi, you must be Louie. I'm Frankie. So nice to meet you. Give me five minutes to put on clothes that aren't covered in paint, all right?"

"I'll get the food ready," Monica says, nodding at Louie and Ryan. "You boys look like you're great at carrying plates."

And there are so many plates. And bowls. Ryan's mom has made two charcuterie boards—one with meats and one with cheeses, she's made a chicken salad, a tortellini salad, a fruit salad, and tiny BLT sandwiches. There are bowls with dips, with olives, with tomatoes, and stuffed mushrooms. She also made sourdough. She bought a baguette.

Ryan laughs at the dining room table that is covered in colorful bowls and plates and trays. "Mom," he says, "this is so much."

"So?" Monica says, surveying the scene. "Isn't this great? I can't wait to eat all of this."

Honestly, Louie has never in his life been this excited for lunch. He wants to try everything.

"Oh, I forgot the focaccia I got at the bakery," Monica says and once again disappears into the kitchen. "I also have pickles. Do you boys want pickles? They're the good ones from the farmers market."

"Sure, I'll have a pickle," Ryan shouts.

Louie feels like he's fallen into an alternate universe. He obviously spent time at his friends' houses when he was younger and he's sure they were exactly like this. Normal. But during the past few years, he's really only been around his own family. At their house in Boston. With its minimalist furniture and its white-and-gray color palette. Can you even call that a *color* palette?

His mom would never serve lunch like this. She hates charcuterie boards. She says that's not a meal. But when most of the bowls and plates are empty less than an hour later, Louie is so full that he's scared he'll explode.

No one really expected him to say anything. Monica and Frankie updated them on all of Ryan's sisters, although Louie can barely keep track of the names. Ryan's mom is photographing a wedding on Saturday—"It's a barn wedding. But a fancy barn. They bought flowers for five thousand dollars if you can believe it."

Ryan's dad has started painting book edges and his Instagram followers are all over them—"I have more followers than Ryan," he tells Louie proudly.

"Well, you actually post cool stuff that people want to look at," Ryan says as he dunks a piece of sourdough bread into his mom's homemade tzatziki. "Did you make a gallon of this like always? Because I want to take some."

Louie also wants to take some. Actually, he wants to stay here. He wants to stay here and not talk about hockey.

Frankie does ask how the hockey is going because he and Monica couldn't come to the game in Philadelphia, but there's no analysis of plays. No one is grabbing their phone to look at anyone's stats. No one is telling Ryan that he has to work on anything. They do go through their entire schedule, but only because they're trying to figure out when Monica and Frankie will come to Hartford to watch a game again. They talk about which day is most convenient, not which game is the most exciting one to watch.

After lunch, Ryan's dad cleans up and loads the dishwasher, then he takes them to his garage to show them what he's working on. Louie will have to look up how expensive that furniture is—he's not the least bit surprised that rich Manhattaners are all over this stuff. Ryan takes Louie upstairs later to show him the hockey dresser in his room. It's small, under the roof, but it has a big, round window just above the bed. A hockey stick that has been too small for Ryan for at least a decade is leaning against the wall by the door.

This is where Ryan spends his summers. Or part of his summers. In this bed, with a mom who makes sourdough bread, and a dad who loads the dishwasher, and at least half a dozen cats. Probably more. Louie isn't sure if the black cat on the stairs was the same one he saw in the living room earlier.

They have cake in the afternoon and then they get back into Ryan's car, a basket full of leftovers in the trunk.

And Louie doesn't know what to say. He should say thank you.

He can't. He's afraid that it would split him right in half.

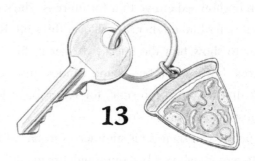

13

Maybe Ryan didn't actually do Louie a favor when he took him home.

He's been—he doesn't talk.

Which is definitely down to the fact that Louie isn't much of a talker in the first place, but sometimes it just seems like he's all caught up in his head. Like he gets stuck there.

Ever since New York, Ryan has been keeping track of Bastien Hathaway. Louie's mood gets worse whenever Bastien does something impressive. Unfortunately, Bastien does something impressive every other game. The league posts about him all the fucking time; there's no escape.

Ryan's kind of starting to get annoyed, even though he's never met the guy.

Even worse than Bastien, though, is Dad Hathaway.

Admittedly, Ryan was excited as hell to meet him, but that was before he found out that he failed Parenting 101 big time.

Ryan isn't new. He knows hockey parents. He grew up with guys who had the worst hockey parents. It's kind of funny, though—a lot of the guys whose parents would stand by the glass and yell at them because obviously they knew better than their coach anyway didn't even get drafted.

Dad Hathaway isn't that kind of hockey parent. He probably never stood at the glass and yelled at Louie. He watched. He yelled after, in the privacy of their home. Maybe he didn't even yell. The way he talked to Louie after that game against Minnesota made Ryan's intestines turns themselves into knots. It was the most casual *you're not working hard enough* that Ryan had ever heard. It stung like a bitch and Ryan wasn't even the one it was directed at.

The worst part is that Louie would literally kill himself working out if he thought it'd please his dad. He already kind of does.

Ryan has never worked as hard as Louie does. He wouldn't get up early to go on a run. He wouldn't stay until the very end of practice. He's never been the guy who picks up all the pucks before the Zamboni gets on the ice. Through Louie, Ryan has become one of the guys who stays late, but he would have never gotten that idea by himself.

Maybe that says something about his work ethic.

Louie is out there doing the most at all times. When Ryan suggested they order pizza from a place on Main Street tonight, Louie got pasta and a salad instead. Ryan did get the pizza and when he offered Louie a slice, he took it, but still. That guy just won't let loose, not even for a second.

"How's your pasta?" Ryan asks.

Louie holds out his plate because, yes, he got himself a plate and took the pasta out of the container. "Wanna try?"

Ryan stares at the eggplant for a moment. "Nah…"

"It's good," Louie says. "The salad is amazing."

Ryan takes another slice of pizza. He went to Italy with Ivy last summer and this is real Italian pizza. When Ryan ordered earlier, the lady on the phone told him that they had tiramisu to go today and he almost went for it. Now he's mad he didn't because if the pizza is actually Italian, the tiramisu would have been too.

"Hey, is it okay if we watch the Knights game?" Ryan asks. They're playing against the Ravens, so it's obviously going to be a good one.

Minnesota is back on the road, Chicago this time, and Ryan wants to keep Louie away from that game.

He gets that look on his face when he checks his brother's game stats. It's slightly different from the look he gets when his dad texts him. Which happens almost every day, even when they didn't have a game the night before.

"Yeah, should be a good one," Louie says.

"Brian Kelly is my hero," Ryan says softly when he turns on the game. One of these days he's going to retire and Ryan will not know what to do with himself when it happens. "I was so bummed out when the Knights didn't draft me."

"Really, you had a favorite team going into the draft?" Louie asks in this *sweet summer child* voice.

"I grew up watching them because my grandparents lived in Newark. They took me to my first ever hockey game there. Of course I wanted to play for the Knights." If someone were to grant him a wish, Ryan would ask to play with Knights captain Brian Kelly as his d-partner at least once.

"So, do you wish the Knights had traded for you?" Louie asks.

Ryan laughs. "The Knights don't go for problem children." Every player on the Knights has *stellar work ethic* and *a pleasure to have in the room* written all over him. The Knights don't take a chance on a guy that may or may not work out for them. They don't have to.

Louie spears the last lettuce leaf in his bowl, then a halved grape tomato. "Except you're not a problem child. You're a top defenseman whose personal life was more interesting than his play for about a week."

"I don't think they miss me in Toronto," Ryan says with a shrug. When a team trades a guy, they obviously don't want him anymore and have someone at the ready to replace him. It's different when one of your stars has had enough and decides to leave and try his luck elsewhere. Greener pastures and all that.

"Does it matter if they miss you?" Louie asks and starts gathering up his dishes.

"It's nice to be needed," Ryan says. It's nice to be *wanted*, but he doesn't say that out loud because it sounds pathetic.

Louie gets up and takes Ryan's empty pizza carton as well. "You are needed," he says. "Here."

He doesn't leave for the kitchen just yet because the Knights and the Ravens are having a disagreement on TV, but the refs untangle them pretty efficiently. No penalties. Ryan may have argued that there was some goalie interference before the whistle, but what does he know.

Louie huffs, like he's disappointed in the outcome as well, and shuffles away.

"Hey, Louie, can you bring me the Reese's Pieces?" Ryan shouts. The broadcast just went to commercials, but he's too lazy to get up. He's full of pizza.

Louie does toss him the bag with the Reese's Pieces when he returns. "I can't believe you put that shit in your body."

"Uh-huh, Louie, but you didn't say no to that second slice of my mom's cheesecake the other day."

"That was homemade cheesecake," Louie says, indignant. "It's not the same."

Well, he's not wrong. Ryan still rips the bag open and eats a handful.

Louie bends over the back of the couch so his head is right next to Ryan's. "You should eat more vegetables."

"There was basil on my pizza."

"That's not a vegetable."

"What the fuck is it, then?"

"It's an herb," Louie whispers and pulls back. He wanders back into the kitchen and the sound of dishes being put in the dishwasher accompanies the TV timeout.

Ryan's mom would adopt this guy who puts dishes straight in the dishwasher instantly. She texted him after Ryan and Louie had come to visit and told him to bring him back in the summer. Their house, in the summer, is more like a hostel—his parents' friends, his sisters and their friends, their boyfriends and girlfriends and many, many others who don't fit into any of those categories. Ryan's grandparents; other relatives. The occasional foster cat. In any case, it seems like Mom sensed that Louie could use some family time.

Louie's dad's version of family time is probably more like a never-ending coaching session. Ryan didn't ask if Dad Hathaway is *always* like that. He knows the answer.

Louie returns with a glass of water and grabs the fluffy knit blanket from the back of the couch, wrapping himself up like a burrito before he sits down.

Ryan talked to Petrov yesterday. He's skating and close to coming back—maybe just days away from joining them for a practice. Maybe in a no-contact jersey, but still. At that point, it's just a matter of time before he's back in the lineup and the Cardinals will have one guy too many on the roster.

Then that spot on Ryan's couch will be empty.

Then it'll be really fucking quiet.

Then he'll have to figure out how the dishwasher works because Louie always starts it.

He'll have to actually load the dishwasher.

Ryan glances at Louie, burritoed, in his corner of the couch. He starts yawning when the second intermission rolls around. He rests his head on one of the fluffy throw pillows. (So soft but terrible to sleep on because you'll wake up with fuzz in your mouth and nose.)

It takes Ryan a second to realize that he was about to say something but then couldn't figure out what, so he just stared.

He grabs his phone and pulls up Slaw's Instagram. He got a puppy last summer, chocolate lab, named it Pickle, and now he posts pictures and videos of him every day. Unless he's on the road. Then his girlfriend sends him pictures to post. Today's picture is a very good Pickle with snow on her nose.

"Look," Ryan says and shows it to Louie. "This is what I'm missing out on."

Louie makes a noise that's neither here nor there.

"Right, I forgot you don't like dogs," Ryan mutters.

"I don't—" Louie sighs. "Dogs are fine. I'm not as passionate about them as other people, but as long as it's not a wiener dog, I don't mind." He side-eyes Ryan's phone. "It's not one of those weird accounts where the owner pretends that the dog is writing the posts, right?"

Ryan snorts. "No, it's just Slaw saying how cute Pickle is over and over again."

"Good. People who are acting like their dog is a person are so weird." Louie rolls his eyes. "*Doggo* is the worst word in the English language. I don't even know if it actually is a word. Oh, and *pawrents*. And *pupper*. What the hell is wrong with those people?"

Fuck, Ryan is trying so hard not to laugh. He has nothing against people who use those words, but Louie seems to be very passionate about this and that doesn't happen a lot. Louie is so calm. He takes it all in; he watches quietly. He doesn't get pissed, doesn't throw shit, and doesn't break his stick when he gets mad.

Ryan once broke a stick during his rookie year because he essentially scored on his own goalie with his skate blade. He wasn't paying attention and should have moved out of the way. His mom called him the next day to remind him how expensive a hockey stick is and how many parents can't afford to buy their kids equipment. Ryan hasn't even thought about breaking a stick since then.

But Louie? Louie would never. And now he's sitting on the couch, red-faced, complaining about people who call themselves their dog's *pawrents*.

"You're laughing," Louie says. "But it's ridiculous. All of that..." He waves his hand at Ryan's phone. "Those videos with that annoying as shit music? Oh, and you know what I hate the most? Those guys with the kindness tests. Like, they're out there pretending that they need help and then they say, oh, actually, I don't need help, I just wanted to see if you were gonna be kind to me and then they give them a thousand bucks. Hate those guys."

"You hate the guys who give nice people money?" Ryan asks, still laughing. "Why?"

"Because if you have a thousand bucks to give away, just give it to someone?" Louie sits up and leans closer to Ryan. "Just go to Applebee's, eat some chicken fingers, drink a margarita, and give your server the tip of a lifetime. Even if they're having a bad day and aren't groveling at your feet."

"Wow," Ryan says. "Okay. Good point."

"All of that bullshit just for clicks. Annoys the hell out of me."

"It's like you and my Uncle Artie are the same person. He takes three to five business days to reply to my texts and thinks the videos on his phone are too small and refuses to watch them. Same goes for pictures."

"Can we visit him next time? I think we'd get along."

"Sure, but he has a big dog," Ryan says. "Like, absolutely humongous."

"Hm," Louie says.

"What about cooking videos? I love those, they're so soothing. Have you ever watched someone ice a cake? Or when they pipe flowers?"

"Only if they don't use annoying music," Louie says. "And if they don't have an annoying voice."

"Hey, people can't help their voice."

"Oh, uh-uh, I mean, when they do the social media voice that is extra cheerful and high-pitched," Louie says. "Makes my skin crawl."

"Guess now I know why you never update your Insta."

"I haven't looked at it in weeks."

"Ah, so that's why you haven't followed me back," Ryan says, nodding to himself. "I was starting to think you secretly hate me."

Louie stares at him. Just stares. Like this is high school biology and he's about to dissect Ryan like a frog. He sits up and says, very gently,

"Ryan, social media follows don't matter. At all." He turns away and picks up his water. "I washed your stinky socks yesterday. Do you think I would have done that if I didn't like you?"

"Um," Ryan says. When Louie is gone, he'll have to wash his own stinky socks. Sometimes he just loses a pair somewhere in the house and then Louie takes pity on him.

"Do you think I'd live with you?" Louie goes on.

"I mean, you only said yes to living with me because you didn't want to live in the same house as Santa's dog."

"Are you arguing with me right now?"

Ryan is, isn't he? He fixes his eyes back on the TV because the game is about to start up again. "No."

"Good," Louie says, sheepish. "Watch the game."

"I am, I'm watching the game." They drop the puck and the Ravens score pretty much immediately, tying up the game. Very Raven-y of them. Ryan glances at Louie, who is smiling at the Ravens being Raven-y. "It's just that—" He cuts himself off. Louie wouldn't lie to him. He's sitting on the couch with him, isn't he?

Louie shoots him a look. This time Ryan doesn't feel like a frog but like an annoying lab partner who's about to get stabbed with a dirty scalpel.

Ryan keeps his mouth shut until the game is over. It goes all the way to a shootout, with the Knights walking away with the win in the end. "Wanna switch to a West Coast game?"

Louie shakes his head and struggles to get out of his blanket. "I'm getting up early tomorrow."

"Hm," Ryan says and turns off the TV.

Louie folds his blanket and puts it back where he found it, takes his empty glass, passes by the piano, and pushes down one of the keys as he walks by, like he just can't help himself. He keeps doing that.

"You know, you can play if you want," Ryan says.

"I don't want to."

"I can leave the room if you don't want anyone to listen."

Louie laughs and shuffles into the kitchen, leaving Ryan without a reply. The glass clinks quietly when Louie puts it in the dishwasher. Ryan makes a mental note to put his own glass in the dishwasher before he goes to bed. For now, he sits on the couch and watches videos of people making the most unhinged-looking Crock-Pot recipes. They put entire blocks of cream cheese in there like it's a pinch of salt.

Ryan kind of wants to try it.

He could buy a Crock-Pot. He's an adult and adults buy Crock-Pots.

His mom has one. He could ask her for recipes, although she probably doesn't have any that use entire blocks of cream cheese. She always made this really good stew in the winter. That's what he'll make.

Before he can close the app and fully commit to becoming a Person Who Owns a Crock-Pot, a notification pops up: *louiehathaway18 has followed you.*

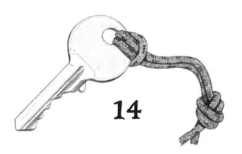

14

"You wanna go somewhere?"

Louie opens the NHL app and pulls up the standings. The Cardinals are one perfect game away from sliding back into a wild card spot. Not that it should matter to Louie. He'll be gone, back in Springfield, by the time the playoffs start. Petrov is days away from coming back. Skated with them today. No contact, but still. He was there, reminding Louie that his days with the Cardinals are numbered.

"Maybe to the mall? I want a new suit. I guess I won't buy that at the mall, though," Ryan says as he pulls out of the rink parking lot. "Liam gave me his tailor's number. His suit game is off the charts."

Louie checks on the Bears. They're not doing well. Bastien scored another goal last night, but he's not even close to catching up with the league leaders. He's still leading all rookies in points and goals, though. If he doesn't win the Calder, the world will end for Martie Hathaway.

"I haven't bought shoes in a while. I think I need new shoes."

Now is probably a good time to start thinking about ways to get out of flying to Vegas for the NHL awards. Louie could fake an illness at the last minute. Obviously, his dad will tell him to come anyway. A little touch of the flu has never hurt anyone, he'll say. Louie once missed two games because he was puking his guts out and his dad texted him that he'll never make it to the NHL if he doesn't learn to play through it.

He always played through whatever life threw at him. *He* made it to the Cup finals with a fucked-to-hell shoulder. *He* didn't go home to be with Mom when Dominic was born because he had a playoff game to play.

Dominic was badly timed, Dad always says. Louie was born in the summer, but still too early for Dad's liking. Just after the playoffs. Bastien's birthday is in early August. Perfect.

"Earth to Louie?"

"Huh?"

"Do you wanna come to the mall or nah?" Ryan asks. "I can drop you off at home."

Does he want to go shoe shopping with Ryan? Absolutely not. Does he want to sit around at home and think about packing his stuff and going back to Springfield? Sounds even worse. "Yeah, shoes, okay."

The thing that Louie expects the least is that he'll be the one to buy shoes. They're red Converse, Cardinals colors, that he eyes while Ryan tries on his third pair of Nikes.

"I just didn't *love* any of them, you know?" Ryan says when they head out of the store.

Louie does not know. He doesn't spend a lot of time thinking about shoes. Sometimes he doesn't hate shoes and he tries them on and he buys them. End of story. He had no idea that they'd come here looking for Ryan's soulmate. Solemate, even.

"But you found something, that's great," Ryan goes on. "You wanna get Froyo? Ice cream? I want ice cream."

"You can get ice cream," Louie says, a little distracted by Diane's Chocolate Manufactory. Diane has a *make your own chocolate bar* offer and it sounds… fun.

"You wanna get chocolate?" Ryan asks.

"No," Louie says, still looking at the window display. "But I want to look."

"That's no fun, but okay."

Ryan pulls his phone out of his pocket while Louie considers the salted caramel pralines and the rose chocolates and the tricolor box with tea-infused ganache, whatever that means. This is the kind of chocolate you get your girlfriend for Valentine's Day or your mom for her birthday. For some people it might be a treat yourself kind of chocolate. But it's not something you buy for yourself to eat on the couch for no reason.

"Oh, for fuck's sake," Ryan says.

Louie tears his eyes off the chocolate that's decorated like little penguins, which is probably for kids. "What's wrong?"

"Nothing." Ryan glares at his phone. Taps it once—probably an emoji response because that's his go-to. Then he locks it. "Just… it's really stupid and you don't want to hear about it."

"Let's get that ice cream," Louie says.

He's very practical about food. Healthy and nutritionist-approved is good enough for him. Ryan gives maybe half of a shit about what their team nutritionist says. He likes a little treat. He likes grilled cheese. With a lot of butter. And it's delicious and Louie enjoyed it when Ryan made one for him, but for Louie that's a cheat meal. For Ryan it's just a meal.

When Ryan asks him if he wants ice cream as well, Louie is about to say no but ends up getting dark chocolate with white chocolate curls and raspberries on top. Ryan's is pink and has M&Ms in it. Louie can't look at it. It makes him smile for some reason and he just can't condone pink ice cream.

They sit in a deserted corner of the mostly empty food court and Ryan looks at his phone again, his face clouding over like it did before. Then he puts it away and picks up his ice cream and it's like sunshine after a rainstorm.

"You wanna try?" Ryan asks and holds up the pink abomination.

"Nah," Louie says.

Ryan nods. "You're a chocolate guy."

"I guess."

"You should have bought some of those fancy chocolates."

"It seemed more like… special occasion chocolate," Louie says and carefully scoops up a raspberry with some ice cream. "I didn't need it."

"No one *needs* chocolate," Ryan says, rolling his eyes. "That's not the point of it."

Louie laughs and keeps eating his ice cream. They fall silent—Ryan only ever really gets silent when he eats. He twitches when his phone buzzes.

"Are you sure everything's okay?" Louie asks.

"Like I said, you probably don't wanna hear about it." Ryan leans forward and whispers, "It's kinda gay."

"I can deal with that," Louie says. He doesn't know why, but it bugs him that Ryan assumed he wouldn't want to hear about it. "Did you meet someone?"

Ryan laughs. "I fucking wish." He puts the ice cream down. Means business. "Remember when my car slid into a ditch in Toronto?"

"Yeah," Louie says.

"I was on the way to see the guy who'd just broken up with me over text, I told you that part, remember?" Ryan goes on. "And I wanted him to break up with me in person."

"Still seems like a fair request," Louie says. Ryan told him the guy's name, but now he can't remember.

"It is a fair request. We're not fourteen fucking years old," Ryan says. "So. The guy." He shifts in his seat. "I blocked him everywhere. I didn't wanna talk to him and I didn't want him to keep texting me."

"He kept texting you after he broke up with you?"

"Yeah. Well. He's like that. Clearly, he wanted me to never ever get over him."

"But you blocked him."

"Unfortunately, that only works on Instagram," Ryan says and pulls the spoon out of the ice cream, considering the blue M&M that is clinging to it for dear life. "He'll be in town next week."

"He's coming to see you?" Louie asks. "Or he'll be here and wants to see you?"

Ryan scratches the back of his head. "I don't know if he wants to talk to me or whatever, but seeing him will be kind of unavoidable."

Louie frowns.

With a sigh, Ryan shifts in his seat again. "He's from *Toronto*."

Louie narrows his eyes at him. Why is Ryan saying it like that? He's from Toronto. Obviously. He's from Toronto and he'll be in town next week and—"Oh."

Ryan nods.

"He's on the team," Louie says. "And you're trying not to out the guy who broke your heart. That's very decent of you."

"He didn't break my heart," Ryan grumbles.

It just kind of sounds like he did.

"He didn't," Ryan adds.

He definitely did.

That's why Louie doesn't date. Because the person you date will break up with you via text and you'll get in your car to demand an in-person break-up and you'll get into a snowstorm and wreck your car and you'll get traded to a team you don't like. Actually, Louie has no idea if Ryan likes the Cardinals or not. But he didn't want to get traded here, that's for sure.

"Anyway," Ryan goes on, "he'll be here."

"But you knew he was going to be here, right?" Louie says. "You knew this game was coming."

Ryan makes a noncommittal noise.

The schedule is pinned to their fridge. Louie put it there. Maybe Ryan doesn't have the thing memorized, but Louie also overheard Liam asking Ryan if he's nervous about Toronto coming to town and Ryan laughed and shook his head.

He wasn't in a bad mood. Something has changed.

Louie tilts his head, thinking. "He was on the farm team."

103

Ryan doesn't answer, but the face he makes tells Louie everything he needs to know.

"And he's not on the farm team anymore," Louie ventures.

"Please don't look up which moves they made today," Ryan says, voice quiet. He pokes at his ice cream. "I shouldn't have told you any of this."

"I won't tell," Louie says. "And I won't look up which moves they made today. And I also won't try to remember the guy's name."

Ryan shoots him a glance, jaw set. "Thank you," he finally says.

Louie will eventually, inevitably, find out who Ryan's ex is. He knows the AHL's rosters too well, and he remembers the people he regularly plays against when he's in Springfield. He won't tell Ryan. Won't mention it. It doesn't matter to him, although he understands why Ryan was being cagey. Because Ryan is decent and wants to do the right thing.

That doesn't mean he always does the right thing—he nearly set the house on fire yesterday when he tipped over a candle in the living room, even though Louie told him not to put it there because he'd tip it over. But Ryan tries. He tried not to tell Louie about this absolute bag of dicks.

"Either way," Louie says, "you deserved better."

Ryan snorts. "I really didn't, but thanks for saying that."

Louie narrows his eyes at him. "Why?"

"What?"

"Why don't you deserve better?"

"Because I was a shitty... whatever I was to him. I get why he broke up with me and, honestly, I kinda saw it coming. I should have broken up with him—probably a month before he decided he had enough. That's why I didn't deserve him, you know? I was so scared of not having anyone that I couldn't bring myself to break up with him."

Louie stares at him. He's never had any issues with being alone. On most days, he prefers it. He considers the things he knows about Ryan, with the big family that loves him, and the hockey career that makes it impossible to love someone without conditions. That makes it impossible for someone to love him out loud.

"Sorry"—Ryan says and scrapes together what's left of his ice cream—"too much information. It doesn't—I'll just ignore him."

Louie nods.

"I guess I shouldn't have started dating him in the first place, but…" Ryan sighs. "Too late now." He leans back in his chair; tilts his head. Then he grins. "Aw."

Louie looks over his shoulder but doesn't find anything Ryan could be awwing about. "What?"

"Chocolate," Ryan says, and touches the corner of his mouth.

Quickly, Louie grabs his napkin and wipes his mouth. "Is it gone?"

Ryan laughs, then taps the side of his chin. "It's down here now."

Louie folds the napkin and tries again. "Now?"

"I'd do it for you, but I think the homoeroticism of it all would kill us both," Ryan says off-handedly. "Try further down."

Louie, slightly exasperated, wipes his cheek and his chin. "*Now?*"

"Here," Ryan says and points at his jaw.

Louie wipes again. "Please tell me it's gone."

"Actually, you have a little more…"

"No way."

Ryan points at his forehead. "Up here."

"I do not, you absolute walnut," Louie says and chucks his dirty napkin at him, Ryan still laughing at him when they get up to throw their empty cups away.

15

Kaden is so fucking hot and Ryan resents that.

"I resent him," Ryan says to Louie in the locker room after warm-ups. Quietly because he does not want to alert Nick or Liam to his resentment. Although Nick is so in the zone that the world could end around him and he wouldn't notice.

"Can you turn the resentment into goals maybe?" Louie asks, also quietly.

"You're always thinking about work," Ryan says with a sigh. He swears, Louie only has hockey on his mind. Hockey, and his hockey brother, and his hockey dad. And how much protein is in his food.

The other day, they got smoothies after practice and a girl tried to hit on Louie. She really gave it her all. So Ryan thought about what Ami said, although it doesn't make much sense. Louie's had girlfriends— several—he's told Ryan about them in passing, like an afterthought. He doesn't seem like the kind of guy who deludes himself out of being gay. Louie just doesn't care whether or not he's in a relationship. He's married to hockey. That's his one true love.

Ryan loves hockey, but he still wants a person. He wants to be someone's person.

He's not sure if that's what he and Kaden were to each other, but in the end, they were something, and maybe Ryan would have really, properly fallen for him if they'd ever gotten past the dating stage. They just didn't see each other enough to get there and didn't end up working.

And then Kaden turned out to be the kind of guy who breaks up with people over text.

And *then* he had the audacity to be called up and come to Hartford and still be hot. He tried to talk to Ryan at the Cardinals' practice rink yesterday, but then Carrot came to steal Ryan away for a chat (and to save him from himself, probably).

Coach put Ryan in the starting lineup, which he may not have done if they weren't playing against Toronto, but this is basically him saying, *look at this guy, we like him, he's working out for us and doing good work.* Or at least that's what Ryan tells himself when he takes his spot on the blue line.

Carrot's out on the ice with him, in a white jersey, on the other side of it all. And Ryan has been here for weeks, has not even been thinking much about his former team, and has mostly settled in, but this is when it really hits him. He's left; he's not going back. They don't want him back. They don't miss him. Not the team, not the friends he made, but the organization.

"Hey, Rye," Carrot says, bumping into him after a whistle. "How about a little bet?"

Carrot loves a little bet. Carrot also once made him dress up as Tinker Bell for the team's Halloween party so he could be Peter Pan. Ryan rocked that Tinker Bell costume, though. So, obviously, Ryan says, "For sure."

"Winner gets to—" One of the refs comes over to usher them away from the net.

They'll talk terms and conditions later. Although the further they get into the game, the more worried Ryan gets. Because at the start of the third, they're down 3–5 and while they still have time to catch up, Ryan's getting nervous.

"I just had the best idea for what I'm gonna make you wear when we win," Carrot says with four minutes left on the clock. Score's 3–6. It's not looking good for Ryan.

"I hope it's something I'll look unbearably sexy in," Ryan says.

"Of course, babe," Carrot says and blows him a kiss before he skates away.

Ryan is so fucked.

"Ryan."

Oh, for the love of fuck. Kaden did not hide in the fucking tunnels to sneak up on Ryan. He did not ignore all the signs that pointed to Ryan not wanting to talk to him.

Nope, he absolutely did.

"Ryan, can I talk to you?" Kaden asks. Looking like an absolute snack in his gray suit.

Ryan wants to punch him in the face. But maybe then even the Cards would take a long hard look at him and decide that he's not worth the trouble. "No, sorry," Ryan says. He should have waited for Louie in the locker room.

Kaden takes a step closer, reaches for him, but then thankfully changes his mind. He's right in Ryan's path now, though. "Please? I get that you were mad at me when you left, but we never talked things out."

"We never—" Ryan laughs. "Kaden. Seriously?" He waits for Nick to pass them—a bunch of his friends are waiting for him a little further down the tunnel with Waldo, so he's not really paying Ryan and Kaden any mind. Still, what Ryan has to say is for Kaden's ears only. "You broke up with me. What the fuck is there to talk about?"

"I know where you crashed your car," Kaden says. "You were coming to my place."

"No, I wasn't," Ryan says, rolling his eyes.

"Don't bullshit me."

"No, I will, I will bullshit you. You have lost the right to not be...

bullshat by me."

Kaden folds his arms across his chest. "Look, this is—I feel bad."

"That's not my problem," Ryan says, maybe a little too loudly. "As far as I'm concerned—" He cuts himself off when someone steps up to them.

Louie. *Finally.*

"Let's go," Louie says to Ryan, his eyes firmly fixed on Kaden. Not in a death glare and not in a way that'd give away that he has a problem with Kaden. Not in a way that would tell Kaden that Louie knows exactly who he is.

"Can we just have another minute?" Kaden says. "We were talking."

"Sorry," Louie says, his voice betraying no emotion, "but I think I left the oven on."

"Bye, Kaden," Ryan says pointedly. They're done here.

They wordlessly head to the parking garage, Ryan fiddling with his keys. When they've made it to Ryan's car, he says, "You didn't actually leave the oven on, right?"

"Of course not," Louie scoffs. When they're in the car, he puts on his seatbelt and before Ryan has even put the key in the ignition, he adds, "You didn't look happy, so I figured you wouldn't mind being rescued."

"Didn't mind at all," Ryan says and takes them home. The highway is blessedly empty, at least. Ryan turns the volume on the radio all the way down and Louie doesn't ask any questions, just stares out the window.

Louie isn't the kind of guy who feels the need to share every single thought he's ever had with the people around him. That's probably why he hates TikTok. But the less he says, the more Ryan wonders what's going on in that head of his. Does he have thoughts? Is it just elevator music? Ryan's head is so full from the second he wakes up to the second he falls asleep that he can't imagine silence inside his head.

Back at the house, Louie shuffles right into the kitchen and gets a glass of water. Ryan follows him for a piece of chocolate from the candy drawer.

Louie tilts his head. "Wanna watch a game?"

"Don't you need to go to bed so you can get up at the ass-crack of dawn to go for a run?" Ryan asks. Louie never stays up with him after a game. Never. Which means Ryan must be visibly pathetic.

"It's going to rain," Louie says. "So?"

"Actually, I'm…" Today, Ryan just wanted to go to bed. "Wanna come hang in my room?"

Louie blinks at him, like the concept of hanging out somewhere other than the living room is completely foreign to him. Did Ryan overstep? Did he finally stumble across the Big Gay Boundary? Carrot would hang out in Ryan's room all the time. Ryan barely ever hung out in Carrot's because every inch was covered in clothes at all times. No wonder Carrot never brought home girls (or guys, although Carrot would have definitely told Ryan if he did, in fact, swing that way).

"Sure," Louie finally says. "I'll just…" He tugs off his tie.

"Same," Ryan says and makes for his room to get out of his suit.

He's just put on sweatpants and an old shirt his sister brought him from a trip to Yellowstone when Louie gently raps his knuckles against Ryan's door.

"Come in," Ryan says and sits on his bed.

Louie does come in but hovers at the end of the bed for a moment.

"Sitting on my bed will not turn you gay," Ryan says lightly.

"I wasn't—" Louie cuts himself off and puts his glass of water on Ryan's nightstand. "I didn't bring a coaster."

"That's fine," Ryan whispers.

Louie sits on the left side of Ryan's bed and leans back against the headboard. It's covered in this fancy velvety black material and Louie touches it with the tip of his pinky finger and an appreciative hum.

"Are you jealous of my fancy bed frame?" Ryan says. "Maybe I should get a different one for the guest bedroom."

"Nah, it's a perfectly fine bed," Louie says. He grabs Gustav the bear and hugs him to his chest. Then he looks at Ryan. "Sorry, did you want him?"

Ryan laughs. "It's fine, I can mope without cuddling my ginormous stuffed bear." He chews on his bottom lip, wondering if he should talk about the weather or the elephant in the room. "He probably thinks I told you about him," is what he settles on.

"But you didn't, not really," Louie says. "So you shouldn't feel guilty about it."

"I will anyway, but thanks."

Louie presses his lips together, fiddling with Gustav's ear. "I didn't like his attitude. And I didn't like the way he talked to me. *And* I didn't hear what he said to you, but I probably didn't like the way he talked to you either."

"That's a lot of things to not like," Ryan says, feeling weirdly vindicated. When he was still seeing Kaden, he very often didn't like the way he talked to other people. Carrot, for example. Carrot, who was Ryan's roommate and actually really good at minding his business. Carrot didn't exactly love Kaden, so Ryan didn't invite him over much anymore and that's how things kind of started to fizzle out. Not Carrot's fault. If Ryan had cared enough, he would have found a way to make things work.

Louie gives a halfhearted shrug. "I'm sure you'll find someone better."

See, Louie definitely means well. It's the plenty of fish in the sea kind of thing that you say when someone's sad about a break-up, but when you're a gay hockey player, the fish are not as plenty. And the sea is more like a swamp. "Hm," Ryan says.

"I know it's tougher for you than for most of the other guys," Louie says.

"No shit." Ryan scoots down the tiniest bit to get comfortable. "After all of this…" He waves his hand, which hopefully encompasses the whole ordeal sufficiently. "I kinda wonder if I should just stay single. It's working for you, right?"

"I mean…" Louie says. But that's all he says.

Ryan tries to read into the silence. It works for him, but maybe sometimes he thinks about dating? It actually doesn't work for him? He's seen right through Ryan and knows that staying single will turn him into a pathetic puddle of sadness?

"Maybe it's not ideal," Ryan says. "I don't like being alone."

Louie's lips twitch the tiniest bit.

"It's not—" It's not funny. Except maybe it's kind of funny. Ryan, who hid at his friends' houses when he was younger because home seemed too crowded and too loud. And now he can't stand an empty house. "You know, when I first started playing in the NHL, I kind of figured I'd be alone a lot, and then I wasn't. It was nice."

"I'm sorry," Louie says. He hands over Gustav. "But, Ryan?"

Ryan buries his face in the bear's fluffy stomach. "Hm?"

"You play a team sport. That means you're never actually gonna be alone."

"I know," Ryan mumbles. "But I just know I'll watch all those guys get married and have kids. Or they already are married and have kids. And I just… I at least wanna adopt a dog with someone. Or a cat. I'll even settle for a… turtle. Or a bearded dragon."

"A bearded dragon," Louie echoes. "That can't be a real thing."

"Dude, it totally is. Slaw's sister has one." Ryan grabs his phone from the nightstand and scrolls back through his pictures. Shit, he took so many selfies with Carrot. He misses that. He misses going out. He misses the bakery down the street from their apartment. He misses the Ryan he was before he got traded. Because he distinctly feels like a different Ryan and he doesn't know how to get the old one back. Anyway. He makes it to the pictures they took in Ottawa last fall. "Here. She let me hold it."

"That does not look like something you should let into your house," Louie says.

"He was really chill." Ryan pats Gustav's head. "Maybe I should get a pet."

"Not during the season," Louie says.

"Do you ever think about something that's not hockey?" Ryan asks. "I mean, I am impressed by how much you think about hockey. But... I worry."

Louie looks him straight in the eye. "Well... don't."

It's probably none of Ryan's business how Louie spends his free time. They sometimes hang out in the living room when they don't have games in the evening and then Louie will just watch tape he got from their video coach all day. And he goes on runs. He runs so much that Ryan is starting to wonder what he's running from.

"Can I ask you something?" Louie says after a moment. "It's kind of personal."

"This can't be worse than Carrot asking me what come tastes like."

"He did not," Louie says flatly.

"Sure did. Anyway, after we had that conversation, I thought a little too hard about what's in come and then I couldn't swallow for like a week."

Louie stares. His eyes are so wide. "Oh my God." Something cracks and he starts laughing, loud and bright and happy, in a way Ryan hasn't heard him laugh ever since he met him. "Was he drunk?"

"Totally sober," Ryan says, grinning. "And I did answer the question. Although, honestly, I can't believe he's never—"

"Don't say it."

"I mean, come on, a lot of guys have. Even straight guys."

"Stop," Louie says, still laughing. There are tears at the corners of his eyes. "This is the worst conversation."

Ryan nudges him. "So, what was your question?"

Louie takes a deep breath to calm himself down. "I was..." He shakes his head. "I don't know if we know each other well enough for this, but I was wondering... Dominic said he didn't figure out he was gay until he kissed a girl and noticed that it wasn't..."

"Oh," Ryan says, "I actually didn't have to kiss a girl first. Not that I didn't try. But I definitely already kind of knew at that point."

"You just knew."

"Yeah. And then I eventually, uh, interacted with a penis that wasn't mine. And I was like, yeah, that *definitely* works for me."

Louie stares at him.

"You know, a dick? A schlong? A... meat wand?"

"Don't call it meat wand."

Ryan cackles. "What's your favorite word for it, then?"

"I don't have one." Louie rolls his eyes. "I would say most people don't."

"You would be surprised."

"Huh," is Louie's contribution to that. He's still looking at Ryan, like he's not done asking questions, like there's something else he's looking for.

"What?" Ryan says.

"It's just that you don't talk about it like Dominic does," Louie says.

"Us gays actually tend to have personalities besides being gay."

"That's not what I meant," Louie says. "You know that's not—" He kicks at Ryan's shin. "Stop making me look homophobic."

"Hey, it's just us here." Ryan winks at him. But he thinks he does know what Louie meant. "I get it, though. People's journeys are different. And some aren't delighted to be gay." With a dad like Dad Hathaway, Ryan would guess that maybe Dominic was not delighted. Although it also took Ryan a while to come out to his family, not because they're homophobic, but just because Ryan is terrible at making big announcements and terrified of people looking at him differently.

Or he used to be.

He told Carrot first and when Carrot, the straightest man alive, didn't look at him differently, he figured that telling his parents wouldn't be so bad.

What really helped when he was still a teenager was having friends who understood the situation he was in. Not only did they—cough, his teammate Adrian, cough—understand, they were also willing to make out with him. Which was *very* helpful.

"Dominic would be fine if Dad wasn't…" Louie scrunches up his nose. "I don't think Dad hates gay people. He just wishes Dominic had stayed in the closet."

"Please tell me he didn't say that to your brother's face."

"No, but if I know it, Dominic knows it, too." Louie tips his head back against the headboard. "There's a reason he doesn't live in Boston." He waves his hand, shooing those thoughts away. "I was gonna make you feel better, but I don't think I'm doing that."

"No, you did," Ryan says. "Really distracted me for a second there."

"Good, okay," Louie says.

His eyelids are starting to flutter. Ryan should tell him to go to bed, but he wasn't kidding when he told Louie that he hates being alone.

He'll have to get used to it sooner or later.

"It's okay if you wanna go to bed," Ryan says. "I'll just hang with my bestie Tracy Chapman."

"Tracy…" Louie frowns. "Who's that?"

"'Fast Car', Louie."

"What?"

"Um. 'Talkin' Bout A Revolution?'"

"I—"

"Oh my god," Ryan says and grabs his earphones, handing one of them to Louie. "Sorry, but you can't go to bed yet."

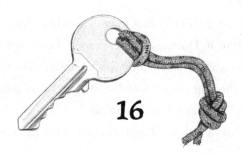

16

Something about Louie's bed is really weird.

He rolls over to see what time it is and bumps into something soft and squishy.

That's—he blinks.

Gustav.

"Ugh," Louie says and sits up, expecting to find Ryan on the other side of Gustav, but save for the stuffed bear, the bed is empty.

Morning has started to crawl into Ryan's room, but the world is only just waking up. Louie sits up, considering the comforter that is slung around him like he's the filling of a calzone.

He slides out of bed and tugs the comforter back into place.

Ryan's bathroom door is open, but the light's off, so he's not in there. The house is quiet as Louie sneaks into the hallway and checks the kitchen. Also dark, equally empty. He squints at the living room, where Ryan's phone is sitting on the end table by the couch.

Louie approaches as quietly as he can, peering over the back of the couch.

There he is.

Wrapped into the cheap blanket he got at Target, not the nice fluffy one Louie always uses. Doesn't look like he's cold, though. He's grabbed about five pillows and has made himself comfortable. Has he been here all night?

Louie doesn't remember falling asleep. Ryan made him listen to a few songs and he must have dozed off during one of them. Louie will leave Ryan be; the couch is more comfortable than some beds he's slept in, so Ryan will be okay. Once again as quietly as possible, Louie retreats, puts on his running clothes and heads out, down the street.

In the few weeks that he's lived here, he's learned the names of their immediate neighbors. Like on most mornings, Mrs. Horowitz is walking her labradoodle. Louie waves at her as he passes. Ryan told him, about two weeks after they'd moved in, that he once saw Mrs. Horowitz stop and look at Louie's butt. She probably wasn't, but Louie's also too embarrassed to turn around now and check. What if the nice 70-year-old lady *is* checking out his butt?

When he gets back to the house, the smell of something fried hangs in the air. Probably Ryan making himself a breakfast bagel. He eats so much bacon. Ryan would probably tell him that every other week is not actually "so much", but Louie eats bacon maybe once a year, so he doesn't look at it the same way.

"Hey," Ryan says when Louie comes walking into the kitchen. "Sleep well? In my bed?"

Louie was about to answer. Really. Except Ryan is cooking in a towel and nothing else. "Did you run out of clothes?"

"Listen, I could have just put my dirty underwear back on, but I didn't," Ryan says.

"I'm so proud of you."

"Hey, easy on the sarcasm," Ryan says, pointing a whisk at Louie. "Anyway, I hope you didn't need to do any laundry today."

He didn't. When he went to Springfield, he picked up all of his dirty clothes and washed them as soon as he got back, so now he has way too much underwear and socks.

He glances at Ryan and his tiny white towel. Maybe he should go out and grab some boxers for Ryan. And a shirt. Seriously, he doesn't have any shirts? How? Louie's eyes get caught on a thin silvery scar just under Ryan's collarbone that he's never noticed before. Probably because he doesn't usually look very closely at Ryan's chest.

Louie turns away and grabs the blender. He was actually going to jump in the shower. He doesn't know why he did that. He's been feeling weird since he woke up in a bed that wasn't his this morning.

"Strawberry?" Ryan asks with that hopeful tone Louie has come to know very well.

Louie was going for mango, but it doesn't really matter. "Okay," he says. He pats the top of the blender. "I'll just shower first, yeah?"

"Sure," Ryan says.

Louie gets some water from the fridge, which was what he came into the kitchen for in the first place, and leans against the counter. "You know," he says, "you could have woken me up."

"Please," Ryan says and starts scrambling the eggs he's cracked into a bowl.

Ryan won't open a Michelin star restaurant any time soon, but he knows his eggs and he knows his grilled cheese. Even though he puts so much butter on there. Louie can't even think about it.

He kind of wants one right now.

"It's fine," Ryan goes on. "Honestly."

"You didn't have to sleep on the couch," Louie says. He should just let it go. It's not like he wants to *argue* about this, but it doesn't sit right with him.

"Eh…" Ryan shrugs. "Didn't wanna, uh…"

"I get why you thought you had to," Louie says quietly. He still wishes Ryan would stop waiting for him to turn out to be some kind of douchebag. He doesn't say that out loud because he knows exactly why Ryan is waiting for him to turn out to be some kind of douchebag.

"I—" Ryan shakes his head. "Yeah. Well."

Louie has never really spent a lot of his time thinking about dicks.

He didn't expect that he'd ever start thinking about dicks.

And he doesn't know why his conversation with Ryan comes back to him while he's in the shower but—

Okay. Louie knows he isn't—

No. He almost tricked himself into thinking he's not normal, but what's normal anyway?

He's not the kind of person who'll just jump into bed with someone he's just met. He likes to go out on dates first. Actually, all the girls he ended up dating were his friends first. Dominic says Louie is demi and he's probably right about that. He let Dominic explain it to him once and it made sense, so Louie accepted it as a fact and moved on with his life. He does like to get to know people and he wants a connection. Yeah, that's him, that's fine.

But dicks? Those were never even on Louie's radar.

Should they have been? He's not sure.

He always knew exactly who he was and was comfortable with it, even when he didn't have a label like *demi* to stick on it. He didn't need to think any further than that. Maybe he should have anyway. Maybe he should have gone through the mental gymnastics.

Maybe then he wouldn't have ended up here, in a house that he's a guest in, in a shower that has revealed all its little quirks to him during the past few weeks, jerking off, thinking about dicks. The more he tries not to, the more dicks pop up in his mind.

He'd call Dominic because he knows a thing or two about this, but he can't say the words "I can't stop thinking about dicks" out loud to his brother.

He can't say them to Ryan either.

Although it's technically Ryan's fault that Louie is hurtling down this road. It's like he's in a car with a cracked windshield and a missing tire. And it's making weird noises. Brakes aren't working. Louie is well aware that he'll crash at the end of this, he just doesn't know when and how.

Ryan didn't turn him gay. It doesn't work like that. The conversation they had just unlocked something at the very back of his mind and now Louie isn't able to put it back.

He tries. Not because he doesn't want to be bi or whatever the fuck this means. It's distracting. It steers his thoughts into directions they shouldn't be going. What he really needs to focus on is his game. Petrov is so close to coming back and when it happens, Louie will be going back to Springfield. The best he can do is leave a good impression.

He stays late at practice. He books extra ice time at a local rink that's not too far from here. It's the one Ida's team plays at. Nick helps him out and gives him the manager's number.

"You need to take a break," Ryan says when Louie comes back after a two-hour session at the rink. "At some point. You just need to… chill."

"Chill," Louie repeats.

"Yeah. You know… sleep in, sit on the couch all day, eat food that is bad for you."

"What if I don't want to do any of that?"

Ryan's eyebrows shoot up. Calling bullshit.

Louie sits on the piano chair. "Listen," he says because sometimes he feels like Ryan doesn't. "I'm not you."

"I… yeah. Obviously."

"No, clearly it's not obvious to you," Louie says, waving his hands at Ryan, who is subscribing to the whole couch-and-junk-food philosophy today. He's got a beer open on the coffee table next to an empty burger box and a handful of leftover fries that have probably gone cold. "You're good at hockey."

Ryan's frown only deepens. "So are you."

"Maybe I am, but which one of us is playing on an NHL team?"

"Both of us are?"

"Are you being like this on purpose?" Louie snaps. "I'll be back in Springfield in less than a week."

Ryan sits up, fully committing to this conversation now. "You don't know that."

"I do. I know that." Louie shakes his head. "Petrov is coming back. When he does, I go. That's how it works. Ever heard of cap space? They can't keep me, not even if they want to."

"Well, yeah, but… you've been playing really well. I'd bet you'll be back in no time if there are any other injuries."

"That's just it, isn't it? If," Louie echoes.

"Someone's always injured," Ryan says. "Come on. You're not a bad hockey player just because you're—"

"Clearly, I'm not good enough."

"You're just saying that because that's what your dad has been spoon-feeding you all your life," Ryan says.

He's right.

That doesn't make it okay.

"Don't," Louie says. Something in his chest feels weird. Too tight. Too hot.

"Why not?" Ryan asks. "You are good enough. You've been showing us that you're good enough for weeks."

Louie stares at the floor. He doesn't want to hear any of that. "You don't have to say all that crap to—why are you even saying all that?"

"Because it's true."

"It's not, though. I'll go back to Springfield and when the new season starts, I'll work my ass off, like every year, and someone will pull me aside and tell me that they saw that I want it but that I'm just not ready yet. They'll call me up a few times and that'll be it."

"You really believe that," Ryan says.

Louie looks up and regrets it a second later because Ryan is looking at him with so much pity that it makes Louie want to throw up. "Just stop," he says. "I—I'm gonna go to bed."

"Lou."

"What?"

"It's, like, seven. Come on. I'll give you my leftover fries."

"I don't want your leftover fries," Louie says. As soon as it's out of his mouth, he realizes it was too loud and too harsh, but the tight, hot something in his chest is about to explode.

"Fine, go to bed," Ryan says and he says it kindly and that makes it worse. "I just think someone should remind you that you're not trash. Because you aren't."

"Why do you even care?"

"Uh, because I'm your friend and caring is kind of part of the whole friend deal."

"Well, stop," Louie says and stands up. "Just fucking stop. I didn't ask you to care."

If Ryan says anything else, Louie doesn't hear it. He stomps down the hall and locks himself in his room. He doesn't slam the door. Not his house, not his door to slam.

He doesn't talk to Ryan the next morning.

He doesn't even go to the rink with him.

Petrov is ready to rejoin the lineup and they're sending him back to Springfield.

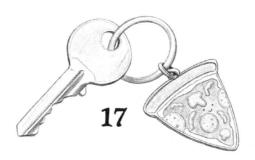

17

The house is so fucking quiet.

Ryan doesn't like how Louie left—without even saying goodbye. Although that's partly his fault, probably.

He did it again. Ruined a good thing.

He was trying to be supportive and took it a step too far. He thought Louie was aware of what his dad was doing to him with his constant criticism, and maybe he is on some level, but he wasn't ready to hear someone else say it. The only time he brought it up was when he was drunk. Ryan should have tiptoed into that conversation, but he went in with a bulldozer.

He texts Louie, but he doesn't reply.

Ryan does keep an eye on Louie's numbers in the AHL. Two goals in his first game back. Two weeks later, he's got a streak going. Because he's good. It's too bad that his dad most likely isn't watching. If it's not the NHL, it's beneath him. He's got that vibe.

After his first text to Louie sort of vanishes in the ether, Ryan doesn't text him again, even when Louie pulls an absolutely filthy move that would have rocked Dad Hathaway's world if only it had happened in Hartford and not in Springfield. That's what he was talking about. Louie is good enough. It's not his fault that the Cardinals are fucking stacked.

At the rink, the stall next to Ryan's gets taken by Petrov. He's nice, but he's an in-the-zone kind of guy. He wears headphones most of the time, listening to screaming with guitars. Before games, he sits in his stall and closes his eyes, still with his headphones on. No screaming with guitars, though.

Louie was focused before games, too, but not like that. Louie talked. Mostly about their opponents' weaknesses.

But now Ryan is stuck between in-the-zone Petrov and in-the-zone Nick and it's weird. Nick at the very least talks to him during intermissions and after games. Mostly about plays that worked out for them. Sometimes to thank him for a good pass.

The difference between Louie and Nick is that Nick, who also lives and breathes hockey, does it fully for himself. Nick also ditched a bunch of the guys to get tacos with his friends. His non-athlete friends. Ryan has exactly one, *one* non-athlete friend (that would be Ami, although she was a track-and-field star in high school).

Louie is—

He's gone and Ryan needs to stop thinking about him and wondering why he is the way he is or why it was so hard for him to believe he's worth something. If Ryan knows one thing, it's that you can't force someone to open up to you.

He still calls Carrot about it.

"So his dad fucked him up with his expectations," Carrot says. "And then this guy fucked you up because he's unapproachable and you just... love to approach everyone around you. I get it."

Ryan, on the couch, wrapped in the fluffy blanket, stares at the piano that Louie refused to play, even though he clearly wanted to. "I don't— why'd you have to make it sound so dirty?"

"You're a people person," Carrot says. "One sec." He disappears out of frame, followed by the telltale sound of a fridge opening. "Look," he says, now back with a can of Coke, "you don't need a lot of time to yourself."

"Are you saying I'm clingy?" Ryan asks. Shit. He's clingy, isn't he?

"Yeah, but not in a bad way." Carrot shrugs. "You just need to be around people who also don't need a lot of time to themselves. You know… extroverts."

"Slaw's not an extrovert and he still liked to hang out with us."

"Yeah, but you know how he wouldn't go clubbing with us? Slaw's a guy who knows his limits. He goes home when he's had enough." Carrot sighs. "And…"

"And?" Ryan prompts when Carrot holds the rest of that sentence hostage.

"You're the kind of person who always wants everyone to be happy," Carrot says. "But sometimes being happy isn't on the agenda, you know?"

"So I'm clingy *and* pushy."

"No, you're not pushy." Carrot rolls his eyes. "Pushy is a completely different thing. You want to help and it's tough for you when you can't. I guess you just need to accept that you couldn't help in this case."

Ryan sighs. "Fine, I'll accept it."

"Uh-huh."

Yeah, okay, Ryan also knows that was bullshit. "I'll work on accepting it."

"That's my boy," Carrot says. He grabs the phone and takes Ryan on a shaky walk to his own couch.

Ryan misses that couch. It was better. For no reason. He just wants it back.

"What's with the face?" Carrot asks. "Are you—oh my God, were you fucking this guy?"

"No, what the hell, dude," Ryan says. He has no idea why he feels like he's lying to Carrot when he's telling him the absolute truth. He was definitely not fucking Louie.

Carrot's eyes narrow. "Did you want to?"

"Contrary to popular belief, gay people do not want to fuck every single guy on the planet."

"Hey, that's totally not what I'm saying. I know you didn't want to fuck *me*, which I'm still pissed about, by the way, because I'm very handsome. I'm a catch."

"Yeah, so why do you still not have a girlfriend?"

"Low blow, man, low blow."

Ryan rubs his eyes. "Let's just talk about something else."

"Sure. How are the Cards treating ya?"

"It's a good team," Ryan says.

"But?"

"Does there have to be a but?"

"I thought I'd heard one," Carrot says knowingly.

Ryan stares at the fake Netflix fireplace he's pulled up because he has no idea how to light the real fireplace. "I don't think I fit in."

"Why?"

"I don't think they like me."

"But why?"

"I don't know. It's different here."

"Oh, really? The new team you got traded to is not exactly the same as your old team? Shocking."

"Right?" Ryan says. He's so glad he called Carrot. Carrot is a voice of reason, which is always very helpful in countering all of Ryan's... unreasonableness. "I just want things to be like before. I want friends, not just teammates."

"Well, you only just got there a few weeks ago and you spent most of your time with a guy who got sent down, so essentially you're starting all over again. It's tough. Remember when you first came to Toronto? We weren't friends immediately either."

"It still felt easier back then."

"Rye, honestly, you're overthinking this."

"Am I?" Ryan says. "Or do they maybe actually hate me and wish the Cards had never traded for me because I'm a clingy and pushy mess who ruins everything he touches?"

"Wow, you're deep in it," Carrot says. "What about Hellström? He seems like a good guy."

"I mean, he's like ten years older than me."

"Kinda ageist."

"That's a thing?" Ryan asks. "Anyway, he's got, like… kids and shit. They don't want me hanging out there."

"Have you asked?"

Ryan sticks out his tongue at him.

Carrot laughs. "Listen, I know you want a friend on the Cards who's exactly as great as I am——"

"I'm not trying to replace you."

"And I love that for me," Carrot says. "Want my advice?"

"That's kind of why I called you."

"You are where you are. And, quite frankly, I think you're better off there. Your numbers are great. You're playing a good game. If you keep this up, they may want to keep you around for a good, long time."

Ryan nods. "Santa is probably coming back, either for the playoffs or next season."

"Yang's retiring soon, maybe after this season, and I don't think they'll re-sign Russell when they have you."

"Okay, good point."

"So, you may be there for a few years at least. If you don't find a new bestie on the team, find one somewhere else, but maybe give those guys a chance to get to know you before you write them off?"

"Ryan, you look hungry," Liam says to him after practice two days later. "Come over for dinner. Maja misses you."

What, did Carrot call him and tell him to take care of Ryan? He says yes to dinner anyway. The Hellströms make great food. And Maja loves to play with dinosaurs with him, so his best friends are a couple in their thirties and a child who's maybe… two? Is she even two yet?

Anyway, he's not sitting around at home playing Minecraft, he's getting out of the house, he's doing something.

The week after, he googles gay bars in Hartford.

He won't go. But he stares at the addresses on his phone and thinks *maybe one day*. Thinks about New York. It's not far and it's definitely a safer bet. Safer, but not safe. He locks his phone and chucks it at the other end of the couch where it bounces off one of the fuzzy throw pillows.

The Cardinals clinch a playoff spot in late March and the guys decide to go out to celebrate after. They know a place and all Ryan has to do is tag along. He buys himself a strawberry daiquiri, which is maybe a step too far, too *girly* in the guys' eyes, but then Sami sits down next to him with something called Pink Passion Party Punch, so Ryan stops worrying.

Some fans are milling about the bar; it's not too far from the arena. Two of them ask Ryan for pictures and one of them is even wearing his jersey. He asks the girl if he can take a picture of it to send to his mom and she says, "Aww, that's so sweet", and poses for him.

He does send the picture to his mom. (And to Carrot.)

"Should have asked for her number," Liam says.

"Seriously," Sami adds.

"Nah," Ryan says, which is his standard answer and could mean literally anything. Nah, she wasn't his type. Nah, he's already seeing someone. Nah, he's actually a flaming homosexual.

She waves at him and walks away, returning to a girl at the bar who smiles when she leans in to tell her something. She laughs. They kiss.

"Ohhhh," Liam and Sami say at the same time.

"Hm," is Ryan's contribution to that conversation.

Liam heads out early with a few of the older guys in tow, and eventually Ryan ends up at his little table all by himself, the stools around him empty. Sami and Mikko are at the bar having an intense conversation that involves a lot of pointing, and Yoshi, Lucky and Nick are at a table together, probably talking playoff odds.

Waldo is talking to the lesbians. Presumably lesbians. The girls who were kissing earlier. Ryan kinda wants in on that conversation, but he doesn't want to be a dick who interrupts others either. So he stares. And feels sorry for himself.

He eventually scoots off his chair and says goodbye to the guys.

"Hey," Sami says, "when you are coming by to meet Koira?"

Mikko laughs about a joke Ryan clearly didn't get.

"Uh, soon?" Ryan says.

"Maybe I'll bring him to the rink," Sami says.

Mikko nods approvingly.

They let him go. Yoshi tells him to get home safe when Ryan says good night and asks if he's okay to drive. He'll take an Uber home, pick up the car tomorrow. He's not taking any chances. Nick says he'll give him a ride to practice in the morning.

Ryan wanders out into the night. He really wants some fries. He was thinking about grabbing a bite, but there are no bites to be grabbed. If he wanders about for a bit, though, he'll probably come across a takeaway place that's still open.

"Oh my God, Ryan!"

Ryan looks around and finds himself face-to-face with Louie's brother Dominic. He's got a handsome dude in tow. That's probably Cameron, the elementary school teacher fiancé.

"Hey, hi," Ryan says, eyes getting caught on the bits of bright red under their coats. "Were you at the game?"

"You sound surprised," Dominic says. He nods at most-likely-fiancé. "This is Cameron. He's been a Cardinals fan since he was—"

"Since I was born, actually," Cameron says and shakes Ryan's hand. "Nice to meet you."

"His family has season tickets," Dominic says. "They sometimes let us have them."

Ryan was not expecting that. "Oh."

"I don't tell my parents how often I go to games," Dominic goes on. If Ryan is reading this right, he's silently asking him not to mention it should he ever come across the Hathaways again. "It's complicated."

"Yeah, it, uh… it sounded like it is."

Cameron laughs.

"Babe, come on," Dominic says and nudges Cameron's side.

Cameron turns to Ryan. "You've met them, yeah?"

"Briefly," Ryan says, eyeing Dominic.

"Louie lived with Ryan before the Cards sent him back down," Dominic says to Cameron.

"Ah," Cameron says, nodding, "so you get it, right? You know that their family is completely insane?"

Ryan frowns at him. "Louie's not—"

"He's talking about my dad," Dominic says.

It's probably rude to agree with Cameron because the Hathaway's mess is not Ryan's mess and Dad Hathaway's impossible standards are not his problem and what he's doing to Louie is—it's fucked up. And Ryan is still pissed on Louie's behalf, even though they haven't talked since he went back to Springfield.

Ryan clears his throat. "Have you heard from him? Louie, I mean?"

"I haven't," Dominic says but doesn't sound too concerned. "He's pissed because he got sent back down, even though it was inevitable when Petrov came back. He sulks. It's what he does. You just need to, you know, keep the door open for him."

"I sent him a text," Ryan says. "He didn't reply."

"Give it some time," Dominic says. "All Louie's been told since he was a kid is that whatever he does isn't good enough. He doesn't get that sometimes saying sorry is actually all it takes. And he doesn't get that people who aren't our dad want to be around him even if he's not the best hockey player of all time." He nods at Ryan. "He liked living with you."

"Yeah, I, uh… I liked having him there."

"He'll be back," Dominic says.

"Next season at the latest," Cameron says. "Calling it now, he'll be on the roster full-time."

Dominic gives Ryan a gentle pat on the back before they part ways. "Thank you for caring about him," he says.

That sentence eats its way through Ryan like acid on the way home. His Uber driver isn't talkative, so Ryan spends most of the ride staring at the text he sent to Louie. Still unanswered.

Slowly he starts to type. Deletes. Types something else. Tries to find the right words. He hits send just before they make it to his place.

To: Louie

I know I overstepped when I said all that stuff about your dad

Then:

I'm sorry

And:

hope you're okay

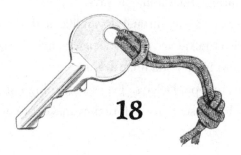

18

Springfield and Hartford get eliminated from the playoffs almost at the same time.

They both make it to six games, both lose at home, both don't live up to the expectations the fans had for them. The Cards may have made it to the second round if they hadn't lost two d-men: first Russell, then Yang. Louie isn't expecting either of them back, although that doesn't change anything for him. He'll have to wait and see who decides to leave, how many forwards the Cards sign once free agency rolls around, and if they trade for anyone.

After the game, after their season is essentially over, when they've done their exit interviews, Louie starts to pack. Their lease is up at the end of the summer and his roommates both want to move in with their girlfriends, so Louie will have to find a new place to live. He'll worry about it in a few months.

The optimistic part of him doesn't even want to start looking until he knows whether or not he'll make the Cardinals' roster in the fall.

His phone lights up with a text. Family group chat.

From: Dad

Louie, when are you coming home?

Louie stares at it. Until his phone screen turns off again. He taps it. Stares at it some more.

The thought of going home makes his stomach roil. Technically, he could go home today. It's not that late yet. He could be in Boston by dinnertime. He does not want to be in Boston by dinnertime.

One of his roommates comes upstairs to say goodbye. He's getting on a flight to Calgary in a few hours. They'll see each other in the fall, or at least that's the expectation right now.

Louie is almost certain that the Cardinals will not want to get rid of him during the summer. He played well in Springfield, and he played well while he was in Hartford, at least toward the end of his time there. The question is: does he want to stay?

It's not a contract year for him, but he could always ask them to trade him. Give him a chance somewhere else. He may finally make an NHL roster. Except he wants to make the NHL roster here. He worked hard and he wants someone to see it.

But what if there's not enough to see? What if he wasn't impressive enough? Six playoff games and his dad sent him clip after clip—*you were too slow* here, *that play was a mess* there. Louie wishes his dad had stuck to not watching AHL games at all.

Anyway, Louie shouldn't expect to make the Cardinals' roster in the fall. He knows better than to go into a new season with expectations. He did that exactly once. When he was twenty. He thought he was ready back then. Three years later, he's smarter.

He unlocks his phone and goes to the group chat. *I'll be there in a few hours*, he types.

Considers throwing up in his bathroom as a final farewell to this place.

He deletes the message instead.

Bastien is already home; the Bears didn't even make the playoffs. Dad has been posting videos of them skating together for days. If Louie goes home tonight, he'll be on the ice with them tomorrow.

His stomach throws another tantrum about it.

I don't know yet, I have some things left to take care of here, is what he finally sends.

Louie piles his things into the car.

He doesn't own a lot of stuff. Stuff is for people who are expecting to stay in the same place for a good, long time. Clothes. Hockey gear. A few milestone pucks. His leftover food. They ate most of what they had left in the fridge and the freezer after they did their exit interviews.

When he gets behind the wheel, he knows two things: he's not staying here and he's not going home.

He thinks about Liam Hellström and his kitchen table with the crayon marks and his wife's meatballs and the guest room with the hockey pictures drawn by little Ida on the walls.

Obviously, Louie can't show up at the Hellströms' house unannounced. So there's absolutely no reason for him to get on the interstate. South. Toward Hartford.

There's nothing there for him.

He still drives all the way to Cedar Mills because he wants pasta and the local Italian place has the best fettuccine Alfredo he's ever had in his life. Louie would have never ordered from Giuliana's if Ryan hadn't come home with a pizza and a takeout menu a few days after they'd moved here and insisted they support local businesses.

Louie feels kind of pathetic sitting at a table for two by himself. At least the pasta is exactly as amazing as he remembered.

He leaves. He thinks about going back to Springfield, even though he doesn't have keys to the house anymore. If he rang the doorbell, they would let him in. He could stay for a few more weeks, until summer is over. But then he'd have to explain why he didn't go to Boston. Actually, he never said he was going to Boston. He just said, "See you at training camp" and left.

Louie drives to Ryan's neighborhood, now on autopilot.

The lights are on at his house, so he hasn't gone home for the summer yet. He's got the curtains drawn. He may have fallen asleep on the couch.

Louie can't bug him.

He parks the car in the driveway.

He can't just show up here without a warning.

He gets out of the car and slowly walks up to the door.

He can't ring the doorbell.

He can't.

He rings the doorbell.

Footsteps approach almost immediately and a moment later Ryan opens the door in sweatpants and a shirt that says *Davis Carrolton's #1 Fan* above a picture of Ryan's former teammate Davis Carrolton. Ryan wore that shirt for practice once and of course everyone asked him about it. He lost a bet, he said. A few days later, Carrolton posted a picture of himself wearing a shirt with a photo of Ryan wearing the other shirt.

"Hey," Ryan says. He's holding half a Dorito bag in one hand and a fork in the other. If he's surprised to see Louie, he's hiding it well.

"You're eating Doritos with a fork?" Louie asks. He knows he should have said hello. It only occurs to him a second too late.

Ryan tilts the bag. The Doritos are mostly crushed, with ground beef and sour cream on top. "It's a taco in a bag."

"That's so not a taco," Louie says.

"Anything can be a taco." Ryan grins. "I saw a video of some lady making pancake tacos the other day."

"Sounds weird."

"Hm," Ryan says. And that's it. He doesn't say anything else.

Louie was kind of expecting a *get the fuck out* or something along those lines. It doesn't come. Ryan just looks at him. Eats a bite of his taco abomination. Waits.

"I—I don't even know why I'm here," Louie says.

Ryan picks a big piece of Dorito out of the bag. "You're here," he says, "because you needed a friend."

Louie bounces on the balls of his feet. He mostly needed to not go to Boston. And he—he didn't want to go to just anyone's house. He didn't need some *random* friend.

"Wanna come in?" Ryan asks, stepping aside to let Louie in.

Louie nods and takes his shoes off by the door, slowly shuffling into the living room, where Ryan left a nest of blankets behind on the couch.

"Want some water?" Ryan asks.

"I…" Louie sits down in his spot. He has a spot here. He doesn't even have that at his parents' house in Boston.

Ryan sets down his not-actually-a-taco next to a can of Coke.

Louie's dad would drop dead instantly if he saw a hockey player eat that. Even though a lot of the guys love their cheat days. And then for some guys, every day is a cheat day. They eat a ton of pizza and are still better hockey players than Louie.

"Can I have a Coke?" Louie asks.

A second ticks by before Ryan moves. "Sure," he says. "Anything else? Have you eaten? I'll order you something that's not a taco in a bag, although you're totally missing out."

"Yeah, I had dinner before I came here," Louie says. Slowly, he reaches out to snatch his favorite blanket, even though Ryan is still in the kitchen and won't stop him. He probably wouldn't even stop him if he was sitting right next to Louie.

Ryan returns with a Coke, cracks it open for Louie, and hands it over.

Then he sits back down in his nest.

Then he stares at Louie.

He has a playoff game on TV, but he's muted the broadcast, so the players are moving around in total silence. Boston's still in the playoff race and it looks like they're winning the first game of Round 2. Louie looks away.

"So," Ryan says.

Louie understands that he's supposed to tell him something, that he's supposed to explain how he ended up here. Instead, he asks, "When are you going home?"

"Oh, uh, not immediately," Ryan says. "I'm not going home for the whole summer. I'm training here, with Nick and Santa and Waldo. They've got a guy they like. Well, Santa isn't training, but he's getting back into it, so I guess he'll join us every now and then."

Louie is maddeningly jealous. "But you're still gonna go see your parents?"

"Obviously," Ryan says. "Gotta go home for Ami's annual summer potluck. It's a legendary event. Highlight of every summer."

"Sounds nice."

"You can be my plus one," Ryan says and picks up his Doritos bag.

Louie frowns at him. Because of the plus one thing—he can't just go to Pennsylvania with Ryan to some potluck where he'll know exactly one person, maybe one and a half—and also because he's still so confused about that taco situation. He points at the bag. "Why?"

"Saw it on... Insta? TikTok? Not sure," Ryan says. "Seemed like a great idea, though."

"Horrific," Louie says. "Did you throw an entire block of cream cheese in there, too?"

Ryan cackles. "Hey, I am thinking about getting a Crock-Pot and I will be throwing entire blocks of cream cheese in there like there's no tomorrow. I'm becoming a real culinary... something."

"I'm not sure that's a culinary anything."

"Don't shit on it until you've tried it," Ryan says.

Louie rolls his eyes. He takes a sip of his Coke. He hasn't had one since—yeah, he doesn't remember the last time he had one.

"I, uh, I was gonna switch to one of the Western Conference games in a bit?" Ryan says and holds up the remote. "Or we can watch something that has nothing to do with hockey. What about... *Top Gun*? We have to go see the new one, by the way. Or maybe something happier. *Paddington*? Or maybe we need something like... oh, I know, we should watch the show where people guess if stuff is cake or not."

"Hockey is fine," Louie says.

"Sailors, then," Ryan says and pulls up the game.

Louie isn't sure if Ryan actually wants to watch the Sailors or if he's doing Louie a favor because he knows that his dad used to play for the Grizzlies and has deduced that Louie doesn't have the greatest relationship with his dad and therefore doesn't want to see anything Grizzlies-related.

For a few minutes, they listen to what the commentators have to say about the Sailors, Ryan noisily munching on his terrible culinary creation. Louie hates to admit it, but it smells good. Like tacos. Which is kind of the point of it.

Louie pulls the fluffy blanket all the way around himself. It smells like Ryan. He stares at the TV for a few more minutes, the commercials getting more and more obnoxious somehow. Then he says, "My dad asked when I was coming home and I panicked."

Ryan turns to him. "You panicked. Because he asked when you're coming home," he repeats slowly.

"I know it sounds stu—"

"No, it doesn't," Ryan interrupts. "It's not stupid. He treats you like shit, so obviously you don't want to go home." He clears his throat. "Sorry. Shouldn't have said that."

Louie picks at one of the tassels on the throw pillow next to him. Ryan texted him a few times while he was back in Springfield. He apologized for overstepping. Louie never replied, too caught up in making the playoffs. He mostly looked at the texts when he couldn't sleep. At two in the morning. He couldn't reply to them in the middle of the night and three weeks too late.

"It's fine," Louie says now. "It's not really about him, though."

Ryan's eyebrows shoot up. "It's not?"

"It's..." Louie shakes his head. Maybe he doesn't enjoy being told what he's doing wrong every single day, all summer long. But his dad just wants him to become a better player in the end.

It's the dinners. Dad, Mom, Bastien, Louie. Not talking. Or talking about hockey.

It's that he has no one else in Boston.

It's his childhood room that makes him feel like he's still a stupid kid.

It's that he doesn't have a spot on the couch.

"Point is," Ryan says, "you didn't want to go home yet."

"Yeah."

"So you didn't. Good for you."

"I—hmm."

Ryan puts down his now empty Doritos bag. "You can stay here tonight."

"Thank you," Louie says. If Ryan hadn't offered up his guest room, Louie would have asked. Other than Boston, he has nowhere to go.

"You can also stay here tomorrow," Ryan adds.

Louie stares at him.

"You know," Ryan goes on, waving his fork, "in case you need another day. A buffer, if you will. I've been thinking about going to Salem. The one with the witches?"

Louie laughs. "Why?"

"Because it sounds cool as fuck," Ryan says. "And, hey, if you want to stay here all summer, the room's all yours."

"What?"

Ryan shrugs, like it's not a big deal. "Yeah. Train with us, it'll be fun."

"But… I have to go back to Boston."

"No, you don't."

Louie stares at him. He doesn't know what it is about Ryan that is just so completely incomprehensible to him. Part of it is that he says stuff like that. Stay here. Sleep in the guest room. Train with a bunch of Cards players.

"You don't have to go to Boston," Ryan says. "You're an adult. You can do whatever the fuck you want. That includes staying here."

All of that is objectively true. But Louie honestly can't imagine what his dad would say if Louie told him he wasn't coming home at all this summer. He'd be so disappointed. A quiet voice at the back of his mind whispers, *So what?* "I don't know, I—"

"Sleep on it," Ryan says. "A trainer that is good enough for Nick is good enough for the both of us."

For the first time today, Louie doesn't feel nauseous.

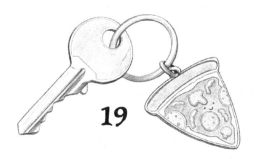

19

"Hey."

"Urgh," Ryan replies.

Something pokes him in the side. "Ryan."

"I'm sleeping," Ryan grumbles. He *was* sleeping until Louie started poking him. Why the fuck is he poking him? "Is the house on fire?"

"No," Louie says, his tone suggesting that he thinks that question was ridiculous.

"Then what's on fire?"

"Wanna come to the rink with me?" Louie asks.

So it's Louie who's on fire. He's been here for two days and he already wants Ryan to get up and go to the rink with him? It's probably six in the morning. "No, I'm sleeping, actually."

"Nick invited both of us."

Of course Nick invited him. Both of them. Whatever. Ryan curls around one of his pillows. "Have fun with Nick."

"Come on. It's not that long of a session. You don't even have to put on your gear. Just skates are fine. Nick's bringing a friend who coaches college hockey and he said the guy's a stick-handling wizard."

Louie has issues. His dad is one of them for sure. And being a workaholic is another one. Those two things might be related.

"Yeah, but I don't want to get up," Ryan says.

Louie's voice is much closer to him all of a sudden when he says, "You don't want to meet the stick-handling wizard? That guy must be ridiculously good if Nick is taking pointers from him."

That is a correct assumption and Ryan is kind of curious, but he's not used to jumping back into hockey this soon after the season ended for him. He needs some time to recuperate. Sleep until noon. Be as lazy as humanly possible. Wear the same sweatpants every day. Order takeout. (Okay, he orders takeout all the time anyway. Order *more* takeout.)

"It'll be fun," Louie whispers.

That is also correct, but—"Ugh," Ryan says, still unwilling to open his eyes. "Five more minutes?"

"Okay," Louie says and a moment later the mattress shakes.

"What the—"

"Take your five minutes," Louie says, making himself comfortable next to Ryan. "I'll wake you up."

Yeah, Ryan is not going back to sleep for five minutes. He'll take them, though.

Next to him, Louie heaves a sigh.

"What?" Ryan asks.

"Nothing."

"Totally sounded like nothing."

"I thought you were going back to sleep?"

"No, I just wanted five more minutes," Ryan says. "They're for... you know, getting used to the idea of getting up."

"That makes no sense."

Ryan turns over and looks up at Louie, who is essentially a personified frowny face. "So, what's wrong?"

"Nothing's *wrong*," Louie insists. He locks his phone. "My dad keeps asking when I'm coming home."

"You still haven't told them that you're staying here?"

"I—" Louie cuts himself off. "Maybe I shouldn't stay here all summer."

"Why?" Ryan asks.

"I should at least go there for a weekend. Say hi to my family." Louie stares at the ceiling. "Right? That's... I should do that."

"You don't have to if you don't want to," Ryan says carefully. He will not overstep again; he's learned his lesson. He will not tell Louie that his douchebag father doesn't deserve a weekend visit. Maybe Louie wants to see his mom. She seemed okay. Ish. She's chosen to stay out of all the hockey stuff, which may actually not be that okay. Maybe she should have told Dad Hathaway to calm his tits at some point.

"Right now, I don't want to," Louie mumbles. "Which makes me the shitty son."

"What about Dominic? He's not going home," Ryan says. Assumes.

"He doesn't have the entire summer off." Louie gives the most minuscule shrug. "I guess I'll see them at the Awards?"

"You're going to the Awards?"

"I mean... I kind of have to."

"But they're on your birthday," Ryan says. "I guess there are worse things than being in Vegas for your birthday, but still..." He was so close, *so* close to putting his foot in his mouth again. He's getting really good at not doing that, though. Practice truly does make perfect.

Louie frowns. "How do you know they're on my birthday?"

"I googled you before you moved in with me," Ryan says.

"And you just memorized my date of birth?"

"I didn't memorize it, I just... like to know when people's birthdays are. It would have been so awkward if I'd let you move in with me and then it was your birthday, like, four days later."

"Hm." Louie frowns at him. "When is your birthday?"

"Google it," Ryan says. He sits up with a groan and gives his phone a tap. It's eight. Way too early to get up on a day off. "Anyway, I say don't go to the Awards. Fuck Vegas. I'll throw you a party back home."

Louie stares at him for a moment. "Why?"

"Because I'm going home in June and you're coming with me, remember?"

"I said I *might* come with you."

"If you get to drag me to the rink at ass o'clock in the morning—"

"It's not—"

"—then I get to take you back home and put a little party hat on you and make you blow out some candles."

Louie blinks at the ceiling. "Maybe."

"Liam's not replying," Ryan says.

Louie drops an ice cube into his water. It's going to melt in seconds, even though they've turned up the air conditioning. "It's been five minutes."

"Yeah, so…" Ryan shrugs. "Maybe you should have asked."

"Why?"

"Maybe he likes you better."

Louie reaches out to flick at Ryan's temple. He must have learned that from Ami. "Give it at least an hour." His lips twitch the tiniest bit. "You should have texted his wife."

"I don't have her number," Ryan says. He's not sure he should have any of the WAGs' numbers.

It's approximately five thousand degrees outside, so Ryan and Louie decided to invite themselves over to Liam's house. He has a very nice pool with a slide and a waterfall. He's in town until school ends for Ida in a few days, then he's taking his family to Sweden.

For once, Ryan actually wouldn't have minded staying at the rink, but Nick had places to be—he's going to the beach for the weekend. Ryan thought about hiding in his trunk for a second, then Louie casually mentioned Liam's pool. Technically, Ryan knew about the pool, he lived at Liam's house for a bit, but back then they didn't exactly have pool weather. It was more of a wrap yourself in five blankets and wait for the sun to return kind of weather. He misses that weather a tiny bit today.

He needs to call the rental agency so someone can check that A/C because it's struggling. Fighting for its life. And it's not even real summer yet. It's just a particularly hot day in early June.

Liam finally replies half an hour later, just a very curt *come over* that is followed by a palm tree emoji five minutes later.

"See, he doesn't hate you," Louie says. Ryan made Louie check his phone because he was driving. They jumped in the car as soon as Liam got back to them. "He never texts me emojis."

"Liam isn't a big texter, I don't think," Ryan says. "He's too busy being a dad."

"Good for him," Louie mutters. He definitely means that. He probably means it more than he realizes.

Ryan would bet that Louie's dad never fled the rink after practice so he could pick him up from school. He probably also didn't bow out of the plans his teammates were making because he promised the kids he'd watch a movie with them and didn't want to disappoint them.

When they get to the Hellströms', Liam is indeed busy being a dad. He's in a gigantic donut float that looks like someone took a bite out of it with Maja in his lap and a drink floating next to him in a smaller donut.

"Maja, look who it is," Liam says and points at them.

"Rah-rah!"

"Yeah!!"

Louie laughs softly.

"And who else?" Liam asks. "Say... Louie. Loouuu-iiieeeee."

"Rah-rah."

"She'll get there eventually," Ella says and hands both of them red cups with a wink. "Enjoy."

Ryan smells the drink. Berries? Alcohol. Definitely a lot of that. "I drove here."

"Sleep in the guest room," Liam says.

"Yeees, is Ryan staying for a sleepover?" Ida has appeared out of nowhere and starts bouncing around him. "Are you staying for dinner?

Do you wanna jump off the deep end with me?"

"Um," Ryan says, a tiny bit overwhelmed. Not even his own nieces are this excited to see him.

Ida peers around Ryan. "Hi, Louie."

Louie waves at her. Then he turns to Ella. "Should we be drinking before getting in the pool?"

"I'm not drinking, so I can pull you out," Ella says with a smile.

"You're not drinking?" Ryan asks. He realizes a second too late that he shouldn't have asked. Louie elbows him in the side. "Forget I asked."

Liam laughs. "Tell them. It's fine."

"We only found out two weeks ago, so don't put it in the hockey group chat," Ella says. "We haven't even told Liam's mom."

Ryan gasps. "You told us about Baby Hellström before your mom?"

"My mom cannot keep a secret," Liam says. "All of Sweden would know within a day."

"Less than a day," Ella says. She gives Ryan a pat on the back. "Grab a float. And do stay for dinner."

"Yeeesss," Ida says, then yells something at her mom in Swedish and pulls Ryan around the pool to the deep end.

She's delighted when Ryan tells her that he wants to try out the slide. Ryan loses track of how many times he climbs up that weird fake rock formation with Ida. A billion times at least. Then she makes him get out of the pool and reminds him to put on more sunscreen because it wears off after a while and grabs him a popsicle.

Louie is fast asleep on a beach chair in the shade but does wake up when Ida loudly asks if anyone else wants ice cream.

Ryan's almost twenty-five years old, but sitting at the side of the Hellströms' pool with his feet dangling into the water, popsicle in his hand, he kind of feels like a little kid. Louie sits down next to him in his boring black trunks that make him look even paler than he is already, sunglasses sitting low on his nose.

He leans in close, his hair tickling Ryan's cheek, and out of the blue something zaps through Ryan, there one second and gone the next. The heat, Ryan tells himself. Because it has to be the heat. He can't let it be anything else. "We're staying for dinner, right?" Louie whispers.

"Duh," Ryan says. He's not saying no to dinner with the Hellströms, even though Ella said she'll *just* be ordering food. And he's pretty sure he shouldn't be driving. He's still not taking any chances with that. He's done fucking up good things.

Liam slowly paddles closer to them. "So," he says, "what are you kids doing this summer?"

"Training with Nick," Louie says.

"And what else?"

Louie shrugs.

"Come on," Liam says, looking to Ryan. "Where are you going? Bahamas? Côte d'Azur?" He grins. "Disney World?"

"Ew," Louie says.

"You don't like Disney World?" Ida asks, shocked.

"I'm just not going anywhere," Louie says.

Ryan elbows him in the side because they've talked about this. "We're going to my parents' place actually."

"Yeah?" Liam asks. "Both of you?"

"I'm throwing Louie a birthday party," Ryan tells him. He's made a whole plan. The plan involves his whole family. It'll be great.

Louie makes a face at him. It's not his fault; he hasn't experienced a Harris birthday party yet. "I haven't actually agreed to going with him."

"What the fuck are you talking about?" Liam asks. "You're just not gonna go to your own birthday party?"

"Papa," Ida says. "Mom says you're not supposed to say fuck."

"Right, I'm so sorry, sweetheart," Liam says and smiles at his daughter. "Still…" He points at Louie. "Go to your fucking birthday party."

"Yeah, Louie," Ryan says. "I throw great parties. And if Ivy's home, we'll make you a sandwich cake."

Liam whistles. "Saying no to that would be a huge mistake."

Louie shifts, clearly still not convinced.

Somehow, this is his family's fault. Him thinking he doesn't deserve nice things, like a birthday party with a sandwich cake. Ryan doesn't know how they fucked him up exactly, but they did.

"Even Nick takes time off," Liam says. "You know that, right? You know that the hardest-working guy on this team goes on vacation and visits his parents, yeah? Sometimes he even takes his parents on a vacation."

"Yeah, but Nick is... he already has a roster spot."

"Louie, I didn't make the team immediately either," Liam says. "We're not the same person, not the same player, but I promise that taking a week or two off will not ruin your chances. You know what I did the summer before I made the roster?"

"No," Louie says, almost a little pouty.

"I went to four weddings in four weeks. I got drunk with the boys. I met Ella. No hockey the entire time," Liam says. "Live a little. Not even for four weeks. Just a little."

Louie is quiet for a long moment, then he gently takes Ryan's popsicle stick and stands up, presumably to throw it away with his ice cream sandwich wrapper. "Fine. A little."

"Yeees," Ryan says, grinning at Liam. He's so glad they came here; Liam always comes through. "Thanks for the assist."

"Always," Liam says. "Make sure he has a good time, yeah?"

Ryan glances at Louie, who is trying to high-five Maja. Louie has been working out. And that's all Ryan's going to say about that. He'll stick to the plan: no more ruining good things.

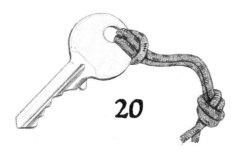

20

Louie's palms are sweaty. The air conditioning in Ryan's car is on full blast. It's a million degrees. The cold air is making goosebumps prickle on Louie's arms. He's about to melt into a puddle.

He doesn't know what the hell is happening to him. Actually, it is some kind of hell. His own personal hell.

It looks like this: Ryan is wearing shorts.

It's summer. And a lot of people wear shorts in the summer. The thing is, Ryan has hockey player thighs. Which are, objectively, good thighs. Louie has spent his life around hockey player thighs and maybe, on occasion, he was a little bit jealous of other guys.

Jealousy is not what draws his eyes back to Ryan's thighs over and over again. He's figured out that much.

Louie checks his phone to distract himself. Missed call from his mom. *Shit.*

"You're very twitchy today," Ryan comments.

True. And Louie would love to stop being twitchy. He'd rather not think about thighs. Ryan's thighs. Louie shifts in the passenger seat. Honestly, the thighs are just the tip of the iceberg.

"Wanna just tell me what's going on?" Ryan glances at him. "Is this about the Awards?"

"Kind of," Louie says. The NHL Awards are part of the iceberg, at least. He holds up his phone. "My mom called. She texted this morning to ask when my flight to Vegas was landing."

Ryan's lips twitch.

This isn't funny.

"I can't do this to them," Louie says, even though he is very much doing it. He's not on a plane but in a car and he's not going to Nevada but to Pennsylvania. "I can't—"

"You can," Ryan says. "You are doing this to them. Because…"

"Because?"

Ryan shakes his head. "Because you're an adult. And you can make your own choices."

"That's not what you were going to say."

"Hm."

Ryan has been very careful about what he says about Louie's family. None of the things he's said so far were lies. It's just that Louie didn't want to hear what he had to say. Now that he's crossed some invisible line by not going to the NHL Awards, he kind of does.

"What were you going to say?" Louie asks.

"I was going to say it's about damn time you put yourself first," Ryan replies without missing a beat.

"I should tell her I'm not coming," Louie says.

"You do that. Give me your phone afterwards."

Louie frowns at him. "Why?"

"I'll turn it off for you."

"I can turn it off," Louie says. He turns it off all the time. Before important games, for example.

"Will you, though?"

Louie doesn't reply. They both know he wouldn't, not today. He can't even bring himself to text his mom back yet. He lied to his family two weeks ago when he said he'd forgotten to book a flight. Too busy training for next season.

And he has been busy—the trainer Nick works with every summer is not taking it easy on them. Louie likes that about him. Ryan keeps calling him a sadist, but at the same time, the training gave him thighs like that, so he has no reason to complain.

For once, Louie didn't mind that Ryan posted pictures from their workout sessions on Instagram. Whenever his dad mentioned that Louie was in Cedar Mills, slacking off, Louie had proof that he was, in fact, working hard. His dad didn't say much when Louie eventually texted the family to tell them he was training with Nick and several other teammates. Just: *If you think that's the right move.*

Dad didn't think it was the right move.

He's punishing Louie with his silence. He's not saying much in the family chat anymore. If questions are asked, it's Mom who sends them. And now it's also Mom who's asking when Louie is joining them in Vegas. The thing is, his dad's silence doesn't bother Louie. It probably should, but this is the most peaceful summer he's ever had.

Mostly peaceful. He does have an unexpected thigh problem.

Louie doesn't get that about himself. How he never noticed that maybe he was a person who's into other guys' thighs. Who thinks about dicks occasionally. More than occasionally during the past few weeks. Maybe there were some guys he thought were attractive, but more in a *this guy has a nice face* kind of way. Possibly, things got muddled in his head because he just isn't attracted to people the way most others are.

Whatever the case may be, he won't do anything about this. It's awkward, it's inconvenient, but Louie knows where the line is. This one isn't invisible. And under no circumstances will he cross it.

The Harris house looks different in the summer.

First, there are about three times as many cars parked on the gravel at the end of the driveway.

Second, there are flowers everywhere.

Third, there are more cats than last time. Louie counts six on the way to the door and Ryan's cat Chicken isn't even with them.

Ryan opens the front door for them and steps aside to let him through. Louie hesitates. "We're just walking in?"

"I live here," Ryan says with a shrug. "I mean, I don't, but this is home. When you go home, you just walk in, too."

Actually, Louie doesn't have a key for his parents' house and they'd never leave the door unlocked, so he always rings the doorbell. He doesn't tell Ryan that. Anyway, lots of people probably don't have a key to their parents' house, especially when they moved out years ago.

Louie steps inside and looks around the quiet, empty foyer.

"Hello?" Ryan shouts when he follows him. "Anyone home?"

"HOLY FUCKING SHIT, IS THAT RYAN?"

A whirlwind of colors and purple hair comes flying down the hallway and into Ryan's arms. One of his sisters, Louie would guess. She squeals when Ryan spins her around and then, without missing a beat, turns to Louie once Ryan has set her down.

"You must be Louie," she says and pulls him into a hug as well. "It's so great to meet you. I'm Ivy."

"Hi," Louie says, shooting Ryan a helpless look over Ivy's shoulder.

"Please let go of him," Ryan says.

Ivy does let go, smiling brightly. "It's so great to see you guys," she says. "You have to go upstairs first."

"Why?" Ryan asks. "Where's Mom?"

"In the kitchen," Ivy says. "She'll say hi later."

Ryan frowns at her. "Why not now?"

"Because it's someone's birthday tomorrow and she's busy." Ivy gives him an exaggerated wink. "So why don't you go get settled in?"

"You guys really don't have to do anything special for my birthday," Louie says. He barely knows the Harrises' and it seems weird that they'd make such a huge effort just because of him. Ryan told him they were having a barbecue with his family, no big deal, just a little party, but now Louie is worried they're making him a cake.

"Uh-huh," Ivy says. "This is not a 'nothing special' household, unfortunately. Dad's been working on your present for a week."

"I—"

"Shhh, Louie," Ivy says, and starts steering him toward the stairs. "We are so happy you're here. We love a party, all of us, and you're giving us a perfect excuse. Ryan will show you his room, okay?"

"Okay," Louie says, resigned.

Ryan shrugs at him in a *no way to stop them* kind of way and heads up the stairs to the small room under the roof with Louie at his heels. The air conditioning unit by the window is doing its very best, but it's still warm up here.

"Take the bed," Ryan says and flops down on the mattress—not an air mattress but an actual mattress—on the floor. "What if I just take a nap?"

"I don't mind," Louie says and sits down at the end of the bed. Ryan's bed. He doesn't like that Ryan doesn't get to sleep in his own bed while they're here, but Ryan would never agree to switching. "My mom would actually kill me if the first thing I did when I got home was sleep."

Ryan grins up at him. His shirt rode up when he threw himself on the mattress, revealing a sliver of skin and a trail of coarse brown hair on Ryan's stomach, which is where Louie's eyes get caught.

"Hey," Ryan says.

Louie snaps out of whatever trance he was in. That cannot happen again. "What?"

"You won't be weird about the birthday cake, right?" Ryan asks. "There's only one correct answer."

"I will not be weird about the birthday cake," Louie says because that's the correct answer.

"Ivy and I are still making the sandwich cake, I think."

"That's a lot of cake."

"The sandwich cake is mostly for me anyway."

Louie laughs. "Okay."

While Ryan does or doesn't nap, Louie unlocks his phone and pulls up the text his mom sent. Slowly, he starts typing, considering every word. *Something came up, I don't think I'll be able to make it to Vegas. I'm really sorry. I hope you all have a good time and good luck to Bastien!*

He's not sorry for not going. Or for lying. He's sorry that he didn't say he wasn't coming in the first place and that he dragged this out for so long.

Ryan would probably tell him off for saying sorry, which is why Louie doesn't tell him. He just locks his phone and drops it on the mattress next to Ryan's head.

"Here," he says.

"Oh, I see, we're really growing as a person, huh?" Ryan says, then gets up and puts Louie's phone on the dresser that's covered in painted hockey sticks and pucks and other equipment. Ryan's phone ends up next to it. "Okay. Let's go."

"Go where?" Louie asks.

Ryan shrugs. "For a walk or something. Until they're done with the cake. Maybe we can say hi to Dad, although I guess he won't let us into the garage either if he's working on your present."

"You did tell them I didn't—"

"Yes," Ryan interrupts, "I told them that you're allergic to presents and that you will die if you get any. They do not care. They're obsessed with birthdays. Honestly, I think that's why my parents had so many kids. More birthdays. Don't worry about it. They're loving the extra birthday."

Louie sighs. He just didn't want to inconvenience anyone. He's already staying here for free and he'll be eating the Harrises' food and he doesn't want to annoy them. A barbecue seems like enough work already. But if Ryan says that his family is having a good time, Louie will believe him. And he does hear the excitement in Ryan's voice when he talks about that sandwich cake, so Louie won't tell him not to make it, even if it sounds weird.

It's kind of—

Endearing.

And Louie will stop thinking about it right now.

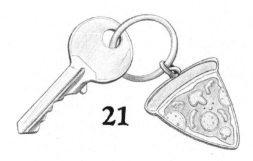

21

Ryan knows that he and his family are walking a fine line between overwhelming Louie and making him happy.

The party hat that Ryan makes him wear in the morning stays on during breakfast. Ryan would guess that Louie forgets all about it because he's too busy trying to remember everyone's names. Almost all of Ryan's sisters are here, and some are with their partners. Emery has two kids and she's only staying for a few days while her husband is on a business trip, but her visit also adds tiny humans into the mix.

It's a lot, which is why he eventually extracts Louie from the house and takes him into town for lunch. They do birthday sundaes for dessert and Louie only looks horrified by the suggestion for a second.

He's different. Has been different ever since he showed up at Ryan's place and decided that he wasn't going home. It's almost like he realized that he has choices. He smiles more, too. Now that Ryan has learned that Louie does smile, he's developed a strange obsession with cracking that shell of his even more. Whenever Ryan makes him smile, he feels like he won something.

On the way home, they stop at Ami's parents' place to say hello to their alpacas. Ami gives Louie socks that he won't be able to wear until winter, but since Louie keeps petting the alpacas and saying "They're so soft" over and over again, Ami probably hit the jackpot with this gift.

"He's cute," Ami whispers to Ryan.

"Stop," Ryan whispers back.

If he chose to be self-aware, he might figure out why making Louie smile is so important to him. Needless to say, he will not choose to be self-aware. He watches Louie pet alpacas instead.

He snaps a few pictures, just for Louie. Ami also takes one of the two of them with several alpacas looking over their shoulders. That one's going on the fridge.

"Don't post those, okay?" Louie says in the car. "I don't want my family to see."

"Have you——"

Louie's phone starts buzzing just then. "Oh, it's Dominic," he says and actually answers this time. "Hey, what's up?"

Ryan hears Dominic laugh at the other end of the line, hears the loud *happy birthday* of two people. At least one person in Louie's family cares about him having a fun birthday.

"Thank you," Louie says. He listens to whatever his brother is saying. "Yeah." He huffs. "No. I just told them I wasn't able to make it."

Ryan isn't eavesdropping, and he's not even sure it counts as eavesdropping since he's only able to hear half of the conversation anyway, but he knows what this is about. Louie was supposed to fly to Vegas for the NHL Awards yesterday. Or maybe today if he'd hopped on an early flight.

He is extremely not in Vegas.

"I texted Bastien afterwards," Louie says, "I told him I'd cheer for him from afar and he said it's fine. He even sent me a birthday text this morning."

Ryan will go out on a limb and say that Louie isn't actually going to cheer for his brother to win the Calder, but that's a mean thought that will stay locked away forever and always.

"You're not there either," Louie adds.

A pause.

"Yeah, well…"

A longer pause.

"I went home with Ryan. His family is throwing me a birthday party."

Ryan pulls into the driveway of his parents' house, keeping an eye out for cats. He parks in his spot. Because even when everyone is home, he still has a spot and he has his chair at the table and he has his room with his bed. Although he's sleeping next to his bed while Louie is here with him. Point is, there's room for him here.

"All right," Louie says. "I gotta go, but… thank you. And I'll come see you when we're back." He rolls his eyes at whatever Dominic's reply is. "Yes, I promise. Bye. You too. Yeah. Bye."

"Everything okay?" Ryan asks. He probably shouldn't.

"Yeah, Mom called Dominic this morning to ask what's going on with me and he had no idea. Apparently, Dad is *very* disappointed that I'm not coming and has correctly deduced that I'm off somewhere celebrating my birthday."

Ryan genuinely hopes that he never runs into Martie Hathaway again because he may punch him in the face.

"Am I a bad person because I didn't go?" Louie asks. He glances at Ryan but quickly looks away again. "My brother may win the Calder tonight and I won't be there."

Aw, fuck, what the hell. "Can I ask you something?"

Louie shrugs. "Sure."

"Would you be genuinely happy for him if he won?"

For a long moment, Louie thinks on that. "I don't know," he says eventually.

"Honestly, if that answer isn't a quick and easy yes, you have no business being there anyway."

Louie stares straight ahead and finally says, "Yeah. I guess you have a point there."

"Are you good?" Ryan asks. He'll sit in this car with Louie for another ten minutes if he needs to.

"I'm… yeah. Sure."

"Okay." Ryan holds up his phone. "Because I'm about to text my mom a sloth emoji and when I do, the party starts."

"Uh, why a sloth emoji?"

"Because she likes it," Ryan says.

Louie frowns at him. "It's two in the afternoon."

Ryan frowns back at him. "So?"

"Isn't it a bit early for a party?"

Ryan's family has started parties much, much earlier than two in the afternoon. He shrugs. "No?"

Louie seems to come to terms with that answer astoundingly quickly, nods and hands his phone back to Ryan because he apparently doesn't want to look at it for the rest of the day. "Okay, send the sloth."

Ryan's mom has outdone herself. The woman loves a party, has always loved a party, but usually Ryan and his sisters aren't around for their birthdays anymore, so she's taken years of pent-up birthday energy and put it all into today.

She's pushed two tables together in the backyard, decorated them in greens and blues and has brought out actual plates. She's folded the napkins, set up candles for later, and put small pink flowers into shot glasses. One of the chairs has over a dozen balloons tied to it.

"There he is!" Mom shouts as soon as Ryan turns the corner with Louie in tow.

Going by the excited hollering, Ryan's dad has already started mixing drinks. "Louie, I didn't ask, do you drink?" he asks and holds up a pink cocktail that matches the flowers on the table.

"Uh, sure, yeah, kind of sometimes," Louie says, his cheeks matching the cocktail. And the flowers. "Just don't make me drink beer."

"Right?" Ivy says and holds up her fist for Louie to bump.

This is almost as good as making Louie smile.

The two of them played cards until midnight yesterday, talking about their favorite songs to play on the piano. She almost got him to play something for her, but then one of the cats decided to dramatically meow at Louie and he started petting Pancake instead.

Ryan gets his own Cherry Colada and settles in for the presents. It's a whole thing and Louie's face has gone from pale pink to cherry red because all the attention is on him. He still says thank you every time he's handed a new gift. Pictures of Louie playing hockey, drawn by Emery's kids. The cake Mom baked that has big bees and flowers piped on it—it says HAPPY BEE-DAY LOUIE! on top. Ryan's sisters hand over a potted basil plant, a mug with an *I'd rather be playing hockey* print on it, and a plush chicken. "I hear hockey players love protein," Ivy says with a shrug, "but I wasn't going to show up with raw chicken."

The entire time, Ryan watches Louie's face. There's that fine line again. He has no idea when someone last threw a birthday party for Louie. He has a feeling it wasn't a priority in the Hathaway household. About two weeks ago, Ryan asked Louie if there was anything in particular he wanted to do on his birthday, any traditions, anything that couldn't be missing. Louie shrugged. He thought about it for at least ten minutes and then came back with, "Anything is fine, honestly. We never did anything special. Just dinner."

"So, we'll do dinner," Ryan said—hence the barbecue they have planned for later. He called his mom and they made plans. She didn't even let Ryan make too many suggestions. She just said she'd take care of everything.

Ryan's dad has disappeared in the meantime and eventually shows up with a small coffee table that's painted just like the one in the living room. "Monica said you liked it," he says. "It's not as big, but that just makes it easier to find a nice place for it."

"Thank you," Louie says, his voice soft, full of awe. "This is... you really didn't have to get me anything."

He needs to stop saying that. It's his birthday—*of course* they had to get him something. And, honestly, Ryan's sisters love buying presents. All of them. Even the one who isn't here today. Ryan would bet they all had a great time. He, too, had a great time when he made Louie's sandwich cake this morning. That one is for later, though.

All he really wants is for Louie to have a good day. And that he forgets about his shitty family and the NHL Awards and whether or not his brother will win the Calder. He's almost sure they did it.

"Too late to return all of this, I'm afraid," Ivy says and picks up the biggest knife Ryan's parents have in their kitchen. "Now cut that cake. I'm starving."

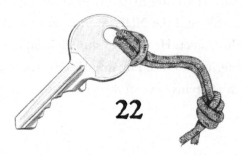

22

Louie is sitting in a chair on the back porch with a plush chicken cradled to his chest and a plate with a piece of sandwich cake in hand.

It's almost midnight.

The mosquitos are relentless.

Louie does not care.

He cares about his sandwich cake and the chicken he has named Agatha. Ryan has pretzeled himself into another one of the chairs and is staring out at the quiet backyard. All traces of Louie's birthday party have vanished. Monica left them with two glasses of water and the last two slices of sandwich cake. "You'd better eat that. It'll just be soggy tomorrow," she said.

Louie's own mother would never encourage him to eat anything in the middle of the night. She'd probably hate the idea of a sandwich cake. Ryan and Ivy used a crap-ton of cream cheese to stick those layers together. There's some mayo in there, too. Louie never eats mayo.

He's eating mayo today. And buttercream. The chocolate Ryan got him that he once stared at when they were at the mall. Things wrapped in bacon. So many things wrapped in bacon.

He drank cocktails in the afternoon.

He doesn't know who the fuck he is right now.

"What are you smiling about?" Ryan asks. "Is it my sandwich cake?"

"Yeah," Louie says and eats another bite.

Ryan smirks. "Aren't you glad you're here?"

Louie glances at Ryan. For a second, actually, for much more than a second, he forgot that he was supposed to be somewhere else. "Do you still have my phone?"

"I do," Ryan says. "I'll give it back if you want. Technically, your birthday is over."

"Keep it," Louie says. He has no idea if the Awards are over. Maybe not. Who knows. If Bastien has already won the Calder, he doesn't want to know yet. He'll check before he goes to bed.

Ryan nods and leans back in his chair, looking out at the dark backyard.

On the horizon, lightning flickers. The roll of thunder is faint; far away. It's still pleasantly warm. Maybe that storm isn't even headed their way.

Ryan hums. "Have you ever thought about..."

"What?"

"Lightning and, like, ponds. Rivers. The ocean," Ryan says slowly. "What happens when lightning strikes the ocean? Do all the fish die? Are they like, the fuck, who just turned the lights on?"

"Is this one of those 'do pigeons have feelings' kind of things?" Louie asks.

"Huh." Ryan is quiet for a moment. "Okay, but do pigeons have feelings?"

"Of course they do," Louie says. "Probably not like we do. They have... pigeon feelings."

"Maybe pigeon feelings would be better than human feelings."

Maybe Ryan has a point there. Louie doesn't know what to do with the human feelings he's been having.

This entire summer has been an absolute fever dream.

He didn't go home.

He didn't go home and now he doesn't know who the hell he is anymore. Who is Louie without the rest of the Hathaways? It's only starting to dawn on him that he's never had a chance to find out before.

All his life, he practiced the way his dad told him to, he ate what his dad told him to, he held his stick and skated the way his dad told him to. He spent his life trying to be exactly the way Dad wanted him to be. More like Bastien, that is. Louie was never going to be that, though. He knew, Dad knew, Bastien knew. And Dad still tortured him about it summer after summer. Louie let himself be tortured. Bastien watched and was glad that wasn't him.

Training with Nick has been feeling wrong because Nick's trainer tells him when he does something well. He says, "Good." He says, "Time to stop for today." He says, "I want to try something else with you." It has been feeling wrong because Louie is so used to being told that whatever he does isn't good enough.

Thunder rumbles gently, a little closer now.

"You were right," Louie says.

Ryan doesn't reply right away. "About what? The sandwich cake?"

"That too." Louie puts down his empty plate. "And what you said about my dad."

"Oh," Ryan says. "That's… uh. I'm sorry."

"You're sorry for being right?"

"Yeah. Because that means your dad has been treating you like shit your whole life and you definitely didn't deserve that."

"I—"

"You didn't deserve that," Ryan says again.

Possibly, Ryan is right about that, too.

Louie keeps staring out at the dark backyard. Something is moving through the grass. A cat with white spots. "I don't think he did it on purpose," he says. Before Ryan can protest, Louie adds, "He just never understood me as a player. He wanted me to play like him. Bastien did. He thinks like Dad when he plays."

"Permission to share a thought?" Ryan says.

"Sure."

"Don't say *sure*." Ryan huffs at him. "It's not a fun thought. And it's kinda still your birthday, even though it's after midnight, and I don't want to ruin a good thing."

"Just say it," Louie says. "I promise I won't let it ruin my birthday."

"Hm. I'm thinking maybe it's been holding you back. You know, trying so hard to be like your dad? Maybe you should have just… played your own game. You weren't ready because you weren't you. You were trying to be whatever your dad was trying to make you."

Louie sighs.

"I'm sure he taught you good things. He was a great hockey player."

There is absolutely a *but* coming.

"But he never let you be your own person," Ryan goes on. "Right? He thought you had to become a certain kind of player to be successful and he never considered you could be just as successful if he let you go your own way."

"I think it's too late to try to be someone else," Louie says.

"You sure about that?" Ryan says. "I've seen you with Nick. You're different with him."

"Am I?" Louie says, although now that Ryan has said it, he thinks of all the things he's been working on with Nick that his dad would call a waste of time. Like how to pull off a Michigan goal. "Maybe I am."

"Maybe you are."

Louie lets him have this one.

Ryan yawns.

Raindrops are starting to fall and the cat that was sneaking through the grass joins them on the porch. Louie grabs it and hugs it to his chest.

"That's Clover," Ryan says. "Because she's lucky."

Louie scratches Clover's head and she takes that as an invitation to make herself comfortable. Somehow there are still cats around here he hasn't met yet. He could use some luck for next season. Or just for his life in general.

As much as he hates it, making it in the NHL isn't always just talent and attitude. It's also luck and being in the right place at the right time.

Louie glances at Ryan, who has tipped his head back and closed his eyes. He still has a smile on his face.

"Wanna go inside?" Louie asks.

"Nah, I don't think this storm will go right over us," Ryan says.

"It looked like you were going to sleep."

"I was just… enjoying that I get to sit here." Ryan laughs under his breath. "I feel like there's never enough time to just sit somewhere. You have to really… make yourself sit. And not think about the next thing and the next thing, you know? Like, I don't need to plan how I'll entertain you tomorrow."

"You really don't," Louie says. "Today was enough entertainment."

"Good entertainment, yeah?"

"Yeah," Louie says. "I…" Oh, this is going to hurt to admit, but Ryan deserves the truth. "I've never had a birthday like this. You know, one that was just for me. When I was a kid, my birthdays were more for my mom's friends and when I was older, I wasn't supposed to care about my birthday anymore."

"That's bullshit. Birthdays are awesome," Ryan says. "By the way, I still have your gift upstairs."

"You already gave me a gift."

"When?"

"The party? And lunch. And the sandwich cake. And the chocolate."

"Okay, if you're counting those as gifts, what I'm giving you will be really fucking boring."

"What is it?"

Ryan nods at the back door. "Let's go upstairs. You can bring the cat."

Louie does bring the cat, who clearly doesn't mind being carried through the entire house (with a detour to the kitchen to put away their plates) and up to Ryan's room. Clover immediately goes to sleep on Louie's pillow.

"Okay, here it is," Ryan says and hands over a gigantic bag.

Louie reaches in and finds something soft. He pulls at it.

Ryan bounces on the balls of his feet. "It's a blanket. Like the one we have in the living room that you like so much," he says. "Except it's black because I know you like dark sheets, so I figured—you know, you can still use the one in the living room, but now you have one for your room."

Not for Springfield. For his room. To match his bedsheets.

"You hate it," Ryan says. "I'm—"

"No, it's great," Louie says. "I—thank you."

"I still have the receipt. I can totally take it back if you hate it."

"I don't hate it."

"Are you sure?"

Louie puts down the bag and pulls Ryan into a hug. "I really like it, okay?" he says.

And, *oh*, big mistake.

Because Ryan is a hugger, so obviously he wraps his arms around Louie and gives him a tight squeeze. And he's so warm. And he smells like summer, like the grill and faded sunscreen and the cherry cocktail he spilled on his shirt earlier. It's so much. Louie's heart is about to explode in his chest with how fast it's beating and he doesn't even know why, except he knows exactly why.

It's always been like this. Well. Not always, not with everyone he's ever met, but with the people he ended up dating. The feelings just sneak up on him.

Louie doesn't want these. Not because Ryan's a guy. The whole guy thing is inconvenient, but Louie could deal with it. Maybe. Actually, he'd most likely choose to ignore it if it was anyone else.

But this is Ryan.

Shit, this is Ryan.

Ryan, who gently rubs his back and says, "Okay, you're welcome."

"Okay," Louie says again and takes a step back. He takes the blanket and wraps it around his shoulders, even though it's summer and too warm. He's just trying to get rid of the awkwardness that has taken possession of him.

Ryan seems completely normal at least, so he must have not noticed the existential crisis Louie went through in the past thirty seconds. He grabs a shirt to sleep in and disappears to the tiny en suite bathroom his parents had built so Ryan's sisters wouldn't have to share with him, Ryan told him earlier.

Louie snuggles up to Clover while he waits for Ryan to be done and falls asleep without even meaning to.

23

Ryan is slightly worried that Louie will get bored of his hometown about three days in because Louie is the kind of person who wants to do stuff. He's not a sit-still-and-do-nothing guy.

While Emery is still there, Louie plays street hockey with her kids in the driveway with an old net and sticks that he and Ryan's dad dug up from the shed. By the time they leave, the kids are begging Emery to get them Louie's jersey. Louie promises he'll take care of it.

Ryan takes him to Ami's annual potluck—they bring three dips because not even Ryan fucks up a dip. He'd bring grilled cheese if he could, but his specialty doesn't travel well. Still, he might end up making some on the grill later on.

When they get to the Kurodas' place, the backyard is already filled with people Ryan went to elementary school with, mixed with people he's never seen before in his life. The wives, the husbands, the partners, the just-passing-throughs, the occasional cousin. Finally, for the first time, Ryan is also bringing someone these people have never seen before in their lives. Except for Ami, who's obviously met Louie and gives Ryan this look he'd rather not try to read.

He meets Ami's girlfriend Valeria, who is sweet and kind and all around wonderful, so Ryan can't even be mad that Ami broke up with him for her. Although some of their friends have some things to say about her dumping Ryan for a girl. Ryan only rolls his eyes at them and says something about him and Ami never being that serious and that she can date whoever she wants and when he gets annoyed, he takes a plate full of leftover pasta salad and hides behind Ami's parents' little gazebo.

When Louie finds him, Louie has a plate full of mini burgers.

"Since when do you eat that kind of crap?" Ryan says.

"Well, you took all the pasta salad."

"I'll give you some if I can have a burger."

Louie gently sets down a tiny burger at the edge of Ryan's plate. "It's fine, just take it."

Ryan sighs. "Have you correctly deduced that I'm being pathetic?"

"Why are you—" Louie cuts himself off and shakes his head.

"What?" Ryan asks. Louie once told him that he hates people who don't finish their sentences, so he'd better follow through on that one.

"Nothing's changed between you two, right?" Louie asks.

Technically, no, nothing has changed. Except everything has changed. "This is going to sound selfish and shitty because I am selfish and shitty," Ryan says, "but for years now, I felt pretty safe because every summer, I came here and took a few pictures of Ami kissing my cheek and us holding hands and sharing ice cream sundaes or whatever and people kind of backed all the way off and didn't ask about my girlfriend or whatever. And when they did, I showed them a picture of Ami and said, look, this is her, I don't see her a lot, but she's amazing."

"And now you don't feel safe anymore?" Louie asks, voice low.

"I… no, that's not it. I just don't know what it'll be like and if I'll have to pretend to hook up with girls on the road or whatever."

"I don't think the guys will care if that makes you feel any better," Louie says. "No one's ever even asked me if I have a girlfriend."

"Well, you're straight, that's different."

Louie doesn't reply.

Ryan suddenly feels like he stepped into something. He thinks about what Ami said when they came to see her at the firehouse. Ryan tells himself to stop thinking about what Ami said. Louie isn't—he's off limits. Part of the *don't ruin good things* agenda is not sleeping with teammates or potential teammates. He made that mistake once; he won't make it again.

"I know none of this will matter when we go back to Hartford," Ryan goes on. "It's just weird right now. Everyone here has been... you know, they've seen the photos I posted, too. And I haven't missed that some of them thought I was stringing Ami along or whatever. Some definitely think I cheated on her. Which... I guess I kind of did."

"I don't think it counts when she's in on it," Louie says.

Ryan shrugs. Sure, she's in on it, sure, it's all a lie anyway, but only Ryan and Ami (and Firefighter Alvarez and some other people who know Ryan is actually very gay) are in on that secret. "Doesn't change what everyone thinks," he says.

Louie shifts a teensy bit closer, which is almost too close, except it's perfectly acceptable. It's just in Ryan's head. It's just that, when they met, Louie never sat this close to him.

"Can I ask you something?" Louie says.

Ryan considers Louie's knit-together eyebrows. Then he shrugs again. "It's going to be mean, right?"

"A little."

"Whatever, at this point it doesn't matter. Ask me."

"Why do you care so much about what other people think about you?" Louie asks. "Or why they like you?"

It's such a weird question. Even weirder than Louie asking him if he really needed another pair of shoes when they were at the mall. Doesn't everyone care? Okay, maybe not everyone, but it's not completely abnormal either. "Why wouldn't I care?"

"It doesn't matter," Louie says, like it's the simplest thing in the world.

"It doesn't matter if I'm nice and kind to other people?"

Louie frowns. "That's not the same."

"How is not—"

"You know you're doing your best to be kind and that should be enough for you," Louie says. "Some people will never see that you're a good person and some won't care either. They won't like you for the weirdest reasons. You know, because they think your hair is stupid."

Ryan runs his fingers through his hair. "Excuse me?" What's wrong with his hair? Granted, Carrot laughed at him when he came home with this haircut, but Ryan really loves it.

"I'm not saying your hair actually looks stupid." Louie rolls his eyes. "I'm saying it's enough that you know. Because you can never please anyone anyway. What other people think about you is none of your business. You have to like yourself. Everything else doesn't matter."

"Huh," Ryan says. Does he like himself? Not every day, that's for sure. Definitely not right now. He looks at Louie and his tiny burgers. "Do you like yourself?"

"That's a really personal question," Louie says and eats a burger.

Ryan laughs. He holds out his fork to Louie. "I licked that, but if you want some pasta salad…"

Louie takes it and spears a noodle, then takes Ryan's entire plate, quietly munching on the pasta salad while Ryan stares out at the Kurodas' backyard. The tightness in his chest that he's been carrying around with him ever since they arrived has mostly disappeared.

With a glance at Louie, Ryan says, "Thank you."

He won't just stop wondering what all these people think about him from one second to the next, but Louie has a point. Ryan sees most of them once a year, at this party, and for the rest of the year they practically don't exist. Ami is happy and kissing her girl by the grill, swatting at people with the tongs when they get annoying. And Ryan is—he's sitting here with Louie and a bunch of tiny burgers and maybe that's happiness, too.

Louie starts talking about hockey—about Nick, about how easy he is to play with. "He's amazing," Louie says. "He's better than anyone else

I've ever played with."

"Do we have a little crush?" Ryan teases.

Louie laughs. "No, it's just fascinating, isn't it? Guys who are that good can play with anyone. He's got such a sense for the game. He always knows where I'll be."

"Yeah." Ryan nods. "Just a tiny little hockey crush."

"Says the guy who had a hockey crush on my dad."

"Oh, I've been cured, don't worry."

Louie shrugs the tiniest bit. "He was a good hockey player. I don't think that's—I think that's why I thought I had to do whatever he was telling me. Because he does know what he's talking about. People pay a lot of money to send their kids to his camps."

"And you got all that for the low price of zero dollars and some childhood trauma."

"It's not *trauma*," Louie says. "It's—"

"You guys!" Ami kneels down in front of them with two plates. "You have to try my girlfriend's chocolate cake."

"Oh, absolutely," Ryan says and takes one of the plates. "That's so cute. You're bringing me your *girlfriend's* chocolate cake."

Ami's cheeks go pink. "Shut up."

"Why is everyone telling me to shut up?" Ryan asks. "I speak the truth."

"No one wants to hear the truth." Ami laughs. She hands the other plate to Louie. "Cake is so much better than the truth. Although I've noticed that my dad likes you a lot better now."

"I've noticed that, too," Ryan grumbles. Ami's dad actually smiled at him when he got here, which hasn't happened in approximately five years.

"He didn't think Ryan was good enough for me," Ami explains to a confused-looking Louie.

"Even though I have great hair and I'm rich."

"Not rich enough," Ami says with a wink. "No, really, he doesn't care that much about money, but he didn't think we were being serious."

"Which he was correct about," Ryan says. Maybe it's a good thing their little charade is over. Maybe it was stupid and just helped Ryan lie to himself about what kind of life he was living. It was an easy way out, although for a while he believed he deserved an easy way out.

Ami smiles tightly. "You'll be okay without me."

"We'll make sure he's okay," Louie says and gently jostles Ryan.

Ami seems to approve. "I like you way better than his high school teammates."

It's not hard to like Louie better than Ryan's high school teammates. Whenever some of those guys started talking about girls, Ryan wanted to walk right out of that locker room. Some of them were also deeply decent and Ryan tried to stick with them, even though he never felt as deeply decent as them because he spent his entire time lying to them and pretending he was so straight and so into chicks and really loved boobs. He was never actually Ryan around them.

If someone had told him that he'd one day have teammates that he'd be comfortable enough with to come out to them, Ryan would have— he would have laughed for a million years, honestly. He's never thought much about it before, but he's definitely not the guy he was back then. He's not the guy all of these people think they know. They can't even like him because they don't know him.

Louie knows him.

Louie knows him and he's here anyway.

Ami smirks at him.

Shit.

Shit, shit, shit.

"Enjoy that cake," she says and wanders away, but not without shooting Ryan another look over her shoulder. *I see you*, it says.

Ryan eats his cake.

He will not think about it.

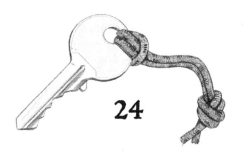

24

Louie can't stop staring at the little bit of chocolate at the corner of Ryan's mouth.

A normal person would hand him a napkin.

Louie does not feel like a normal person. For one completely wild second, he thinks about kissing Ryan right where that bit of chocolate is. Louie isn't Louie right now. He's someone who eats pasta salad with mayo in it and follows that up with a huge chunk of chocolate cake.

Someone who thinks about the corner of Ryan's mouth.

Someone who hasn't thought about making the Cardinals roster in days.

Someone who's remembered how to breathe.

They stay at Ami Kuroda's party until midnight, then Ryan decides he's had enough and tugs Louie over to a tipsy Ami, who wraps her arms around him and gives him a long, tight hug. When she's done with Ryan, she hugs Louie as well, even though Ryan tries to tell her not to.

Something in Louie's stomach tips over dangerously when Ryan tries to come to his rescue. Ami makes it a quick one, since Ryan's protest comes a second too late.

"Sorry," she says and almost falls over when she pulls away. Louie catches her by her elbow.

"You okay?" he asks.

"I was okay two tequila shots ago," she says brightly. She glances at Ryan, who is now talking to her girlfriend, and turns back to Louie. "You're so much better for him than I could have ever been." She gently pats his biceps. "You should kiss him if that's what you want. Maybe I'm just drunk and, yeah, you don't know me, but I see you. And if I know one thing, it's that life is too short to not kiss the people you want to kiss. If they want to be kissed by you. You understand what I'm saying?"

"I—no," Louie says. He does understand that she's telling him to kiss Ryan, except he doesn't... oh, whatever, he won't admit it to her, but he can at least admit it to himself. He wants to. He's been staring at the corner of Ryan's mouth all evening.

"Yeah, you do," Ami says. What is she, a mind reader?

Well, then. He will admit it to her, which is just another not-Louie thing to add to tonight's list. "I do, but—"

"Uh-uh." Ami wags her finger at him. She gives him another pat. "Sometimes you just have to turn off your brain and stop thinking about everyone and everything else and go for what *you* need. You're the most important person in your life." His arm gets a poke in emphasis. "For the record, I'm glad he has you. Thank you for taking care of him."

Then she leaves Louie standing there to give Ryan another hug.

Of course he'll take care of him. That's what you do when you're on a team. Although Ryan isn't the kind of guy who needs anyone else. He thinks he does, and wants everyone's approval, but in the end, he'll always be fine on his own.

He was fine coming to Hartford. He carved out a place for himself on that new team. Everyone thought it was a bad move and then he helped take a struggling team to the playoffs. They didn't make it far, but having Ryan gave the Cardinals a chance.

Louie waits until Ryan and Ami are done saying goodbye, until Ryan has gathered up their empty dip bowls, then they climb over a wooden fence onto a dirt road. It's the way they came, a shortcut, Ryan told him earlier. And one where they won't get run over.

"Is it okay if we head back after lunch tomorrow?" Ryan asks as he turns on his small flashlight. "I really wanna sleep in one more time. Even if you get up at the ass-crack of dawn to go for a run."

Louie went on a run twice since they got here. He's just not very good at sleeping in. On most days, he quietly sneaks downstairs and sits on the porch with Ryan's dad before he goes to work—which is to say, his garage. One time, he got to tag along with Ryan's dad and watch him paint furniture for an hour. He literally just sat there and did nothing but look and he was okay with that.

He almost asks Ryan if they can stay for another day, but they're meeting their trainer bright and early the day after tomorrow, and Louie can't blow up everyone's schedule like that.

"What?" Ryan asks.

"I didn't say anything," Louie says.

"Your thoughts are very loud."

"They're not."

"I wasn't saying I know what you're thinking, don't worry." Ryan laughs. "God, can you imagine? If people could read minds?"

Louie thinks of Ami, who can definitely read minds. He pushes that away with all his might. "Don't want people to know that you think about tacos in bags all day?" he quips.

"Yes. And the occasional penis. You know how it is. I mean, you don't."

"I kind of do," Louie says. He's afraid he's been thinking about 'the occasional penis' more than Ryan has.

"But occasionally," Ryan rambles on, "not at the rink, I'm not thinking about the guys' dicks, I swear, but, like—wait. What did you just say?"

"Nothing," Louie says. Why did he say that? He's not even drunk; he has no excuse. The truth just slipped right out of his mouth because he's not himself today.

Ryan stops walking. "Louie?"

Louie stops walking a few feet ahead. He can barely even see Ryan, just the patch of light on the ground from the flashlight. "Can we just go back to the house?"

"Sure," Ryan says, but he doesn't move. He's looking at Louie differently than he was a minute ago and Louie wishes he could take it all back.

His heart is racing like it does after a long shift. Ami really got to him with what she said; he has no idea how she knew. Possibly, she caught him looking at the chocolate at the corner of Ryan's mouth and jumped to the correct conclusions.

The wind picks up, goosebumps rising on Louie's arms. Leaves rustle all around them. Louie tears his eyes off Ryan to look up. Not a star in the sky. Right then, a raindrop hits him right in the forehead.

"Aw, crap," Ryan says and finally gets a move on, looking back at Louie once before he starts running.

Louie can't do anything but follow.

The rain picks up long before they reach the end of the Harrises' driveway. When they stumble up the stairs to the front door, Louie is swimming in his sneakers and his shirt is sticking to his skin.

In the distance, lightning strikes, the thunder rolling over them a moment later.

"Fucking hell," Ryan mutters and pulls off his sneakers outside the door, where they finally have the porch roof over their heads. "I have ponds in there. Lakes."

Louie wordlessly unties his Converse, the tips of his hair dripping when he bends down. It's gotten messy and shaggy since the end of the season and Louie barely even noticed since his mom wasn't around to nag at him about it. He can barely get his wet shoes off, nearly tripping over himself.

Ryan reaches out to steady him, fingertips cold against Louie's skin. He lets go quickly, without saying a word, but then he just stands there with the house key in his hand and doesn't unlock the door.

"Are we going in?" Louie whispers, the wind almost whipping the words away.

"Yeah, yeah, of course," Ryan says and fumbles the key into the lock.

Thunder hides their footsteps on the stairs up to Ryan's room. The lights seem too bright when Ryan flicks them on. He quietly grabs towels and throws one to Louie, who only barely manages to catch it because Ryan's pale blue shirt with the flamingo pattern, now drenched, is practically see-through.

Ryan goes for his socks first and makes a face. "Is there anything worse than wet socks?"

On a regular day, Louie could probably think of a few things. Except today is not a regular day.

Ryan stops toweling his hair dry and stares at Louie when he doesn't reply. "What is going on right now?"

"Nothing," Louie says and pulls off his own socks.

"You keep saying that." Ryan stops what he's doing to stare down Louie some more. "I'm not buying it."

Louie sighs. He almost made it out the other side of this trip without embarrassing himself, without forgetting who they are to each other and who they will be to each other when they go back home. How did he become this person? He's convinced it's all Ryan's fault. It's Ryan and the way his thighs look in those shorts and his see-through shirt and the corner of his mouth that doesn't even have chocolate on it anymore and the way he looks at Louie when he's worried about him.

Louie's never met anyone who cares this much about other people. People who weren't even that kind to him when they first met. Being around Ryan makes him wonder if he should care about other people more.

"Did I do something?" Ryan asks and takes a step closer. "Did I say something stupid without noticing? I do that sometimes, you know me. I swear, it's all cool, what you said earlier just threw me off, but it's not…

179

what did I do?"

"It's just something Ami said." Louie shakes his head. "It doesn't matter."

Except it does matter. It matters because it struck something in him the way lightning sometimes splits trees straight in half. And now there's a part of him that thinks he can't and there's a part of him that believes her, and one of those parts is just a little bigger than the other.

Ryan huffs. "What did she say?"

"Something about…" Louie looks up at Ryan. He only has an inch and a half on him, but he's just so much bigger than Louie, although Louie doesn't notice much right now. Because there's the corner of Ryan's mouth and Louie's world has zeroed down to just that.

"Oh," Ryan says, like he understood something, even though Louie didn't say a word.

"We should go to bed," Louie says. He can't do whatever he wants. He can't kiss Ryan because he feels like it. Except Ami said—she said something about the other person wanting it, too, and maybe that was supposed to tell him something about Ryan.

"Did you know," Ryan says, his voice a little breathless, "that Pennsylvania is a little bit like Las Vegas? And that whatever happens here—"

Louie doesn't let him finish. He should have let him finish. He should have asked for permission. Scratch that, he shouldn't have come here in the first place. Because coming here led to this: his lips on Ryan's and his hands on Ryan's sides and a tornado in his head.

The lights flicker and thunder rumbles and Louie should take that as a warning, but he doesn't because Ryan is kissing him back like he's been waiting just for this, like he's needed exactly this. And Louie *wants*. He wants to get closer, he wants to grab Ryan's hair, and he wants to feel his skin and he wants to kiss his neck and he wants to get that shirt off him and he wants and wants and wants.

The rain is loud against the big window behind Ryan's bed, but not loud enough to hide the low whine Louie lets out when Ryan grips him just a little tighter. Louie lets go of Ryan's damp shirt, curls his fingers around the back of Ryan's neck, touches his cheek.

Another roll of thunder, another flash of lightning and the power goes out, leaving them in total darkness.

Ryan pulls away, hands still on Louie. "Huh."

Louie tries to catch his breath somehow. He's never felt his heart beat this fast. He can't remember, can't think. What happens now? How is anything ever going to be normal again? He wants to push Ryan away and wants him closer at the same time.

"Not gonna lie," Ryan says into the silence, "I wasn't expecting that."

"I..." Louie shouldn't lie either. He was expecting this. Has been expecting this for weeks. "I think I'm bi." Another truth, a different truth. One he couldn't hold in any longer.

"Congratulations," Ryan says, voice soft now. His thumb gently rubs at Louie's side. "Are you okay?"

"I don't think so," Louie says. He shakes his head. He hasn't felt okay in a long time and it has nothing to do with this kiss.

"Hey," Ryan says, his hand falling away. The flashlight he's been carrying around with him comes back to life and Ryan puts it on the dresser with the hockey sticks and pucks on it. "It's late and we..." He grabs Louie's towel and wraps his around his shoulders. "We should get some sleep."

"Yeah," Louie says. He's suddenly cold all over.

"By the time we get up, the power will probably be on again," Ryan says casually.

Nothing about this is casual. How the hell did he flip that switch so fast? One second they're kissing, the next they're having a completely normal conversation. Louie's world just shifted on its axis and for Ryan it's business as usual?

Louie turns away, peels off his wet clothes, and digs through his suitcase for a shirt that's at least dry. His heart is still fluttering at the thought of Ryan's hand at the small of his back. Like he's never been touched by another person before. Between Ryan being his teammate and Ryan making his heart explode with how much he wants his hands back on him, at the small of his back, or anywhere, really, anywhere else, Louie is completely lost. Unmoored. Adrift. Staring at Ryan in the flashlight's small beam that's pointed right at Ryan's thighs.

This is the universe mocking him. Pointing and laughing at him. Look, there is Louie Hathaway, and he's a total mess. He kissed his teammate because he wanted to, even though he knew better. He can't look at the guy's thighs without fainting like an eighteenth century damsel. He can't talk to him without wanting to ravage his mouth like a romance novel hero. That's not him; it can't be him.

He needs to focus on hockey. He's going to make the roster next season. Everything else doesn't matter; can't matter.

Louie gets into bed, Ryan's bed, and pulls up the sheets and closes his eyes. One more night, then they're going back to Connecticut. They're going back to real life.

Ryan's footsteps move around the room and whenever they get close to the bed, Louie freezes up. Obviously, Ryan won't get into bed with him, but that doesn't make Louie want it less.

When he fell asleep in Ryan's bed last season, maybe he wanted to wake up next to him a little. Louie grips the sheets harder; forces himself to stop. He counts to ten along to Ryan's footsteps.

Then something rustles beside the bed. Ryan's sheets. "Lou?" he says after a moment.

Louie takes a deep breath. "Yeah?"

"I meant what I said," Ryan whispers. "This can stay here if that's what you want."

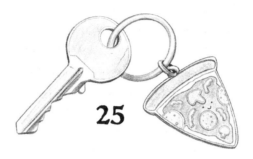

25

Ryan is going to lose his entire mind. He's kind of losing his entire mind already. Maybe he lost his entire mind a week ago when Louie kissed him in his childhood bedroom, with rain-drenched strands of hair sticking to his forehead and his lips cold from the run back and his fingertips burning hot against Ryan's cheek.

Louie's right there in the kitchen, putting together lettuce wraps that are slowly turning into just salad because he keeps ripping the lettuce, cursing softly under his breath every time.

They've been back for a week.

They've been quietly, peacefully existing together at Ryan's house.

And neither of them has said a word about the kiss.

Ryan, in an attempt to not ruin a good thing, told Louie that Pennsylvania was basically Vegas. Except the state of Pennsylvania isn't big enough to swallow up something as monumental as your teammate kissing you. On the mouth. With his mouth. And tongue. There was tongue. There were wandering hands. And Ryan told him it was okay to forget all about it.

He was worried about the look on Louie's face. It was a strange cocktail of wonder and regret. Ryan drank it all in and decided to make things easy for Louie. That, of course, entailed making things harder for himself, but it was all in the spirit of finally having a normal season. When Louie makes the team in the fall—and that's a when, not an if—he'll stay with Ryan and they'll be roommates and they'll be friends and that is where it ends. There won't be any break-ups, there won't be any hard feelings.

Ryan will not ask Louie why he kissed him. The way he sees it, there are two options: either Louie has been suspecting that he's bi and wanted to make sure and Ryan conveniently happened to be there, or he just wanted to kiss Ryan. Both of these options are terrible, horrible, no good at all. So Ryan will write the kissing off as some weird summer fluke.

Considering Louie's life so far, this was probably the first fun summer vacation he's ever had. Which is pretty horrifying, now that Ryan thinks about it, but Louie must have been drunk on the freedom of it all. He wasn't home, no dad to nitpick, no brother to compare himself to, just dozing in porch chairs and eating the snacks Ryan's mom made and going for walks on dirt roads and listening to distant thunderstorms while they were falling asleep.

To Ryan, it was perfect. Including the kiss.

The kiss he told Louie to forget about. Because he wanted to protect him.

Clearly, clearly, he's going through something. He's (badly, adorably) making lettuce wraps, for fuck's sake. When he told Ryan he was bi, it was delivered without emotion. Just another thing he had to deal with like he deals with anything else, with hockey, with lettuce wraps. Silent stoicism.

Ryan asked him if he was okay. Louie said no. And now Ryan keeps hearing that soft little no. Day after day, it bounces around in his head, draws his eyes back to Louie.

"I don't think this is working," Louie says and looks up at Ryan. He wipes at the hair that has fallen into his eyes. He doesn't put product in it, so it's just soft and floppy. Perfect to sink your fingers into.

Ryan clears his throat. "It's fine. Just put it in a bowl."

"I think I… wrapped too hard," Louie mumbles.

"Chop it all up," Ryan says.

"And throw it in a Dorito bag?"

"Not saying no to that."

Louie shakes his head at him and moves to grab bowls from the cupboard by the sink and he's not exactly wearing the tightest sweatpants, so they ride down and—Ryan looks away. He can't stare at the dimples low on Louie's back, he's better than that.

"I can go to the store and grab tortilla wraps," Ryan says to the floor.

"This is fine," Louie says and scrapes the wraps into two bowls. "Sorry."

"I like salad." Ryan takes his bowl and shuffles away to the dining room table, which they started using after they came back without even talking about it. Louie ordered them dinner and when it got here, he put out plates.

To Ryan, it was just another sign that something was off, but now he actually likes it. When he lived with Carrot, they never ate at the table. Ryan isn't sure Carrot is aware of the table as a concept.

"You don't," Louie says and joins him, his bowl meeting the table with an emphatic thunk. "You think salad is a side."

"I mean." Ryan spears a bit of chicken with his fork. "This at least has chicken in it. That's not a side."

Louie's eyes narrow. "Stop trying to make me feel better."

"Fine," Ryan says. "I hate green things. They're bad. Ew. Can't believe you'd make me food. Terrible of you."

Something not entirely unlike a smile makes an appearance on Louie's face before he starts eating his lettuce wrap disaster.

"Enjoying the show, hmm?"

Ryan has been caught. Not literally. Liam, who appeared next to him out of nowhere, has no idea what Ryan was thinking about.

Nick and Louie are on the ice. The ice the Cardinals usually practice on. Summer's almost over and informal skates are starting. In Hartford, it's Nick who gets everyone together as soon as it seems acceptable. Nick, and with him Louie, have been skating, training all summer long, but the fact that they've moved back to the rink in Silver Lakes means the new season is approaching at breakneck speed.

And Ryan can't stop watching Louie. That's what Liam caught him doing. He caught him watching Louie. *The show*, as Liam called it.

Last season, Louie was good. He played well. He deserved to get called up. But the guy who's on the ice with Nick right now is a different player. He moves differently, passes differently, and he's smiling. The laser focus is the same, but last season's Louie never cracked a smile while he was on the ice. Probably thought people (his dad) would say he's not taking hockey seriously.

Ryan will not be so arrogant as to suggest that he did this by telling Louie not to go back to Boston. Louie made his own choices; Ryan didn't make him do anything. But he may have played a part and he's glad he did.

"Nick has been texting me all summer," Liam says, amused. "We do have an open spot on our line."

"You think Nick wants Louie full-time?" Ryan asks, even though the answer is currently on the ice and having a lively discussion by the goal.

Liam clears his throat and does air quotes when he says, "Lee, you have to come to the rink today, this is going to work, I feel it." He shakes his head. "Like Nick will be the one making that choice."

"Pretty sure Coach listens when Nick has a request," Ryan says.

"Nick is very accommodating," Liam says. "He'd never actually *request* that sort of thing. I guess he plans on convincing Coach the conventional way."

Liam doesn't tell him what the conventional way is and gets on the ice. Presumably, Nick's plan is to convince Coach with sheer on-ice chemistry. Louie already played with Nick and Liam for a few games last season and it worked out for them, but now Nick has also spent all summer teaching Louie how to find him in every corner of the rink. Those two are tuned into each other and Ryan highly doubts anyone else will stand a chance at this point.

Good for Louie. He's ready for this.

Ryan lets them have the ice a little while longer, not so much watching the three of them but following Louie around the ice with his eyes. He tries to snatch the puck away from Liam, who promptly puts him into a headlock and pulls his practice jersey over his head.

In the meantime, Nick sweeps the pucks out of the net, smirking at Louie and Liam, who are still wrestling. He comes over to the bench to grab his water bottle, raising his eyebrows at Ryan.

"Just admiring your work," Ryan says.

Nick glances at Louie, who seems to be trying to evade the fighting lesson Liam wants to give him. "I didn't do anything."

It's very *Nick* of him.

Ryan shrugs. "You gave him a chance."

"Because he deserved one," Nick says. "He's the one who showed up every day." His lips twitch. "You showed up every day, too."

"He made me," Ryan says. He would have shown up for training even if Louie hadn't been a pain in the ass about it, but he may have taken a few more rest days.

"Uh-huh," Nick says, like he knows that Ryan, even though he complained a lot about getting up early, looked forward to training or skating with them every day.

Nick puts his water bottle down and skates away. Ryan gives himself another second, breathing in deeply. The closer they get to next season, the more antsy he gets. It's like he's vibrating on the inside. He's not worried about making the roster, but he can't stop thinking about whether or not Louie will stay.

He doesn't know what would be worse—Louie staying with him and being around all day, every day, or Louie going back to Springfield and leaving Ryan on the Cards all by himself.

Ryan is at least sort of friends with Nick and Liam, but he's not friends with them the way he's friends with Carrot and Slaw. Those two knew (know, actually) that Ryan is extremely-not-straight, and Ryan just doesn't see himself telling Nick Rivera that he loves dick. Sorry, Nick, but that's not happening.

Liam is a solid maybe on the coming out agenda. He's nice and he loves the boys, but he's also such a dude. Ryan picks at his stick tape to give his hands something to do while he has his crisis.

"Rah-rah," Liam shouts, grinning at him, "get your ass out here."

Ryan slowly clambers over the boards. He's not making any decisions today. Or this week. He grabs himself a puck and starts doing tricks. It was always one of his favorite parts of warm-ups when he was in high school. He stopped doing them in Toronto after his first game when some reporter called him a show-off. When Nick and Louie started practicing lacrosse goals, Ryan started playing around with pucks. He throws one as high up as he can, catches it, does it again, goes higher and higher until he loses the puck and has to chase after it.

That's when he notices Louie watching him from across the rink.

Ryan picks up the puck and nods at Louie. Then he tosses it. Louie, being Louie, catches it on the blade of his stick without much of an effort.

Ryan wants to kiss him on the mouth. Fuck's sake.

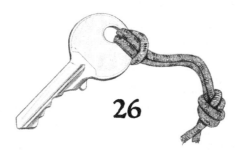

26

Louie is on the roster for the Cardinals' first preseason game.

Hardly surprising. He's been on the roster for the Cardinals' first preseason game so many times that it has lost all meaning to him. Ryan isn't playing—Yang hung up his skates last summer, so there's an open spot for Ryan. Ryan may end up playing with Waldo this season. Maybe Coach will try him with someone else, but he absolutely has a spot on the roster.

Unlike Louie.

His Calder-winning brother obviously doesn't have to worry about making his team's roster either. Dad sent a text in the family group chat, praising Bastien for his hard work this summer. He mentioned he wasn't expecting to see Louie on NHL ice since he spent his time partying instead.

Because Ryan posted one picture of Louie's birthday party on Instagram. He even asked Louie for permission and Louie didn't give a shit at the time. It was a photo Ryan's mom took, with perfect sunset lighting and Ryan wearing a party hat while Louie got a flower tucked behind his ear by one of Ryan's nieces. It's a cute picture. Ryan's mom emailed it to him along with a few others from the party.

Ryan clearly got them too because he printed one out—Louie has no idea where he found a printer—and pinned it to their fridge with a Cardinals magnet. So now Louie can stare at them sitting on the steps that lead up to the back porch, both holding up their pink cocktails and smiling, every day. And every day his heart trips over itself.

Which is better than spending the morning being pissed at Dad because he had one good birthday and Dad won't even let him have that.

It doesn't matter. Summer's over. Louie's playing, and scoring, and Coach doesn't send him to Springfield with the first round of cuts. He doesn't mention it in the group chat. Not getting cut after one game is nothing to be proud of.

"Thank fuck, I'm finally in the lineup," Ryan says before they play against the Ravens in New York. "I was starting to get bored."

Nick sighs deeply because he's not playing. Yet.

Louie actually cannot wait to hit the ice with him. Coach Beaulieu saw how they clicked last season and he took a look at them together during training camp, but that's not the same thing. Last season, Louie filled someone else's spot. This season, he wants that spot to be his and only his. There's a buzz under his skin that carries him from one game to the next, and when they're playing in Boston, he finally gets his wish.

Nick scores two, both with assists from Louie, then Louie scores one himself, and Liam gets the empty netter. This is good, this is right, and Louie can't stop talking about it. He can't believe the Cardinals would give them a day off during the preseason. He needs to get back on the ice. This is it. He knows that this is it.

He practically chews Ryan's ear off all day.

"It's like he's always exactly where I need him to be," Louie tells him at the grocery store.

"It's like he knows where I'll be," Louie says when they have lunch together.

"It's like he can read my mind," Louie whispers when they sit on the couch together.

That's when Ryan says, "That's probably because he can. He's just that good."

"I want to play with him," Louie says.

Ryan snorts.

Louie rolls his eyes. "What, are you five?"

"Sorry," Ryan says. "I do take this very seriously and I understand your wish to play with Nick because he's very good at the whole hockey thing."

"He is," Louie says with emphasis. His face has turned flaming red.

"Look…" Ryan turns away from the TV. "I can see that you and Nick work really well together. And Coach has eyes, so he can see it, too."

Louie sighs. Right. That's what he thought last season. Although Coach didn't give him a chance to play with Nick a year ago.

"If Coach sends you down, Nick will probably cry," Ryan says.

"I don't think Nick cries. He's too good at hockey to cry."

Ryan laughs. "In any case, you're staying."

When Louie got called up in February, Ryan said something like that to him. He doesn't remember exactly. Something about him making the lineup when he'd just gotten called up. And then he didn't. Funny how Ryan believed in him when he didn't even know him. He just decided he would.

It feels like less of a platitude now. Maybe because Louie also believes it. Something is different this season, although Louie can't put his finger on what it is. Could be him. He's different.

The day before their second-to-last preseason game, back home in Hartford, Coach wants to talk to him. This is it, then. Decision time. Louie does his best to feel as little as possible. This isn't new to him. He made it this far last season and then Beaulieu sat him down and told him he's not ready. He could see that Louie wanted it, could see how hard he worked, but it wasn't enough.

"Have a seat," Beaulieu says and nods at the exact same chair that Louie sat in last year. That chair makes Louie sweat waterfalls. That chair haunts his nightmares. He'd rather stand, but that's not how this works.

Louie sits. He waits until Coach sits down as well. His face feels hot like it did after he drank that pink cocktail Ryan's dad made for him. Except this is his life, his career, his future. Louie is going to throw up.

"Look, Hathaway," Coach says, his face not betraying a single emotion.

Crap. That's exactly how this started last year. *Look, Hathaway, I think you're almost there. But not yet.*

"I don't want to beat around the bush or anything," he goes on and holds out his hand. "Congrats, kid."

"I—" Louie stares at Beaulieu's hand. "Yeah?"

"Yeah." Coach smiles. Not a rarity with him, but Louie has rarely been the one that smile was directed at.

Louie manages to kick himself into gear and shake Coach's hand. "Thank you."

"Hathaway, I know it took a while…"

Louie only nods. It did take a while.

"But I've got a good feeling about this." Coach leans back in his chair, looking pleased with himself. "You put in the work. This is your reward. You earned this."

"Thank you," Louie says again. He's sitting ramrod straight in his chair. His palms are sweaty. The little voice in his head is just screaming at this point. On the outside, he politely says *thank you*. His entire body is shaking on the inside.

Coach lets him leave a moment later, probably about to grab someone else to reveal their fate, although there's barely anyone left now.

Louie slowly shuffles out of Coach's office and makes sure not to slam the door. He is calm, he is calm, he is calm. He is a professional.

His entire life just changed.

Down the hall, Ryan is leaning against the wall, looking down at his phone. He shoves it into his pocket as soon as Coach's office door has clicked shut. Ryan stares at him.

Louie nods. Grins.

"Yeeesss!" Ryan shouts and it only takes him a few steps and then he's right in front of Louie and sweeping him into a hug, actually lifting him off his feet. "You did it, I knew it!" He gives Louie a shake. "I fucking knew it."

Louie just holds on.

If he doesn't hold on, he'll scream.

"DID LOUIE MAKE IT!"

A moment later, Waldo joins their huddle, then Liam, then someone else that Louie can't see because his face is smushed into Ryan's chest. It takes at least a minute for them all to let go of him. A minute that feels like an hour because he's so close to Ryan and he wants to keep being close to Ryan, but he can't, and it's ruining the moment.

As soon as the guys have started making plans to celebrate and Louie isn't attached to any other people anymore, someone gently claps him on the back. Nick.

"Rivs, our place tonight," Ryan says. "Everyone needs to bring something, though. I can make about five grilled cheese sandwiches and that's it."

Louie doesn't tell Ryan to knock it off; that he doesn't want the party.

He does want it. And he deserves it.

"I'm never inviting the guys over again," Ryan says as he moves around the living room, shoveling paper plates and plastic cups into a huge trash bag from the coffee table.

Louie gently pushes the piano stool back into place. Some of the guys tried to give them a little concert. Went for Vanessa Carlton, which might have been a bit ambitious for them. Ryan thankfully didn't tell anyone that Louie took piano lessons until he was twelve.

He finds his phone, forgotten on top of the piano. One unread message from Dominic is waiting for him. When Ryan drove them home from practice, Louie sent his older brother a text and told him he made the team. That he and Cameron can have his tickets for the Cardinals' home opener if they want them. The first reply reads *HELL YEAH* with way too many exclamation points, and the next one says: *proud of you, of course we're coming. hope you're partying hard.*

They didn't party that hard because they do have a game tomorrow that most of them will be playing in, but half the team stuck around until two in the morning and Louie will definitely regret staying up this late. Most likely when his alarm goes off in the morning.

"What are you smiling about?" Ryan asks and swipes an empty cup off the windowsill.

Louie shrugs. Puts his phone down. Looks at Ryan. "I didn't tell my family that I made the team. Just Dominic."

"Good for you," Ryan says.

"You think so?"

Ryan drops the trash bag and sits on the piano stool with Louie. It's way too small for the both of them. "Do you feel guilty about not telling them?"

"Yeah," Louie says. "I mean, I… I should want to tell them."

"Maybe. But you don't have to. Just like you don't have to go home for the summer and don't have to ignore your birthday for an event you don't want to go to."

"Isn't that selfish, though?"

"I think everyone should be a little selfish every now and then. It's a fine line, but you're walking it pretty well."

"Dad will find out eventually anyway." Louie shrugs. He just didn't want to deal with the *took you long enough* text today.

Ryan knocks his shoulder against Louie's. "And then what?"

"And then I would love for him to be happy for me," Louie says. "And maybe he will be, in his own way. But he won't say it."

"Well, I'm not your dad, but I can say it." Ryan glances at him. "I'm happy for you."

Louie can't glance back at him. He can't, he can't, he can't. He does. Ryan's eyes are so sincere and his eyelashes are so pretty and it's way too easy to lean in; those two inches between their mouths may as well not exist. This is nothing like the kiss in Ryan's attic room. This is soft. A *hello again*. A huge mistake.

Like last time, Ryan kisses him back. He doesn't touch Louie otherwise, but he's once again this steady presence. Matches him. Moves with him. Whatever this is, Ryan isn't scared of it.

Louie tries to pull away. Really. He just leans right back in. It's only when he catches himself reaching for Ryan, his fingers bumping against Ryan's thigh, that he finally snaps out of it.

"It's late," Louie says. "We have… hockey. And…" Where was this sentence going? Nowhere coherent, that's for sure.

Ryan doesn't say anything for a long moment. Then he clears his throat. "Yeah. I'll just…" He stands up and grabs the trash bag. "I'll just take this out."

"Okay," Louie whispers.

Ryan leaves, the trash bag rustling. He curses under his breath in the hallway.

Louie stays, frozen to the piano stool, his lips still tingling. What did he just do?

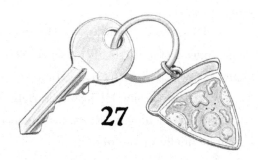

27

Louie needs to stop kissing him.

Ryan needs to tell Louie that he has to stop.

The first time was bad enough. Ryan thought about it for days. He still thinks about it sometimes. All the time. Nonstop.

Still, the first time was easier because Ryan could call it a fluke, an accident. High temperatures, thunderstorms, and the soft chirp of the cicadas just does shit to you. It makes you think you need to kiss someone because it's summer and that's what you were told you're supposed to do when you were a teenager.

But now Louie has kissed him twice. Twice is not an accident. Twice is… something.

Twice is what keeps Ryan up that night. And the night after that.

Louie acts like it didn't happen at all.

And that's probably the best course of action. The season is starting—on the road in Toronto of all places—and Ryan needs to survive that. Maybe he can think about Louie and the way he kisses him like he's the most precious person in the world after that, when they're back home.

He's not sure that Louie understands how he kisses. Ryan has never been kissed like that.

"I have never been kissed like that," Ryan tells Carrot, who proceeds to drive straight off Rainbow Road. Ryan wanted to hang out today because he misses Carrot, but he also needed to talk with someone who isn't a walking disaster.

"Okay," Carrot says and puts down his controller. "Tell me more. Who was on the other end of this life-changing tongue action?"

"Uh, a guy," Ryan says. He looks around for a pillow to grab. He needs emotional support. Unfortunately, this apartment hasn't changed at all since Ryan moved out and Carrot has not yet discovered the many advantages of throw pillows.

Carrot picks up his beer. "Yeah, I figured. Did you meet him this summer?"

"Kind of." Ryan shrugs. "I met him before this summer, but I really, *really* met him this summer."

"You met him with your mouth." Carrot nods, like a mouth-meeting connoisseur. "Did you..." He wiggles his eyebrows.

"No," Ryan says. He doesn't know why he sounds so offended. When he still lived here, he left the premises to hook up with Kaden all the time. And Carrot definitely had to listen to way too much of Ryan's personal shit while hardly ever sharing personal shit of his own.

"Why not?"

"Because he's... emotionally constipated," Ryan says. "He's not there yet. And, honestly, I don't know if I want to get there with him."

Carrot shoots him a look.

"What?" Ryan asks.

"You know that I follow you on Instagram, yeah?"

"Yeah, why?"

"I just... I was also following you on Instagram this summer."

Oh. Shit. Oh, fuck. Did Ryan just accidentally out Louie? That's what Carrot is implying, right? That he saw the photos Ryan posted throughout the summer. And that he's deduced (in Sherlock Holmes fashion) that Ryan didn't hook up with Nick, who is extremely married to hockey, or with Liam, who is extremely married to his wife. Which only leaves one option.

How does Ryan keep doing this? And why the fuck is everything so complicated? He just wants to talk to his friend about his life and it's so unfair that he can't.

"Let's talk about something else," Ryan says. "Are you seeing anyone?"

"Yes," Carrot says, without missing a beat. That's why Ryan loves Carrot. "The guy with the cute Labrador who lives down the hall. I run into him every fucking day when I go to practice. It's like he knows I'm dying to pet that dog."

"Very funny," Ryan says flatly. "It's a cute dog, though."

"Adorable. And always happy to see me."

Ryan sticks out his bottom lip. "I'm also always happy to see you."

"That's because you're actually a golden retriever," Carrot says and reaches out to ruffle Ryan's hair.

Ryan sighs and leans back. He nods at the TV. "Wanna restart this?"

"Or," Carrot says, "you could just tell me."

"Tell you what?"

"Everything." Carrot shrugs. "You know, all the stuff that's bugging you beyond the emotionally constipated guy."

"Nothing's bugging me," Ryan grumbles. "It's more like... I feel... ugh."

"I can relate to that feeling at least. Sometimes you have an *ugh* phase."

"Yeah, but... I shouldn't be having one?"

"Because?"

"Because," Ryan says, "things are awesome in Hartford. I played a good season. I had a great summer. That doesn't add up to an *ugh* phase."

Carrot nods. "But?"

"But things are different. I don't have anyone like you in Hartford. Or anyone like Slaw. I'm part of the team, but I'm not—they don't know me."

"They don't know you're gay," Carrot translates. He's good. That is also why Ryan loves him. "Yet."

"Yet," Ryan echoes.

Ryan is already writing an apology text in his head when he gets off the ice after the game in Toronto. The Cardinals walked in and said, actually, this is our place now. They were tied at one until the second intermission, their first goal scored by Louie, then Nick followed that up with a hat trick in the third. They got two empty netters, one of them Ryan's.

He caught Carrot's eye across the ice after the final buzzer—Ryan definitely owes him a beer after this.

Liam taps his head when he gets to his stall. "Drinks?"

"Drinks," Santa agrees loudly.

Louie refuses to go with them; says he needs to get some sleep. Ryan has an inkling that he probably didn't sleep well during his pregame nap. It wasn't as obvious during the preseason, but Louie has been nervous. Maybe about getting sent down after all. Louie played a perfect game, but knowing him, he doesn't trust that he's with the Cardinals for good.

If he's going to be this un-fun all season, Ryan's going to—he's going to accept it and do nothing because Louie finally made it and Ryan will not ruin a good thing.

When Ryan ended up in a ditch last winter, he thought he'd never be able to go out for a drink in Toronto again, but now it doesn't matter at all. Not his town anymore. He takes a handful of guys to a bar he likes and he sits in a booth with Liam, Santa and Waldo. Three guys who've been on the team for years. They *are* this team. Together with Nick and Yoshi. Obviously.

Ryan wants in. He is in. Only...

"Can I ask you guys something?" Ryan asks, glancing at the guys across from him before he turns to Waldo, who used to be the Cardinals'

You Can Play ambassador. When those were still a thing.

"Always," Waldo says at the same time that Liam says "No" and Santa says "Only if it's about ordering fries."

"Yes, to the fries," Ryan says. "I was wondering, though…"

"Hm?" Waldo prompts when Ryan doesn't immediately go on.

"Oh, he's making it suspenseful," Liam says, nodding at Ryan. "I'm an old man, I might die before you get the rest of this sentence out, have you considered that?"

God, Ryan is so stupid about this. Wrong place, wrong time for sure. Then again, the perfect place and time don't exist. "Have you guys ever had a gay teammate?" Ryan asks. He briefly considered reusing what he said to Carrot all those years ago: *So, what if I was gay?* Seems too bold now.

It's like the world immediately goes dead silent.

It obviously doesn't. People are still chatting, glasses are still clinking, the music is still being terrible. They're still in a bar. Fuck, Ryan shouldn't have asked in a bar with tons of other people around.

Liam is the first to say something. "Why are you asking?"

"Just out of curiosity," Ryan says with a shrug. Playing it cool. He is not cool. He is dying. He knew no one was going to say, *Yeah, duh, we love gay teammates*. And yet he somehow still expected it; was surprised when the answer was a different one.

Santa nods. "It doesn't really matter to us, you know? If a guy shows up and plays his game, we don't care."

Ryan does not love that answer. They should care. They should want that hypothetical guy to be safe on their team.

"What Santa is trying to say," Waldo cuts in, "is that we accept everyone."

"Yeah, that," Santa says.

That's better.

"We also don't name names," Liam says, suddenly sounding strict, like he does when Maja tries to eat crayons.

"Yeah, that's fair," Ryan says quickly. "I wasn't asking... I was just wondering." He wiggles in his seat and picks up the small menu with the sparse offering of snacks. "So, fries?"

Coming out is, unfortunately, a journey that never ends. It most definitely doesn't end easily and with fries.

"Why do you want them to know?" Louie asks when Ryan confesses that he almost... confessed. Three games on the road and they barely talked, which isn't that weird, but Ryan was starting to think that Louie might be avoiding him.

Because of the second kiss.

Now that they're back home and he's snuggled into his favorite blanket, he's acting perfectly normal. If normal is the same as pretending it never happened.

"Because," Ryan says. He'd love to look Louie in the eye while they're having this conversation, but Ryan can't anymore.

"Who you sleep with doesn't make you who you are."

"It kind of does."

"How?" Louie says. "Do you think you'd be a different person if you were straight?"

"I'd be less anxious about people finding out who I sleep with, that's for sure," Ryan says. "Maybe it doesn't make me who I am, but it's part of who I am. And I feel like the guy who walks into the locker room is not entirely me. I miss being me."

"Were you ever fully you?" Louie asks. "In Toronto, I mean?"

"You mean, was I out to the entire team?" Ryan laughs. In his dreams maybe. "Hell no. But I had my place on the team and it was a good place."

"And you don't like your place on this team."

"That's not really it either."

Ryan doesn't know how to explain it. It doesn't feel the same. Doesn't make sense to have this conversation with Louie either because he lives in a completely different world. In his world, you can just mind your business. Play hockey and anything beyond that doesn't matter to him.

Ryan sneaks a glance at Louie and finds Louie looking back at him.

Or maybe it's not that easy. It's never actually that easy. Ryan could ask. He would if he wasn't sure that he wouldn't get an answer.

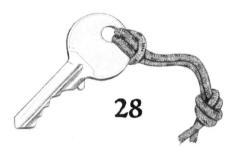

28

Ryan has started throwing a puck to Louie all the way across the ice during warm-ups the way they did at the rink during the summer. Every game, always right before he heads off the ice. It's gotten to a point where Louie wouldn't dare get off the ice before Ryan.

Louie isn't wildly superstitious like some other guys are, but it's part of the routine now. Hopefully, Ryan knows they can never stop doing this. Not because it's working (some of the guys insist that it is), but because Louie likes having this thing that connects him to Ryan.

Yes, he understands that he's absolutely hopeless. He's been very successful in ignoring that fact. Hockey is all that's allowed on his mind.

This is their fourth game of the season, their home opener, and Louie has a point streak going. He's had point streaks in the AHL, long ones too, but they didn't mean as much as this one does. This is the one he's been waiting for and he wants to keep it going for as long as he can.

His mom sent him a text this morning and said her and Dad unfortunately wouldn't be able to make it to the game, acting like Louie invited them. He didn't reply; he was about to walk into morning skate. Then he forgot all about it until he hit the ice that evening and found Dominic and Cameron behind the glass two minutes ago.

The people Louie wanted here came. They're wearing his jersey.

They brought a sign. Louie waves at them in passing and Dominic holds up his phone because he wants a picture. Ryan photobombs them, then tells Louie to wait, only to return with a random phone a moment later to snap another picture from the other side.

"Did we really need that one?" Louie asks, skating back to the bench with Ryan to make sure that picture doesn't end up anywhere Louie doesn't want it.

"Of course we did," Ryan says. "One for him, one for you."

Ryan still tosses his puck to Louie before warm-ups end, only this time Louie doesn't hurl it at the net but passes it on to Dominic afterwards. Dominic grins and waves, and when Louie scores his first goal that evening, he's glad that he invited him.

And when he scores his second goal, he's also glad that Dominic came, even though he tried so hard to leave hockey behind. He came here for Louie. Maybe a little bit for Cameron.

Louie doesn't think about scoring a third one. When you think too hard about it, it doesn't happen.

And, really, it shouldn't have happened.

Louie would have taken the two-goal game. That's good; it's excellent. It's proof that he belongs here. But then Ryan is… well, he's Ryan. And when he snatches the puck away from a Carolina Comet in the third period and takes off with it and finds that Louie has caught up, he doesn't shoot. He passes. The Cardinals are up 4–2, so it's not the worst mistake of his life, but it's still a mistake.

Louie could miss and throw away a damn good chance.

The thing is, Louie didn't just spend all summer training with Nick. Ryan was there, too.

Ryan knows exactly what kind of pass will connect here. He took a calculated risk and it pays off. The puck lands right on Louie's stick blade. Too late for him to properly shoot it, so Louie goes behind the goal with it, scoops it up the way Nick taught him and it's in before Louie can even think too much about what he's doing.

The goal light turns on, the horn blares, the arena erupts.

Ryan barrels into him first, screaming into his ear while hats start raining. The rest of the guys join in. Nick and Liam and Waldo. Santa dumps an entire water bottle on him when he skates to the bench for fist bumps.

This is it.

This is what he wanted. And it's even better than Louie imagined it would be.

"I'm just saying, it would have been a better play if you'd just taken the shot," Louie says, following Ryan into the house. "I'm not mad because you let me have it. But you would have had it, too. You gave away a goal."

"You still scored," Ryan says, his keys jingling as he picks out the house key. "I didn't give away anything."

"I'm talking about your stats," Louie says. "Goals look good on stats. What if, one day, you're about to hit a franchise record, but then you're missing one goal? And it's this one?"

"Then," Ryan says and opens the door to let Louie in, "I'll think of today and I'll remember that the reason I'm missing that one goal is because I wanted my friend to get his first career hat trick and I'll be fine."

Louie doesn't know what to do with that. So he does the only he thinks he can do: he pushes the door shut. With Ryan against it. And he kisses him.

Ryan makes a surprised noise and his keys hit the floor, which is when Louie briefly reconsiders whether or not this was a good idea, but then Ryan grabs Louie's sides and pulls him close. Louie's brain shuts down. He was going to focus on hockey; wasn't going to get distracted. Getting swept up in his personal bullshit was one thing in the summer, but he was going to push all of that far, far away when the season started. He almost managed.

Now here he is and it feels so good.

Ryan's fingers find Louie's and he gently takes the bag with Louie's hat trick pucks to set it down on the small table by the door. That's where their keys usually go. Ryan's stay on the floor while Louie kisses him. Louie completely forgets about them when Ryan's hands start to move, first up Louie's chest, to his neck, where they stay still for a moment. Ryan must be feeling Louie's wild heartbeat, out of control, flying away.

He's giving himself away, but he doesn't care.

Louie holds on for dear life.

He wanted the roster spot. He wanted the hatty. He also wants Ryan.

"Hey," Ryan says as he pulls away. "Hey, hey…" With care, he pries Louie's hands off his suit jacket.

Maybe Louie was holding on too tightly. "Sorry," he says. He doesn't know why he's apologizing. He's not actually sorry. Maybe for kissing Ryan without a warning, *again*, but not for holding on this time.

Ryan's thumb taps Louie's chin. "Look, you could have just said thank you. I wasn't expecting—"

"Thank you," Louie says. Then he leans back in, stops a breath away from Ryan's lips to see if he'll pull away, if he'll stop him. He doesn't. A second later, Ryan is the one who closes that minuscule gap between them.

He pushes himself away from the door, nudging Louie along with him easily. As they go, Ryan pushes Louie's suit jacket off his shoulders. He throws it over the back of one of the dining room chairs together with his own. Ryan's wearing his new forest green suit tonight. Louie already stared at him way too much when Ryan first came home with it, which Ryan at first interpreted as Louie silently telling him that he hated it. It's very much the opposite.

Ryan parks Louie against the big archway between the dining and the living room. He hasn't turned on the lights, so Louie can barely see his face in the glow of the streetlights. Slowly, he runs his fingers down the row of buttons of Louie's dress shirt and Louie squirms, his breath coming quickly by the time Ryan's fingers come to a halt at Louie's belt buckle.

He stills there for a moment, like he's trying to give them another chance to put a stop to this.

Louie doesn't. He wants to know what happens next.

Ryan ignores the belt buckle, pulls Louie's shirt out of his pants instead and steps closer. He kisses Louie, slow and languid, coaxing his mouth open while he undoes the top button of Louie's shirt. He kisses the line of Louie's jaw and all Louie can do is stand there and breathe, breathe, breathe.

With the utmost patience, Ryan opens the next button, then dips his head down to press his lips to Louie's collarbone and Louie's breath hitches in the quiet. Ryan looks up, his nose nudging Louie's chin. Louie wants to tell him to keep going, to do that again, but the words all get jumbled in his throat and come out in a low moan.

Louie feels his control starting to slip. Maybe he should let it. He grabs Ryan by his sleeve. "Let's, uh…" He feels too exposed here, even with the lights off.

"Hmm…" Ryan grabs him by the hips. "Your place or mine?"

"Um," Louie says because he's not exactly prepared for this, although he's not sure Ryan is either. Ever since he moved in here, Ryan's never brought anyone home.

"My place," Ryan decides. "But…" He starts undoing the rest of the buttons, quicker now. "We don't need this."

Louie gets involved now as well, tries to get Ryan's shirt open in turn and makes it as far as two buttons. He gets distracted when Ryan pushes his shirt away and kisses the top of his shoulder. Louie's pretty sure no one has ever kissed him there, has never even thought of anyone kissing him there and it makes him shudder.

Ryan's paying so much attention to him, to making him feel good. Louie has done nothing at all in return. Two buttons. The rest was Ryan, who kisses the top of Louie's shoulder again when he realizes Louie liked it the first time.

They move through the kitchen, Louie's shirt landing on the tile floor and staying there. They bump into the doorway, Ryan too busy with Louie's belt to pay attention to where he's going. Louie laughs when he stumbles over his own feet and Ryan catches him around his waist. For a second, he thinks Ryan's about to pick him up. He doesn't hate the idea, except he doesn't want Ryan to mess up his back by carrying Louie around the house.

Instead, Ryan holds him there, searching his face. "You sure about this?" he asks.

Louie nods. "I'm sure."

He isn't, but he's frayed, coming apart, and he had no idea that coming apart could feel so good. He's the one who opens the door to Ryan's room, he's the one who pulls him inside. Ryan follows, smiling as he undoes the rest of his buttons, shaking off the shirt.

"Lights?" Ryan asks.

He didn't bother opening his curtains this morning. "Okay," Louie whispers. No one's ever asked him if he wanted the lights on. He never asked either.

Ryan plugs in the string of lights he's wound around the curtain rod and it casts a soft glow on him. He's still in his forest green suit pants and they hug him in the exact right places. His thighs are—Louie is staring and for the first time, he feels like he's allowed to.

Ryan doesn't seem to mind in the slightest. He grins and slowly undoes the button, then the zipper, and pushes his pants down. He's got a fading bruise on his left thigh where he blocked a shot a few games ago and Louie suddenly wants to put his mouth right there. Or... Ryan's wearing dark briefs, but they don't hide that he's hard and maybe Louie would rather kiss him there.

"Your turn," Ryan says and comes back to get Louie out of his pants, his hands lingering on Louie's ass when he pushes them down. "Lou..."

"Hm?"

"What do you—I'm assuming you haven't done this. With a guy."

"I haven't." Louie frowns at him. "Is that a problem?"

"Not for me," Ryan says. He walks Louie to the bed and pushes him down, straddling his hips. "Just tell me if—"

"Yeah," Louie says and pulls Ryan down against him, one hand on his back, the other one at the waistband of Ryan's briefs, slowly sneaking under before he pushes them down and they end up somewhere around Ryan's knees. Louie tries to help him get them off all the way, but he can't reach with Ryan on top of him, so he nudges his shoulder. "Can you…"

Ryan moves off him, letting out a surprised huff when Louie gets between his thighs and pulls off his briefs. He gives himself a moment to take in Ryan in the soft glow of the lights: his parted lips and the trail of hair on his stomach and the bruise on his thigh. Louie has been thinking about these thighs. He slowly dips his head down and starts right there.

"Oh, okay," Ryan breathes. "You're… yeah."

"Yeah?" Louie says and kisses him carefully, Ryan's choked-out moan sending shivers down his spine. Ryan here is like Ryan everywhere; he doesn't hold back. He throws his head back and grabs Louie's hair when he kisses every inch of skin between that bruise and Ryan's hipbone.

Ryan's skin is soft, except for that thin scar just under his collarbone that Louie pays some attention to next. "Where'd you get this?"

"I… hmnng." Ryan's fingers dig into Louie's back. "Tree."

Louie makes a noise to tell him that he heard as he moves back down his chest, to his stomach. Ryan squirms.

"I fell," he grits out, "and got caught on a branch. And I…"

Louie hovers just above Ryan's dick and waits for the end of the story. With a deep breath, Ryan says, "Also broke my ar—ghh *fuck*."

Louie kisses the tip, just a quick touch of his lips. He did wonder briefly if it would feel weird—Ryan was right, he's never slept with a man before. It's different, sure, but it's different with everyone. He figured he'd find his way; he knows what he likes anyway and he's sure Ryan would tell him if Louie did something he didn't like.

He'll take it easy tonight, though. He sits up and slowly runs his knuckles from Ryan's pelvis up to his collarbone. "Do you have lube?"

Ryan nods and there's something so eager about it that sets Louie's cheeks on fire. He glances at his bedside table—he got a new one, one with drawers. Now Louie knows why.

"What about you, hmm?" Ryan says before Louie can go for the drawers. He doesn't take any detours, his fingers finding Louie's cock, still trapped in his briefs.

Louie almost tells Ryan to just go ahead and do whatever he wants with him, but he had a plan and he wants to watch Ryan fall apart under his hands. "You first," Louie whispers. He grabs the lube and starts to stroke Ryan slowly. Like this, he can watch the way Ryan's face changes when he changes his grip, when he goes faster, slows down again.

Since Ryan can't grab onto Louie's hair anymore, he grabs the sheets, throws his head back, the words all gone. Someone should paint him. Make a sculpture. Next time, Louie wants to suck him off, and after that, Louie wants him on his hands and knees, or maybe he'll just do whatever Ryan wants, or he'll ask Ryan to—

"Louie, I'm..." Ryan reaches for him, grabs his free hand. "Lou."

"Yeah," Louie says and speeds up. "I've got you."

Ryan's answer is a drawn-out moan as he comes over Louie's hand. Louie strokes him through it, watches him catch his breath. Ryan blinks at him and props himself up on his elbows. "Wow, okay," he says, voice low. His eyes travel from Louie's face down his chest to his dick before they snap back up and he bites his lower lip. "Hi," he says.

Louie can't help but laugh. "Hi."

"That was very nice," Ryan says earnestly.

Louie almost chokes on the noise that gets stuck in his throat at that.

Ryan sits up, reaching for Louie and pulling him into his lap to kiss him. Louie still has come on his hand, but Ryan doesn't seem to give a crap. He grabs Louie, no small feat, and gets him on his back, upside down on the bed. "Your turn," he says and pulls Louie's briefs down just enough so he can get his mouth on him.

Even though Louie was so close already, Ryan somehow manages to draw it out, pulling away just when Louie thinks this is it and then diving back in. Louie can't even say anything; can't think. The heat of Ryan's mouth is all there is, his hands, fleeting touches, Louie's heartbeat in his own ears. Maybe he says things. Maybe he just… feels things.

"Ryan," he says, a warning that has Ryan resurfacing to finish him off with his hand. Louie's breath stutters and he crashes.

Ryan plants a gentle kiss on the inside of Louie's thigh, like a period at the end of a sentence, but doesn't move afterwards, grinning up at Louie, who's not even sure he can move. Featherlight fingertips draw unrecognizable patterns on Louie's thigh, Ryan giving him a moment, his breath warm against Louie's skin.

"You okay?" Ryan whispers.

"Yeah," Louie says, "I just… can't move yet."

Ryan laughs under his breath. "You're welcome," he says and slowly gets out of bed. "Stay here, I'll be right back."

Louie nods and closes his eyes. He's not sure he could go anywhere even if he wanted to. His bones are liquid and his brain is foggy. Ryan returns with a washcloth, gets him cleaned up, tugs Louie's briefs back into place, and then he disappears again. Kitchen cupboards open and close, the door clicks shut, and a low thunk finally has Louie opening his eyes.

"I got you some water," Ryan says, nodding at the bedside table as he climbs back into bed. "You know, if you wanna stay the night."

Louie's still upside down, his lips twitching when Ryan's fingers curl around his ankle. "Thank you." He sits up and nods at the lights. "I'll get those."

He's almost by the window when Ryan says, "I wasn't gonna say this out loud, but you're so fucking hot."

Louie stops in his tracks and looks back at him, finding Ryan smiling at him. He's leaning against the headboard, still completely naked, his hair a total mess. Louie smiles back at him and pulls the plug on the lights. "So are you," he says and shuffles back to Ryan's bed.

Ryan lifts up the covers for him. "Louie," he whispers.

"Yeah?" Louie says.

In the dark, Ryan's arm snakes around Louie's waist. "Nothing," he says and snuggles close. "I'll be asleep in two minutes and then you can scoot away."

He wasn't kidding; he's fast asleep almost instantly. Louie doesn't scoot away. Before he can even think about why he doesn't want to, he dozes off as well, still boneless and content.

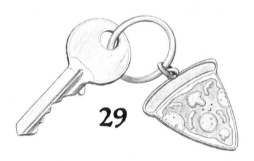

29

It's not that Ryan was expecting Louie to still be fast asleep next to him when he wakes up in the morning. Louie always gets up early, only it's even earlier than *that* when Ryan crawls out of bed.

Ryan grabs some clothes off the floor and shuffles into the kitchen. He doesn't find any of Louie's clothes, only his green suit jacket.

"Louie?" Ryan calls.

Clearly, Louie isn't home. A glance at their pile of shoes by the front door tells Ryan that Louie went out for a run. Okay. That's nothing unusual. For a second, he was worried that Louie might be having some regrets about last night.

Ryan makes himself a cup of coffee and starts cracking eggs for omelets because there isn't much he can do until Louie gets back and they can have an actual conversation. They can't pretend it didn't happen; Ryan won't let Louie do that to him again. He seemed okay last night, at least, but Ryan knows full well that things tend to look different in the morning.

He grabs his phone to check the scores for last night's Western Conference games but gets distracted by the Cardinals' group chat where the guys are asking Louie if his brother is okay.

Ryan's stomach rolls.

It has to be bad. The guys wouldn't be asking if it wasn't.

Louie replied an hour ago, saying he hasn't heard anything yet. Ryan takes a deep breath and checks Twitter. Sometimes Twitter knows too much, but this morning Ryan doesn't mind at all. He searches Bastien Hathaway and immediately finds a clip from last night.

Ryan watches it twice, sick to his stomach. It's a clean hit, which somehow makes it worse. Total accident. But Louie's brother goes into the boards headfirst and he drops to the ice like a sack of potatoes. Ryan can tell, even on his small phone screen, that Bastien passed out before he even hit the ice.

"Shit," Ryan says.

In the video, Bastien gives a thumbs-up as he's stretchered off the ice, so at least he was awake, but that doesn't mean much. Bastien's team posted a statement last night saying he'd been taken to the hospital and was being evaluated.

Ryan waits for the sound of Louie's key in the front door.

It doesn't take long, except it takes an eternity.

Frozen to the spot, Ryan abandons his attempts at breakfast and glues his eyes to the kitchen door, the same door they bumped into last night while Louie was kissing him breathless. Like Ryan said, things tend to look different in the morning.

Louie appears, hair messy, cheeks red from the cold. "You saw."

Ryan nods. "Do you know—"

"I don't know anything," Louie says. "Mom and Dad flew to Saint Paul this morning. Dominic just called me and he doesn't know much either. I think they're mad at both of us."

"Your parents are mad at you because...?"

"Because I didn't go home this summer and shut them out and then invited Dominic for our home opener. And now they're shutting us out and not telling us anything."

"That's fucked up," Ryan says. He's been saying that a lot and it's starting to lose all meaning.

Louie shrugs. "It doesn't matter." He laughs. "Nothing I do matters."

"That's not true."

"No, it is. I scored a hatty last night and it doesn't matter. And I know this is messed up, but I had one good thing happen to me and…" Louie snaps his mouth shut and takes a deep breath. "Nothing matters."

Sometimes, Ryan wants to shake Louie. Not that it'll help. What he's saying comes from a place deep inside him. It's not that nothing matters. It's that nothing he does will ever matter enough for his dad.

"Louie," Ryan says, "your dad is *never* going to see you. And maybe your brother will always be a little bit better than you. But that doesn't mean you're not good. You still matter. And…" Oh, Ryan is so about to ruin a good thing. But Louie needs to hear this. "I know this is tough. Something awesome happened and you thought maybe this time your dad would be proud of you. And now it's all about your brother again. It's okay to be jealous that he's hogging the spotlight."

"He's not—no. I'm not—"

"You're jealous," Ryan says. "It's fine, it's just me. I get it. I see you."

Louie throws up his hands. "Well, I don't want you to."

"Too late for that," Ryan snaps. "What, you think I'm judging you because you're having ugly emotions? Because you're not perfect in every way?"

"Aren't you?" Louie asks quietly. "Judging me?" he adds when Ryan doesn't reply right away.

"No, I'm not. Newsflash, Louie: nobody's perfect. Not even you."

Louie leans back against the wall, eyes closed. "I can't do this right now." He shakes his head. "He's not hogging the spotlight, he's… what if this is bad? What if he's really, really hurt? And it's… for the past few years, all I wished for was that he'd stop being so damn amazing all the time. And guess what happened."

Ryan gapes at him. "You're not actually saying—you can't make someone get hurt with your thoughts."

Louie looks at him. That look says, *Yes, I absolutely believe my brother got hurt because of my thought crimes.*

Ryan tries to reach for him, then remembers too late that Louie isn't much of a hugger. Louie is faster anyway, his hand coming up to keep Ryan at an arm's length.

"That's bullshit, Lou."

"Look," Louie says. And just like that, this conversation becomes about last night.

Ryan doesn't know how. Maybe it's the way Louie's face changed that tipped him off. Deep down, he knew Louie wouldn't jump into this with him. Louie doesn't jump; he calculates his steps. And what he's doing right now is called taking a calculated step back.

"I'm sorry," Louie says in response to whatever is happening on Ryan's face. He doesn't really have any control over it. He won't even try.

"Don't…" Ryan takes a deep breath. "You don't have to apologize."

"I feel like I wasn't honest with you."

"Except we've never had a conversation about this, so you didn't even have a chance to be honest. It's fine, don't worry. I know how it goes. This isn't my first rodeo."

Ryan isn't the kind of guy people want to spend the rest of their lives with. Casual sex? Dudes love casual sex with Ryan. And Ryan's great at casual sex. But everything beyond that is a no. Even the thing with Kaden wasn't an actual relationship that was going anywhere.

He's being unfair—Louie's going through it right now. Ryan can't hold that against him and he knew from the start that being with Louie, in whatever way, wouldn't be straightforward. The more he learns about Louie, the more endearing he finds him. Louie is smart and Louie cares about what he says to other people. He'd never tell Ryan that his dad will never be proud of him. He'd be so much kinder. Louie is good. He'd never go out of his way to hurt someone.

Ryan wants to hug him so badly and it stings a little that he's not allowed. That he's not wanted.

At least Louie had the guts to have this conversation in person, although Ryan still wants to crawl into a hole and die, so maybe a text would have been better. Maybe Kaden did him a favor and Ryan didn't even realize.

"I, uh…" Louie shuffles his feet. "I asked Liam if I could stay with him for a bit."

Ryan looks up. "What? Why?"

"Because…" A shrug finishes that sentence.

Except it doesn't tell Ryan shit. Whatever happened to finishing your sentences? "You're… moving out?"

"I'm not moving out, I just need a break from—"

"Me," Ryan finishes. That one stings a whole fucking lot. "I see."

"No, not you. Just… all of this." Louie shifts again. "I think I… I finally made the roster and I'm doing great. I've been working for this for years and I can't get distracted."

"By me," Ryan says, since Louie won't say the quiet part out loud.

"By my feelings for you," Louie says. "You get it, right? That it's important to me that I don't screw this up?"

"Yeah, of course I get that."

"And you get that this isn't about you."

Ryan only nods. It's probably at least a little bit about him. But the whole *it's not you, it's me* thing never gets old, does it?

"I really am sorry," Louie tacks on.

It's not that Ryan doesn't believe him. It's not that he'd do anything differently. But he did it again. He ruined another good thing.

Ryan should have seen Liam coming.

Liam gives it three days, then he sits down next to Ryan while he's shoveling chicken and rice into his mouth after practice.

"Wanna tell me why you and Lou are fighting?" Liam asks. No *hello*, no *how are you*, no *isn't the weather nice today*?

"Not really," Ryan says, then shakes his head. "We're not fighting anyway." In fact, they had an invigorating chat about the Ravens' mega-lethal power play in the locker room just now. People who are fighting don't have chats, invigorating or otherwise.

Things didn't blow up in a big way. They just kept going, but differently than before. Ryan is starting to wish things had blown up in a big way because that's a real ending. This is something akin to torture. Every day, he resists the urge to poke at it and find a way to blow it up anyway because it'll hurt less in the long run.

"Right," Liam says, "he just showed up at my house because he likes me better than you."

"Yeah, that's probably it."

Liam sighs. "I'm too old for this, just so you know," he says. "Is it about a girl? That would be very stupid."

"It's not about a girl." Ryan rolls his eyes. "Come on."

"You never know," Liam says. "Did he sleep with your sister?"

"What?"

"Did you sleep with his—wait, I don't think he has a sister."

Ryan stays very still. For a second there, he thought Liam was going to ask if Ryan slept with Louie's brother.

"Do you have a sister?" Liam asks.

"I have several," Ryan says. "And Louie didn't sleep with any of them as far as I know."

"Then what's the problem?" Liam asks. "When you kids fight, it's always because someone stole someone else's girlfriend or because someone slept with someone else's mom."

Ryan almost chokes on his chicken.

"He just doesn't seem like the kind of guy who'd sleep with someone's mom," Liam goes on.

"You need to stop saying that," Ryan says. "I was really enjoying this food."

"Did you—"

"Really?" Ryan interrupts. "I mean, seriously?" Liam is just saying all that to get Ryan to spit out the truth, but the truth is even worse than Ryan fucking someone's mom. Well, not worse. Just—more complicated.

Ryan thinks back to the conversation he had with Liam and some of the other guys at that bar about having a gay teammate. It didn't go as planned but it also didn't go badly, exactly. Ryan sighs at his rice and says, "I'm kinda gay, you know?"

Well, shit. Well, fuck. Okay, then. He said it. Didn't happen the way he wanted it to, but when does it ever?

Liam's brow furrows. "Did Louie have a problem with that? Is that why he moved out? Because if that is it, I'll have a talk with him. That's not okay."

"Oh, uh, no," Ryan says. "He's known for a while."

From a few tables over, Waldo is glancing at them. Did he overhear that? Jesus. Shit. This is not how Ryan was going to do this. But he never does it the way he was going to. It always slips out in the worst moments.

Waldo looks away again, distracted by Nick, who's sitting down with him.

"Don't worry about them," Liam says. "Actually, don't worry about anyone on this team."

"Come on," Ryan says, "there's always someone."

"Well, if there is someone, I will deal with it," Liam says, smiling serenely. "If Waldo isn't faster."

"Why?" Ryan asks. "I mean, why do you care?"

"Why should I not care?" Liam says easily. "My daughter would call you a dum-dum for this, you know?"

"Ugh, she'd probably be right."

Liam, lips pressed together, nods sagely. "Come over for dinner?"

"Probably not the best idea," Ryan says.

"Maja will be very disappointed. She said, 'Papa, you need to invite Rah-rah over for dinner and if he says no, I'll cry all evening'."

"She said all that, huh?" Ryan asks.

"Of course she did. I'd never lie to you."

"Rain check?"

"Fine," Liam says and leaves to get himself something to eat.

Maybe Ryan needs to stop trying to find another Carrot on the Cardinals. Maybe his Carrot can be a father of two who calls you a dumdum and invites you over for Swedish meatballs.

Ryan really wishes he could have said yes to dinner. The house is so fucking quiet without Louie there and Ryan is still bad at being alone.

"Everything okay?" Waldo asks from behind Ryan when he's on his way to his car.

Ryan jumps a foot to the left. Totally snuck up on him. "Yeah, why?"

"Lee had the serious face on," Waldo says.

"Yeah, no, it's…" Ryan shrugs. "I came out to him. Weirdly. Over lunch. And I guess now I'm coming out to you weirdly in the parking garage."

"Came out as in…" Waldo trails off and waves his hand at Ryan. "Came out?"

"Yeah," Ryan says and side-eyes Waldo. "I think he offered to kill someone for me if they're mean about it."

"I'm not being mean about it, I promise," Waldo says and claps Ryan on the back. "That's why you asked the other day, hmm? About gay teammates?"

"Yeah," Ryan says. Why lie? It's obvious.

"Wait," Waldo says and stops walking. "Is that why Louie isn't staying with you anymore?"

Why does everyone think that? Louie would never. Except Ryan was also wary before he really got to know him. These guys have been in and out of locker rooms even longer than Ryan; they've heard it all.

"No, it's really not," Ryan says. "He just needed a break from me. I get kinda annoying." It's not even total bullshit. Ryan doesn't understand why it matters. They're not actually fighting and they're not bringing bad vibes to the ice.

At this point, he just wants to go home, lie on the couch for the rest of the day, and mope.

Waldo narrows his eyes at him. "I don't believe you. But okay."

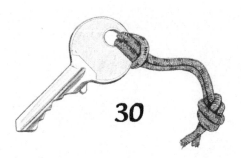

30

"All right, children," Liam says, looking down at the Hellströms' coffee table. "It's almost time to put away the puzzles and get ready for bed. Five minutes, then you're getting your pajamas on, okay?"

"Okay," Ida says. "We're almost done."

Louie is sitting on the floor with her and they're doing a cat puzzle. The cat puzzle reminds Louie of his summer with Ryan's family and their ever-present cats. It's like not living with Ryan makes him think of Ryan even more. He thought it would help him to stay with Liam for a bit. Get away and stop thinking about Ryan and the way he talks to him and the way he looks at him and the way he touches him.

He thinks about Ryan falling asleep with his arm wrapped around his waist. Then the guilt sinks its teeth deep into him. He's well aware that he ran.

Louie doesn't run. Never in his life has he run from anything. When he didn't make the Cardinals' NHL roster, he stuck around and worked on himself until he did, and then Ryan showed up and taught him that running was an option. This summer, he ran from his family. And now he ran from Ryan. From his feelings.

He's doing cat puzzles with Ida so he doesn't have to think. It's not working very well.

When he's giving the black cat its missing eye, the last piece in the puzzle, Ida claps. And just like that, she pushes the whole thing back into its box, some pieces stubbornly hanging onto each other.

"Can Louie read me a story?" Ida asks.

"Actually, Mamma will read you a story," Liam says. "I have to talk to Louie about something."

"Some other time," Louie promises.

Ida says goodnight and shuffles away, doing a perfect cartwheel on her way out of the living room.

When she's gone, Louie turns to Liam. "Are you kicking me out?" he asks. He's been staying here for two weeks and didn't specify for how long he wanted to stay. For a bit, he said. And *a bit* could really be anything. Three days, a week, a month.

Louie didn't really think about it. He absolutely should have. What is he going to do? Show back up at Ryan's in a few days and pretend that nothing happened? Like that worked so well when he kissed him in the summer. He doesn't know what the fuck possessed him when he slept with Ryan. Maybe he was running then, too. Away from hockey.

"I would never kick you out," Liam says. "You can stay for as long as you'd like. We've had rookies stay all season."

"I'm not planning on staying all season, I promise," Louie says. In the end, he'll have to find his own place. He doesn't see himself feeling normal about living with Ryan ever again.

"Hm," Liam says and folds his arms across his chest.

Louie pulls his knees up against his chest. "I saw you talking to Ryan before we went on the road the other day."

"Yes, yes, he told me that he didn't sleep with your mom."

"Uh, what?"

"It's always something like that," Liam says, eyes narrowed. "Except this time it isn't. Threw me off. Or maybe he's better at lying than I thought he was."

"He's a terrible liar," Louie says. Everything's always written all over

Ryan's face. His every thought, his every emotion. That's why Louie is so caught up on the way Ryan looks at him. It's all there.

Liam scratches the back of his head. "Listen, there's something Ryan told me and it's absolutely above my pay grade and none of my business. I don't think he meant to tell me."

"No, he did," Louie says. He already knows what this is about. "He's been wanting to tell… some of you, at least."

"I see." Liam leans back in his armchair, eyes boring into Louie. "Is there anything *you* want to tell me?"

Louie could tell him. The whole story, since Ryan apparently already spilled part of it. He's not worried about Liam knowing something about him that hardly anyone else knows. Liam is a guy who'll mind his business. He's trying to help. But what's the point? Louie ran away. He can't undo that.

That morning, when he woke up next to Ryan, when he found out about what had happened to Bastien the night before, he should have given himself more time. He went on a walk, not even a run, because all he could think about was getting away from his thoughts.

Obviously, his thoughts stayed right where they were.

So Louie had to find another way out. Although it didn't work. The thoughts are, surprisingly, still right where they were. They've become part of Louie's routine.

Get up. Think about Ryan. Have breakfast. Worry about Bastien. Go to the rink. Be normal around Ryan. Focus during practice. Wonder if Bastien's going to be okay. Go home. Think about Ryan. Wonder what Ryan is doing. Then it's Ryan making him a grilled cheese when he's sad. Ryan always letting him have his favorite blanket. Ryan going to the rink early for him. Ryan, naked, smiling, letting Louie take the reins, trusting him completely. And…

"It honestly doesn't matter," Louie says. "I broke things off with Ryan and I won't let it affect the team. Neither will he. I don't even think anyone noticed."

Liam's lips become a thin line. He didn't like that answer. "I understand what you're trying to say." He leans forward. "As your teammate, what should matter to me is that you won't bring your personal bullshit on the ice, yeah?"

"Yeah," Louie says. What's so wrong about that?

"We all have bullshit, though. And we all bring it to the rink sometimes. That's what being a person is like, you know?" Liam shrugs. "Anyway, we're not *just* teammates. How many times have you stayed here, huh? You're my kids' cool uncle. You're family. I want you to be happy. Are you happy?"

"I finally made the team," Louie says. "Of course I'm happy. I worked hard for this and I won't let anything get in the way of it." He sounds like he's in the middle of a postgame media scrum. It's the correct answer, not the true one.

"Anything as in… a relationship?" Liam asks. "Look, I won't tell you that getting with a teammate is smart, that shit can end badly, but… most guys have families. They're married, they're dating."

"Sure, but… I've been trying to get this roster spot for years," Louie says. Liam just mentioned how many times he's stayed here; he should know how long of a journey this has been. "And for years I wasn't good enough. This is important to me."

"Don't take this the wrong way," Liam says, "but do you really think you're the only one who's had to work hard to make it to the NHL? We all had to work hard. Maybe there are some guys who are… they make it look easy. But you were at the rink with Nick all summer. You think he didn't work hard? And, sure, some of us will never be Nick, no matter how hard we work, but that doesn't mean you can't have a life. Or a partner."

Louie shrugs. "Nick doesn't."

Liam blinks at him. Laughs. "Just because he didn't tell you about it personally doesn't mean he's sitting around at home by himself, thinking about hockey all day every day."

It takes a few seconds too long for Louie to understand what Liam is telling him. "What?"

"You need to find a balance, Louie," Liam says. "You can have both. Both is good, hmm?" He gives Louie's arm a pat. "Think on that. I gotta say good night to my kids."

Louie can't sleep.

For once, he's not thinking about Ryan but about Nick. Nick Rivera, who lives and breathes for the game. Louie was convinced there couldn't be anything else for him. Turns out, Nick just thinks his private life is none of anyone's business.

Louie spent years wanting to be like Nick. And now Nick isn't the guy in his head and that's not even Nick's fault. Louie just got everything tangled up in his own mind. This always happens—when Louie makes a wrong move on the ice, when he doesn't live up to his own expectations. Really, a lot of the time, they were his dad's expectations.

When another fifteen minutes have ticked by and Louie is still wide awake, he grabs his phone and gets out of bed, shuffling to the door that leads out onto the lower patio.

It's Thursday, but it's not midnight yet, so chances are Dominic is still awake. Louie thinks about texting him first, but in the end, he pulls up his contact and hits call.

It rings a few times. Maybe he's not home. Dominic is such a moviegoer. He even goes by himself. Louie's about to give up when Dominic says, "Hey, everything okay?" on the other end of the line.

"Not really," Louie says. He wouldn't call Dominic this late if everything was okay.

"Are you hurt?" Dominic asks. "One sec..." His voice is further away when he says, "It's Louie. Go back to sleep, okay?"

"Did I wake you guys up?"

"Don't worry, I was still awake. Cameron just has this weird gift—it takes him like two seconds to fall asleep." Something rustles, then

Dominic says, "What happened? You didn't have a game tonight, right?"

"No, I didn't, it's not… this isn't about hockey," Louie says.

"That's a first."

Funny. That actually tells Louie everything he needs to know. He sits down on one of the patio chairs and stares out at the dark backyard. Liam has put up a bunch of those solar-powered lights, but most of them are dim. "I think I… I messed something up."

"Okay?"

"I don't know if I should fix it."

"Generally, it doesn't hurt to fix things you messed up," Dominic says lightly.

"It's complicated," Louie says. He rubs his forehead, not sure where to take this conversation. "Do you think Dad kind of… screwed up our expectations of what life should be like?"

Dominic snorts. "Honestly, Dad fucked us up in too many ways to count. I've spent years trying to undo all of that and sometimes I still catch myself thinking I threw my life away because it's not exactly the way he wanted it to be."

"But… you're doing great," Louie says.

"And yet Dad was so disappointed that I wasn't even going to go into sports management," Dominic says. "There's a reason I didn't. I wanted out. And you didn't because you actually like hockey, unlike me."

"I just don't even know…" Louie takes a deep breath. "I don't know if I wanted this. Or if I stuck with hockey just to please him. I don't know anything anymore."

"Hm," Dominic says. "I don't think that's true. It was good for you to get away from him and Bastien this summer."

"You think so?"

"Dad always drove the two of you to compete. It would have been easier if he'd taught you how to support each other, but he probably thought he was motivating you when he told you that Bastien was so much better. And then Bastien obviously also thought he had to be keep being better, otherwise Dad wouldn't love him anymore."

Louie doesn't know what to say. His first instinct is to tell Dominic that he's wrong, but Dominic has been on the outside looking in for years now. He's David Attenborough and the rest of them are particularly interesting bugs. "I kept wishing I could be better than him just once. And now he's…"

"Lou," Dominic says. "He's on IR, he's not dying."

"He still got hurt."

"Not because of you, though. Wanna hear my advice? Find a therapist."

"For what?"

"Can't believe you'd even ask me this," Dominic says. "I may have gone to med school and I may be your brother, and I can listen to you, but I wasn't kidding when I said Dad fucked us up."

"What if I'm too broken?" Louie whispers. Something cracks, not just in his voice.

"I honestly don't think it matters how broken you are. You deserve to be happy just like anyone else." A beat, then Dominic adds, "Actually, I don't think that. My therapist thinks that."

Somehow, Louie is and isn't surprised that Dominic has a therapist. They've never talked about this before; Louie always assumed Dominic was fine. He has Cameron. He's always been the smart one, the strong one, and Louie thought he could have made it out on the other side of the mess that their family is all by himself. Possibly, it doesn't matter how smart and strong you are either.

Louie takes a deep breath and stares into the darkness of the Hellströms' backyard. Then he says, "I slept with Ryan."

"Ah," Dominic says.

Just. *Ah.* "What the hell is that supposed to mean?"

"Eh," Dominic says.

"Care to elaborate?"

"When we met him, you were looking at him some kinda way," Dominic says. "And when you talked about him—"

"I was talking about him some kinda way?" Louie asks drily.

"Exactly. I don't think he realized, by the way. I don't even think *you* realized at the time. But you kind of talk about him like you talk about hockey."

"I… what?"

"Yeah. When you text me, it's usually about hockey. And then you moved in with Ryan and suddenly you were talking about him, too."

"Because he's my roommate."

"Right. Except you've had roommates before and I don't even know those guys' names."

"What are you trying to say?" Louie asks.

"I'm not trying to say anything. You told me something, I told you something." Dominic pauses for a second, but Louie can tell he's not done. "It was good, wasn't it? He seems like the kind of guy who'll just completely blow your mind."

Louie rolls his eyes, not giving a damn that Dominic can't see it. "That's not the point. I ran away."

"Ohh, so I guess that brings us to the thing you fucked up?"

"Yeah."

"You want my advice?"

"That's why I called."

Dominic laughs. "Okay. Well. Un-fuck it up. Ryan's a good one. A guy can't fix you, but he can help you fix yourself, you know? We need other people in our lives," he says. After a moment, he adds, "And he's hot. Come on, Lou."

"Well, how do I—I don't know what to do about it."

"You know him," Dominic says, "you'll figure it out."

"That's not helpful."

"I think this conversation was very helpful."

Louie won't disagree. It was. It is. "Hey," he says after a moment, "you're just going to accept that I slept with a guy?"

"Sure," Dominic says. "You did the same for me."

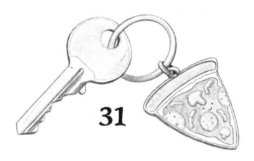

31

Louie keeps looking at him. He can't do that. Ryan doesn't know how to tell him that he can't do that.

They just had a polite conversation about their upcoming roadie to New York, which isn't much of a roadie, but they'll still spend the night in the city, twice, before they head to DC. Louie wants to go to a museum.

Ryan cannot and will not find that adorable.

Louie is still looking and, for the love of fuck, he needs to stop.

"What?" Ryan asks.

Louie blinks at him. "I was just… do you have tape?"

"Just the black one," Ryan says and hands it over.

"That's fine," Louie says and takes off with it.

He so didn't need any tape. But when they hit the ice for morning skate, Louie's twig is taped in black, even though he always uses white. He lied and he took it all the way. Ryan will hand it to him, that's commitment.

During practice, Louie only looks at him when he has to. Ryan watches him then because Louie is distracted. Coach talks to him, gives him a pat on the back. Louie smiles a little. Just a little, but more than Ryan has ever seen him smile at practice. In retrospect, Ryan wonders if Louie may have thought that he'd somehow ruin his chances if he allowed himself to be happy. Or that it'd hurt worse if Coach ended up sending him down.

Louie skates up to Nick after and they do their Serious Hockey Conversation thing until Liam shows up and showers both of them with ice.

Ryan finds out what Coach told Louie only ten minutes later when the assistant coach who runs the power play, Tremblay, calls them over. They're shuffling. Louie's joining the first unit. Which is the one Ryan happens to be on as the lone defenseman. Fun. Okay.

Of course, of fucking course, Louie is annoyingly professional. His passes are beautiful, as always.

"Good work today, Harris," Coach Beaulieu says to Ryan as he heads off the ice.

For a second, it doesn't register that Coach is talking to him.

Which is probably why Coach adds, "Thought you and Hathaway might work well together."

"Oh," Ryan says. Now he's just rubbing it in and he doesn't even know it. "Thanks," he tacks on belatedly.

Back in the room, Ryan quietly pulls off his gear. Louie is doing the same right next to him, analyzing the Grizzlies' injury situation with Nick. Ryan fights the urge to get involved just because he wants to talk to Louie (he's never felt this pathetic about a guy) and turns to Liam instead (still feels pathetic but it's a different kind).

"What are you wearing for the Halloween thing at the hospital?" Ryan asks.

"Ida picks," Liam says. "I'm sure it will be something very dignified."

"She should pick my costume, too," Ryan says. "I have no idea what to wear."

"I'll let Maja pick yours. She's currently obsessed with the trash collectors, so…"

Ryan rolls his eyes at him. "Great, thanks," he grumbles.

Liam considers him for a moment. Ryan feels like he's about to be dissected. Then Liam says, "Hey, what are you doing on Saturday?"

"Uh…" Do they have a game on Saturday? No. That's Friday. Not having Louie around anymore also means he doesn't know when they're going where anymore. He could look at the schedule on the fridge, but it was so much easier when Louie just chewed off his ear about it.

It's one of those teeny-tiny side effects. Ryan hates those teeny-tiny side effects. They're everywhere. This morning he stared at a pair of Louie's shoes that he forgot by the door and considered bringing them to the rink and calculated how much it might hurt and wondered if the other guys would catch on. Because as far as he knows, most of the guys still think that Louie's staying with Ryan. Liam hasn't blabbed, at least not to everyone.

Not about Louie and not about Ryan's gay word vomit.

Ryan probably owes Liam one. "I don't think I have plans," Ryan says and glances over his shoulder. Louie's stall is empty now. "I still don't think dinner's a great idea."

"Actually," Liam says, "I want to take my wife out for dinner and I need someone to spend two hours with Maja. Maybe three. Watch some…" Liam waves his hand. "Cartoons about shapes and colors. Draw a picture. Pretend you're a garbage truck. We'll feed her before we leave."

Ryan shouldn't laugh. "You want me to watch your kids."

"Kid. Just Maja. Ida is going to a sleepover. Our babysitter is out of town and Louie has other plans, so…" Liam's eyebrows climb high.

Liam is seriously trusting him with his kid. Ryan almost starts bawling. He clears his throat. "Yeah, sure."

"Thank you," Liam says and wanders away, buck naked.

Ryan will not spend all evening wondering what Louie is up to tonight.

It's just weird. Louie isn't a Saturday evening plans kind of guy. On Saturday evening—when they're not playing themselves—Louie watches hockey. Maybe he went to the rink with Nick because he's just that obsessed. Wouldn't be the first time. A few weeks ago, Louie would have dragged Ryan along.

Tonight, Ryan is ringing the Hellströms' doorbell.

There are worse things than hanging out with a small child pretending he's a garbage truck and playing that game where you sort shapes into a box if Liam was serious about all that.

"She'll probably fall asleep after running circles around you for ten minutes anyway," Liam said when Ryan asked him how he's supposed to entertain Maja for two hours.

The door opens to Liam carrying Maja, who beams at Ryan. She throws up her tiny arms. "Rah-rah!"

"Hiii," Ryan says and waves at her. It's impossible to be in a bad mood when a tiny child smiles at you.

"Here you go," Liam says and immediately hands Maja over.

"Um," Ryan says. He holds her up. "Now what?"

"Now you do whatever she wants," Liam says, grinning. "I have to go pick up my wife. You have my number if anything goes wrong. And, good news, you're not alone. Seems I was wrong about Louie having other plans." He gives Ryan a pat in passing and off he goes, leaving Ryan and his kid right there on the doorstep.

"Your dad is evil," Ryan tells Maja. "It's so fitting that his nickname is Satan."

"Saaan," Maja says.

"Exactly," Ryan agrees, peering into the house. No trace of Louie. Maybe he's hiding in his room.

Fuck's sake. Liam absolutely did this on purpose. Ryan's been had.

He shuffles into the house, toeing out of his shoes and putting a disgruntled Maja down so he can take off his jacket. She's appeased when he picks her up again and carries her into the living room. Where Louie is sitting on the couch, eyes on his phone. Ryan wonders what he's looking at since he hates Instagram so much. Probably hockey stats.

"Hey," Ryan says.

"Hey," Louie replies, staring at him like he did at the rink earlier.

"Looks like Liam double-booked babysitters," Ryan says.

Louie nods.

"Right." Ryan's going to take a page out of Louie's book and just go away and not deal with this. "We're gonna go play a game."

"Lu," Maja says, pointing at Louie.

"Yeah, that's Louie."

Maja reaches for him. Great. Obviously, Louie is too kind to ignore this small child and gets up to take her to the kids' playroom. Heaving a sigh, Ryan follows them. He's been here before—Ida put little sparkly clips into his hair and took pictures of him in front of the wall that's painted like a magical forest.

Louie puts her down on the soft rug in the middle of the room and grabs the box with the big building blocks. He dumps them out for Maja, who immediately dives for them. Ryan sits on the floor with them and starts helping with the tower they start to build.

"Let's see if we can make it as big as you," Louie says to Maja.

Ryan looks at Louie. That was a mistake. Looking at Louie, here, away from the rink, with only a little kid as a buffer, is a little painful. A lot painful. "Would be more of a challenge if we made it as big as you," Ryan says.

"She can't reach that high," Louie says, deadpan.

Ryan soon finds out that apparently the fun part of their construction business game is not the building part, but the demolition part. Maja has that covered. "Do you want to be a wrecking ball operator when you grow up?" Ryan asks her.

"Rah-rah house!" is Maja's reply and a moment later the Rah-rah house is rubble on the floor.

"I should get her a jersey that says Rah-rah on the back," Ryan says.

Louie's smile appears slowly, tentatively, like he's fighting it.

Maja squeals and starts running around them, jumping over building blocks, and climbing on Louie's back until he flips her over. It's practiced like something they've been doing, probably since Louie moved in here. A few days, and Louie belongs here. It's just one stab in the heart after another.

While the two of them do their gymnastics routine, Ryan collects building blocks and starts constructing a hockey rink. Maja, in the meantime, goes back to running and throwing herself into the pink beanbag chair in the corner.

"Is that… something she should be doing without a helmet?" Ryan asks.

Maja cackles as she lands in the chair for the second time.

"She's fine," Louie says, watching her. "I think."

After the fifth dive, Maja stays where she is and sighs. Exhausted.

"Aww, are you tired?" Ryan asks.

"No," Maja says.

"Interesting," Ryan replies. "You look tired."

"No."

"So, you're wide awake, huh?"

"No!"

"Stop talking to her," Louie whispers. "Just let her fall asleep."

Ryan isn't sure she will—she's definitely fighting it and keeping her eyes wide open. And if she does fall asleep, Ryan will (essentially) be alone with Louie. Does he want that? Maybe not.

One by one, Ryan reads the titles of all the picture books that are lined up on the shelf. Very interesting. So interesting. He actually read some of those to his sister's kids. They're cute. Ryan likes looking at the pictures as much as a two-year-old; he wonders what that says about him.

Quietly, Louie clears his throat. "She's asleep," he whispers.

"Okay," Ryan whispers back, sneaking a glance at Maja. "Do we leave her there?"

Louie nods quickly. Like he knows that moving her would be a fatal mistake.

Ryan narrows his eyes at him. "You've babysat the kids before?"

"Just Ida," Louie says. "Once."

"Hm."

"What?"

"I just…" Ryan shrugs, staring at the pink miniature hockey net in the corner. "I mean, we definitely didn't end up here by accident. Both of us."

"They told me Liam asked you and Ella asked me and they forgot to tell each other, except I live here and I know they tell each other everything, so…"

Ryan nods at the hockey net. "We've been played."

"I told him it wasn't going to affect the team," Louie says.

Oh, good, as long as it doesn't affect the team, it's all peachy, isn't it? Ryan will not let that come out of his mouth. Nope, no way.

A few seconds tick by. The quiet quickly starts to feel claustrophobic.

"Ryan?" Louie says. "Can you look at me?"

"I could," Ryan says. "I don't want to, though, I don't think."

"Okay, well… I wanted to say sorry."

Fuck it, Ryan is going to look at him. Louie is cross-legged on the floor, turning a building block over in his hand. His eyes are fixed on Ryan, and they're looking more green than usual with the magic forest wall behind him.

"It was all a lot," Louie goes on. "You know, that morning…"

"When you thought you'd thought-crimed your brother into getting injured. Yeah, it seemed like it was a lot."

"I know that was stupid," Louie mutters.

"It wasn't, though." Ryan shrugs. "And I'm sorry if I made you feel like it was. Like you said, it was a lot."

Louie finally looks away. "I didn't know what to do with you, I just couldn't stop thinking about you. But I didn't handle it well."

Ryan, the king of not handling things well, definitely understands how that happened. "I guess you didn't," he agrees. "Maybe I didn't either. Maybe things just collectively… weren't handled well."

"Maybe," Louie says.

"I don't…" Ryan shakes his head. "I don't blame you for leaving or whatever, I get that you needed a break. I'm just bad at being left, you know? Because everyone always leaves me."

Louie's face falls. "It really wasn't about you."

"I know that. In my mind, I know that. My heart says I'm unlovable and I suck and no one will ever want me." Ryan shrugs. "But that's a me problem. I'm trying not to take it personally."

"You're not unlovable," Louie says quietly.

Another shrug. "Maybe just easy to leave, then."

"Not that either," Louie says, even more quietly.

"You don't have to say that," Ryan says. He was there when Louie left; he didn't seem to have any trouble with it whatsoever.

Louie chucks his building block on the carpet. "I think I do have to say it. And I think you know what that's like."

Oh, Ryan has felt like he needed to say a lot of things. And he said way too many of them. "Yeah, I do know." He rubs his forehead. "Believe me, I wish I wasn't this insecure and running around, yelling 'Please love me'. My abandonment issues aren't sexy."

"Your abandonment issues don't scare me," Louie says.

What the fuck is he trying to say? Ryan raises his eyebrows at him. "Well, your daddy issues don't scare me either."

Louie doesn't reply. He leans back against the big shelf behind him. Time ticks on. "What do we do now?" he finally asks.

"We wait for Liam and Ella to come back," Ryan says and gets comfortable against a humongous teddy bear. He picks up a random picture book. "Want me to read you a story while we wait?"

"I didn't mean right now, I meant…" Louie waves his hand between them.

"Well, you don't want me to be a distraction, so you either have to stop thinking about us exploring each other's bodies, get over it, and come home," Ryan says as casually as he can manage. "Or you could kill me. I guess then I'd stop being distracting." He gives Louie a moment to roll his eyes about that one. "Or you could... let me distract you a little bit."

"It's a terrible idea," Louie says. "It was a terrible idea all along. We're teammates."

"You're worried it could end badly? I think it already did and, like you said, we didn't take it to the rink."

Louie looks at him like Ryan is tape he wants to analyze for their next game. Having that kind of attention directed at him is cooking his insides like he's sitting in a microwave. Ryan tries to analyze Louie right back, but he only makes it as far as the floppy hair and the forest eyes. Coherent thoughts not possible.

He sticks out his foot and nudges it against Louie's. "Can you just come home?" Ryan asks. "And we'll figure out the rest?"

Louie tips his head back against the shelf. "I don't know."

"I'm not asking you for anything, I swear. Just... the house is really quiet."

Ryan was doing such a great job of not being totally pathetic. Up until now.

A soft sigh is the only answer Ryan gets to that. Louie peers at Maja, who is still snoozing on the beanbag chair like it's the most comfortable place to sleep in the world.

Ryan focuses on keeping his mouth shut. If he says one more embarrassing thing, he has to move into a hovel in the woods and become a hermit. He doesn't want to pressure Louie into anything. If he wants to stay here with Liam, if that makes things easier for him, then Ryan will accept it. And he won't be needy and clingy about it.

After what feels like an hour (but has probably been five minutes), Louie says, "I want to—" He cuts himself off. Shakes his head.

"What?" Ryan asks.

Louie bites his lip.

Ryan nods. "You'll tell me when you're ready."

"Yeah," Louie says softly. Then his foot knocks against Ryan's and stays there, just a small spot of warmth, unmoving, steady.

They don't talk, but it's not awkward anymore. It's like sitting on the couch and watching a game, with Louie paying rapt attention and Ryan scrolling through his phone and looking up when he sees Louie tense and knows something's about to go down.

Ryan eventually starts leafing through the picture book he picked up earlier and things almost seem normal, even though they're in a playroom that is equal parts forest and pink, with a building-block hockey rink next to them, and they're watching a tiny child who is sleeping in a beanbag chair.

"Oh, look, you're all still alive," Liam says. He's appeared in the doorway out of thin air.

Ryan and Louie both jump, sitting up straight. At least Ryan's not the only one who didn't hear him coming. "We know what you did," Ryan says.

"Damn." Liam smiles. "You built an… impact crater? Very creative. Did you play kill the dinosaurs? I thought we were over that, but hey."

"It's a hockey rink," Ryan says flatly and points at the blue lines. Granted, they didn't have a lot of white bricks, so it looks like someone peed on the ice, but he did his best.

"Uh-huh, great job, boys," Liam says. He nods at Maja. "I'll let her mom handle that. Well. Thanks so much, I'll hire you again for sure." He nods at Ryan. "Come on, let me give you your payment."

"We're getting paid?" Ryan asks and follows Liam into the Hellströms' brightly lit and spotlessly clean kitchen. Ella is putting away leftovers from their date. Going by the paper bag, it was the Mexican place in Silver Lakes. "How was dinner?"

"Excellent," Ella says. "Thank you so much for helping us out, Ryan. Louie wasn't sure he was qualified." She smirks at Liam. "But he mentioned you had several nieces."

Wait. Louie said what? "Um," Ryan says, "yeah. I have… yeah." He looks around to find Louie, but he must have stayed in the playroom with Maja. They all sit on a throne of lies.

"Dang, really? I thought he said he didn't have time?" Liam pretends to be shocked. He's terrible at it. "Love, you'll have to carry Maja to bed. She always wakes up when I do it," Liam tells Ella and pulls a huge container out of the fridge that he hands to Ryan. "Meatballs for you. Enjoy."

"Oh my God, thank you," Ryan says. He's going to eat half of these on the couch at home ten minutes from now.

Liam glares at him. "Since you won't come over for dinner."

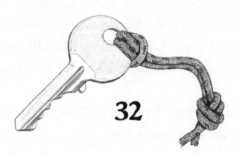

32

"Can I talk to you?" is the first thing Ryan says to Louie at practice the next morning.

Louie managed to escape last night, too embarrassed, too riled up, and too overwhelmed to have any sort of awkward conversation with Ryan before he left. But of course he can't fully escape Ryan; he's still Louie's teammate. "Right now?" Louie asks.

"Later is fine, but I…" Ryan catches Louie by the elbow to keep him from walking out onto the ice. "Ella said *you* told her you didn't want to babysit Maja by yourself."

"Because I didn't," Louie says. "Ida is easier, she can talk."

"And you told Ella and Lee to, what, ask me?"

"I didn't tell them to do anything. And there really was some confusion about who'd ask who." Louie takes a step back, sweating before he even hits the ice. "Can we just…" He takes a few steps to the stick rack and grabs two of his own. "Not now, okay?"

"Fine," Ryan says and takes his own sticks, bumping into Louie before he walks away, "but if you wanted to hang out, you could have just said so."

Except Louie couldn't have *just said so* and they both know it.

He's been a mess. Mentally, that is, not at the rink.

The more he's not a mess at the rink, the more he feels like he might be able to get a handle on the Ryan situation without completely screwing himself over. Now that he thinks about it, he's been a mess a lot off the ice. He never let it affect his performance.

The problem with Ryan is a different one, though. Not because he's a man, or a teammate, or a friend. Louie likes him differently. A few months ago, when they were on the road, Ryan asked him about the last time he'd kissed someone and Louie told him about New Year's Eve, when he kissed his teammate's girlfriend's friend at a party back in Springfield.

"Classic," Ryan said.

"I kind of ghosted her when I came here," Louie admitted. He told her he was leaving, but they didn't talk after because Louie was in Full NHL Mode and thought he didn't have time for a girlfriend.

That's how Ryan is different. Louie wants to make time for him.

But he also doesn't want to hurt him again. Ryan didn't say it outright last night, and kept it jokey, but he is terrified of people leaving him and, well, Louie left him too. And while sometimes that is the reality of life— people leave you and there's nothing you can do—Louie doesn't want to do that to him a second time. When, or maybe *if* he goes back, he needs to be sure he can stick it out. He was going to tell Ryan that last night, but he couldn't find the right words.

Ryan came to his rescue. Said Louie would tell him when he's ready. And he will. He just needs to figure out what ready is supposed to feel like.

Ryan doesn't bug him on the road; doesn't ask if he wants to talk again.

The team goes out for dinner together in Chicago and Louie sits next to Ryan because he wants to and because he misses him. Ryan convinces him to eat the rest of his dessert because he's full, except he's never full. Louie will think about that dessert for the rest of his life.

In Nashville, Louie scores another hat trick. He doesn't know how the hell he did it, but there he is, holding up his three-puck stack for the camera. He pulls Ryan into the picture because he got assists on two of the goals. Ryan hugs him and Louie doesn't want him to stop.

Ryan saves his ass in Winnipeg when the puck bounces off his stick and he almost scores on their own goal. It's so incredibly close and their goalie is so incredibly far out of the net, but Ryan throws himself in there and swipes it out of the crease before it crosses the line. Louie finds him after the game, before they get on the plane, and thanks him.

"I knew I had to. You would have beaten yourself up about it all season," Ryan says.

On the flight home, Louie sits with Ryan. When Ryan has fallen asleep, Louie stares at his hands and thinks about taking them.

It's early morning when they land in Hartford. Louie gets into the car with Liam, watching Ryan the entire time. He's talking to Waldo, not leaving just yet. It's not until they're on the highway and Liam asks him if he wants to grab breakfast somewhere that he realizes he would have rather gone home. With Ryan.

It seems terrifyingly simple in the end.

"Actually," Louie says, "could you drop me off at Ryan's?"

Liam laughs. "Yes, of course I can."

Louie climbs out with all his bags and rolls them up to the front door. He still has his keys somewhere and by the time he's dug them up, Liam has sped off, either because he's really hungry or because he didn't want to give Louie a chance to change his mind.

The key slides into the lock easily and when it clicks open, it welcomes him home. He throws the door open and walks in, the house filled with gentle morning light. A huge plant that wasn't here when Louie left is towering by the table that they leave their keys on. That's where Louie puts his. His bag stays in the hallway for now; he won't move back into his room before he's talked to Ryan.

Who apparently isn't here yet.

Louie shuffles into the living room and takes in the scene—empty glass on the table, next to it a half-eaten bag of candy, a blanket puddled in Ryan's spot on the couch. Louie's favorite knit blanket is folded neatly on the other side of the couch. Waiting for him to come back. For a second, Louie can't breathe. How did he walk away from this?

Like everything's in slow motion, he sits on the piano bench. Back in Boston, he couldn't play anymore when his dad was around. He'd always comment on it and said Louie could have spent that time on the ice. He barely practiced anymore after he'd stopped taking lessons. He's forgotten a lot, but Ida has a tiny toy piano and he actually taught her a few easy songs. He may have not been playing much, but his fingers remember.

He slowly turns around and flips open the lid. His dad isn't here to comment, nobody's listening, and no one has any expectations whatsoever.

Louie starts with one of the very first songs he learned. He doesn't remember the title, and it comes out a little slower and choppier than it ideally should, but he's playing. He tries something harder next, but forgets where that one was going halfway through. He thought it would be harder to sit back down and be bad at something he used to be good at, but he doesn't want to stop. For once, it doesn't matter that he's not absolutely perfect.

What was that song Ryan liked? Louie still has the melody tucked away in his head somewhere. It stayed with him this entire time and played in his head when he tried to go to sleep, even though he couldn't remember the words. He refused to look up the actual song.

He tries to play it now and it almost sounds right. Not quite, though. He starts over, tries again, shakes his head, gives it another go.

The front door's lock clicks again a little while later and Louie should stop playing now, but he's really into it, and he also doesn't want to scare the crap out of Ryan by awkwardly and silently sitting in the living room. He did leave him some breadcrumbs at least—the keys on the table, the bags in the hallway.

Ryan himself appears a moment later, leaning in the doorway with his eyes nailing Louie to the spot. "Oh, it's you," he says. "I was worried a concert pianist broke into the house."

"Hi," Louie says.

Ryan slowly puts down a paper bag and a to-go cup on the end table by the couch and makes his way over, stopping by the bench and sitting down when Louie scoots over. Still not made for two people, so Ryan is once again plastered against him, hip-to-hip, arm-to-arm, but facing the other way.

"You came home," Ryan says.

"If you still want me here," Louie says.

"I always want you here."

Louie nods. Of course Ryan is just letting him come back. Of course he's not throwing a fit or giving him a hard time. Of course not. Because this is home, Ryan's, but also Louie's. Theirs. Louie tips his head against Ryan's shoulder and Ryan's fingers are in his hair a moment later.

Louie allows Ryan's warmth to sweep over him, at least for a little while. Then he looks up. "I'm not going to leave again," he says. "I promise. But you have to hold me to it."

"I will," Ryan says. He reaches up to flip a strand of Louie's hair into place. "I won't make you stay against your will, though. That would be fucked up."

"I just meant... I seem to have developed a tendency to run away from my problems," Louie tells him. He doesn't mention it's his fault and that he taught him how to run. Louie loves him for it. Dominic was right about that: you need other people. They may not save you, but they can show you how to save yourself.

"Uh-huh." Ryan gently combs his fingers through Louie's hair. "That's very human of you, Louie. You're just like the rest of us that way."

"Ryan."

"Yeah?"

"Stop joking about it for one second?" Louie says. "I'm saying I really want to try. I've been thinking about how to apologize and I can't when you won't be serious about it."

Ryan runs his fingers down the side of Louie's neck. "You already apologized," he says. "You came back."

Louie leans into him. "I did, but I need you to understand that I'm not... I'm not a relationship kind of guy. I'm a hockey kind of guy."

"You don't say," Ryan whispers. He drops his hand. "Louie. You wanted me to be serious, so I'll be serious for a second. It's fine if you love hockey more than me sometimes. I can be okay with that. But then you also have to be okay with me being clingy as fuck approximately every five business days. And you have to tell me you still like me, even when you think I'm annoying."

"I can do that," Louie says. "For the record, I don't think you're annoying."

"Not even when I make tacos in a bag?"

"That's more disgusting than annoying."

Ryan's eyes narrow. "But also delicious."

Louie elbows him in the side.

"So," Ryan says, "you'll stay?"

"I will."

"And you won't freak out on me."

"I won't."

"All right, well..." Ryan gently sways against him. "You wanna go out on a date with me later? I'm thinking couch, a game, and I'll order us something really nice?"

"Three-cheese pasta," Louie says, "with garlic bread."

"And maybe a good night kiss?"

"If you still want one after all that garlic bread."

Ryan turns his head. "Maybe I'll eat some garlic bread, too. We'll cancel each other out."

"That works," Louie whispers, although he doesn't actually want to wait until tonight. He reaches up to cup Ryan's cheek and barely has to lean in because they're already touching from shoulder to toe. He waits for a second, gives Ryan a chance to pull away, and kisses him when he doesn't. For just a moment, he lingers, lips still against Ryan's. Then Ryan leans back in for another soft kiss. It barely lasts longer than two seconds but sets Louie's entire body on fire.

Ryan gives Louie's thigh a squeeze. "You want half of my breakfast bagel?"

The correct reply to that is not *I think I'm in love with you*, which Louie thankfully realizes before he says it out loud. "I... yeah. Thank you."

Ryan doesn't move just yet. "Hey..." He turns and gives one of the piano keys a poke. "Were you playing Tracy Chapman?"

"I tried," Louie says, "but I don't think I got it right."

"Try again?"

Louie can't say no to him. He's pretty sure he'll never be able to say no to him ever again.

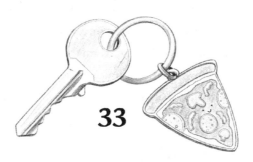

33

Louie is snoring softly into the crook of Ryan's neck. On TV, Toronto is losing against Boston. Just about a minute left on the clock and they didn't even bother pulling their goalie. Score's 1–6.

The camera pans to Carrot, looking like a kicked puppy on the bench.

Ryan texts him a sad face. Not much he can do from afar. Not much he can do period. Even if he was there, he could—what? Turn the whole team around? They didn't even want him there anymore. Getting traded seemed like the end of the world at first, but it may have been the best thing that's ever happened to him.

He's never felt this settled, even though his life is full of question marks. He doesn't own this place and has no idea if he'll be able to renew his lease next summer. It's a contract year and there's no way of telling if he's staying. And then there's Louie.

There's Louie. Ryan will not ruin this. He thought he already had, but it turns out that sometimes people are just... people. Louie left, but then he came back. No one's ever wanted to come back for him, no one's ever given him a second chance. Ryan understands he's not everyone's cup of tea, that he can be annoying (even if Louie says he isn't) and clingy and loud, and Louie wants to give loving him a try anyway.

Ryan kisses the top of Louie's head.

"Hm," Louie says and twitches the tiniest bit. His blanket (his favorite) slides off his shoulder and Ryan tugs it back into place.

They spent all day together. Shared his breakfast, took a nap on the couch. Louie told him he called Dominic one night at Liam's and that they talked about their dad. He got quiet for a bit after that, lost in his own thoughts. It won't be the last conversation about Louie's family. When Bastien goes back to playing, when the next offseason rolls around and Louie has to make another choice, when Louie's dad decides he's had enough of the radio silence and goes back to torturing him with texts, they'll come back to this.

Ryan will take him back to Pennsylvania. Maybe they can go for an extra week next year, or they could get on a plane to Europe and hop on random trains. Ryan's not that passionate about trains, but Louie told him once, in a whisper, that it would be the perfect vacation.

After Ryan had ordered groceries, he made them grilled cheese sandwiches for lunch while Louie played the piano. Well, he *tried* to play the piano. Every so often, he swore under his breath and started over. Ryan watched him from the kitchen and burned his first grilled cheese (he ate that one).

Not every day will be like today, but some of them will be.

They'll order dinner, and Louie will let Ryan pick his food, they'll watch hockey, and Louie will analyze the plays along with the announcers, and sometimes Louie will fall asleep with his head on Ryan's shoulder, wrapped in his blanket.

Some days, hockey will be in first place. When the playoffs roll around, Louie will not be sleeping. He'll sit in his couch corner with his laptop and his headphones and he'll watch the tape he got from their video coach. Ryan already knows those days will be hard for him, but Louie will most likely still let him crawl into bed with him and talk about their power play for half an hour before they go to sleep.

Ryan can deal. He'll share Louie with hockey.

"—someone in the organization may need to ask himself why it is that players suddenly thrive on other teams. We've seen this with Bobby Allen, with Francis Bouchard, with Ryan Harris."

Ryan Harris. That's him. He frowns at the TV. Why are they talking about him when he didn't even do anything tonight other than sit on his couch and kiss the boy who decided to give him—them—a chance.

The game's over, so it's time for hockey opinions that Ryan used to subject himself to before he realized they were tearing his mental health to shreds.

"I'd argue that the Harris situation was different. Harris was playing well in Toronto and continued to play well in Hartford," one of them says.

It never stops being weird when other people talk about you like you're some abstract entity. A player, not a person.

"Hartford seems like a much better fit for him, though. His style of play is exactly what they needed. They made an excellent move there."

"Harris left quite the hole behind."

"That he did."

Ryan laughs.

"What's funny?" Louie mumbles, slowly sitting up.

"Them." Ryan nods at the TV, where the conversation is now moving on to Boston and their current coaching drama. "I was just laughing because... I think they were right for once." At least kind of. It wasn't the Cards who got lucky, it was Ryan.

"Unheard of," Louie says flatly. He takes the remote and mutes the TV, tapping Ryan's jaw. "Hey..."

"Huh?" Ryan, all couch-potatoed, looks up at him. There's intention there, in his eyes, but also in the curve of his lips. "Oh, hello."

Louie moves deliberately, straddles Ryan, and cups his face.

"Sailors game is about to start," Ryan says.

"I know," Louie replies and kisses him, slow, deep. Maybe he knows now how he kisses.

Ryan wraps his arms around him, maps outs his back with the palms of his hands, and counts the ridges of his spine through the thin fabric of his shirt.

Fingers curled around Ryan's neck, Louie stays still, nudging Ryan's temple with his nose. "Do *you* want to watch the game?"

"Um, I don't need to."

"But the Knights are playing against the Sailors," Louie says, smile in his voice.

Yes, the Knights are playing, and yes, Ryan's hockey crush for them and their everything is still going strong. But he doesn't want to take his hands off Louie. "I'll watch it tomorrow."

"Tomorrow sounds good," Louie says. He tugs at Ryan's shirt and slowly pulls it up. He leans in for another kiss but stops a breath away from Ryan's lips. "My place tonight?"

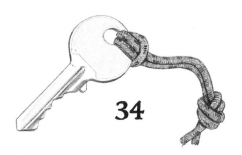

34

"Don't you think it's fucked up that we all assume that every dog is a guy until someone says they're a girl?" Ryan asks. "I mean, isn't that... is that sexist?"

"Please stop," Louie says.

Ryan giggles. "Wow, this eggnog was a terrible idea. I can't..." He holds up the dog stuffie he bought for Maja. He's currently trying to wrap it with snowman paper and has tape stuck to his nose, where he put it so he wouldn't forget about it. He absolutely forgot about it.

"What if you just put it in a bag?" Louie suggests. He always puts everything in bags.

"But little kids love wrapping paper," Ryan says, pouty. "They think bags are boring. It's not fun when you can just pull your present out of the bag." He sighs and lies down flat on his back. "I can't do it."

"Do you want me to wrap your present in wrapping paper?" Louie asks.

Ryan grins. "You got me a present? Even though *you* said no presents?"

"You got me something," Louie says, narrowing his eyes at Ryan. "I know you did. You weren't subtle about it."

"It's just a teeny-tiny thing," Ryan says and pinches his fingers together. "Teeny-tiny."

"Well, mine's just a card, so…" Louie shrugs.

"And you'd wrap that card in wrapping paper? That's so cute. But you don't have to, honestly. Does the card sing?"

"Thankfully, it does not."

"It's fine, I'll sing," Ryan says and starts humming "We Wish You a Merry Christmas." "You can play the piano."

Louie does know how to play some carols on the piano. And he'll play them if Ryan asks because Ryan is extremely hard to say no to. Sometimes, that's a problem.

"So," Ryan says, rolling onto his side to face Louie. "What's in the card?"

"You know, you're not supposed to know what's in there. That's the whole point."

Ryan sticks out his bottom lip. "I need to know why you broke the no present rule."

"It's not really a present anyway," Louie says. "It's more of a… suggestion."

Ryan bites his lip and bats his eyelashes at Louie. "Oh?"

"Not that kind of suggestion, oh my God." Louie rolls his eyes. "You'll just have to wait and see what it is." They spent Thanksgiving with Ryan's family because it's not that far of a drive and Ryan spent half the day snuggling with his cat Chicken on the couch.

Louie checked the local shelter's website on a whim and found a pair of tabbies. He printed out the listing at Liam's house because his wife has a printer and stuck it in a card. As a suggestion. He wasn't going to put an actual cat under the tree.

"Well, I got you a teeny-tiny thing," Ryan says. "And it's not my dick." He smirks. "As you know."

"Uh-huh," Louie says, stretching out his leg to nudge Ryan's side. "Come on, wrap that present, we need to get started on dinner."

"But, Lou, I can't." Ryan grabs Louie's ankle. "Help."

Louie scoots down carefully and joins Ryan on the floor. He takes the half-wrapped dog and carefully folds the wrapping paper so it'll cover the whole thing. He pulls the tape off Ryan's nose.

"Oh, I forgot about that," Ryan says, rubbing the tip of his nose.

"Here," Louie says and hands over the present. He even stuck a bow on it. "How's that?"

"I'm so in love with you," Ryan says and sits up to wrap his arms around Louie.

"And a little bit drunk?" Louie ventures and gives him a quick kiss.

"Yes," Ryan says, "no. Tipsy maybe. A little." He kind of melts against Louie's chest; fits himself there perfectly. "But I also love you when I'm not drunk."

"Love you too," Louie mumbles into Ryan's hair. He doesn't know why he still feels so awkward about saying that. It's like he's admitting something nobody is supposed to know.

"I think I need a nap," Ryan says.

"Hmm-hm." Louie carefully strokes his hair, slowing down when his fingers get tangled. "I'm pretty sure we still need to take care of dinner."

"Five-minute nap?"

"Yeah, okay," Louie says. Five minutes won't delay them too much. And he's still not entirely confident that they'll be able to cook a proper dinner, but they'll try. If the chicken Alfredo is for some reason inedible, they have frozen ramen. And if nothing works out, Ryan will drive to Wendy's. It's a solid plan.

Louie leans back against the couch, Ryan moving with him, sighing softly as he gets comfortable again. His breath is warm against Louie's neck, his fingers at Louie's side curling into the fabric of his shirt.

Louie grabs his phone from the coffee table and considers the family group chat. The last message is from him, replying to his mom who asked him and Dominic if they're sure they can't make it to Boston to celebrate Christmas with them. Bastien's home; he's still on IR and seeing some specialists their dad found in the new year. Then there's Dominic's reply—*sorry, like I said, we've made other plans*. And Louie's. He didn't even say sorry when he told Mom he wasn't able to make it.

With a sigh, Louie closes the chat and pulls up the camera instead. He snaps a picture of their tree—warm white lights and the twenty hockey ornaments Ryan ordered online at the very last minute. Plus the paper candy canes Ida made them. It's the most ridiculous tree Louie has ever seen, but he still stops and looks at it a few times a day because it's *their* tree.

Out of the corner of his eye, he sees something move outside the window. He squints. "Ryan," he whispers.

"Hm, that wasn't five minutes," Ryan grumbles.

"No, but… it's snowing," Louie says.

Ryan shoots up straight. "Really?" He gets up, almost tripping over Louie's foot on his way to the window. "Aw, it's not sticking, though." He smiles at Louie over his shoulder. "You know, I'm so glad I get to stay here and don't have to drive anywhere to demand an in-person break-up."

Louie snorts. "Aren't you lucky."

"So lucky," Ryan says. "Oh, and—"

The doorbell rings.

"—the doorbell's about to ring."

"I'll get it," Louie says and shuffles into the hallway to open the door.

"Merry Christmas!" Dominic shouts and pulls Louie into a quick hug. He's wearing a scarf that has bells on it and he jingles into the house. "Where's Ryan?"

Cameron follows, handing over a bottle of wine. "Thank you for having us," he says, "and for giving us a good excuse why we can't go to Boston."

"You're welcome," Louie says and takes Cameron's jacket. He did feel bad for half a second that he invited them but not the rest of his family, but Ryan threatened to go to Liam's for Christmas if he had to do Awkward Christmas with Louie's parents.

If Louie had invited his parents, he's sure Ryan would have stuck around, but Louie just couldn't deal with having them here. This is his home, the kind of home he never had with them, and they can't come here and ruin this place for him.

"Do you wanna put your stuff in my room?" Louie asks and takes the small suitcase Dominic brought.

Dominic hands it over and follows him down the hall. "Do you even sleep in your room anymore?"

"Shut up," Louie mumbles. He does sleep in Ryan's room on most days. Unless he's nervous about a game, then he sleeps in his own bed where he doesn't keep Ryan awake by... being awake and thinking very loudly. Or at least that's what Ryan accused him of the day before they left for Boston. For the game Louie's parents had tickets for.

"You know, there's nothing wrong with sleeping in another guy's bed."

Louie sets down Dominic's suitcase. "I know," he says. "I don't know why I..." He shakes his head. "It's just new. It's not but it is. I know that didn't make any sense, but..."

"No, I get it. I mean, how long's it been since we last did Christmas together?" Dominic says.

It's been literal years. "Yeah..." Louie says. "Everything's different."

Dominic smiles. "You're growing into the life you chose for yourself. That's not a bad thing," he says. "And, for the record, I'm glad you made a choice that was totally your own."

"Hm," Louie replies.

Dominic ruffles his hair and retreats back to the kitchen where Ryan and Cameron are comparing pots.

"We're cooking," Ryan says. "For real."

"Does Cameron know how to cook?" Louie whispers to Dominic.

"I do," Cameron says and takes the bigger of the two pots. "And, yes, we're cooking."

Dominic grins and steers Louie into the living room. "Good tree," he says.

"Yeah," Louie says, glancing back into the kitchen where Cameron is holding up two knives, probably explaining what they're for. Ryan will have to tell Louie because he never knows which knife to use for what.

Ryan is staring at Cameron with wide eyes, nodding along with rapt attention.

Dominic gives Louie a clap on the back. "Good."

A year ago, Louie didn't have a Christmas tree. Or friends. Or a family he wanted to spend the holidays with. He didn't really care about having any of those things either. All he cared about was that roster spot. Now that he has all those other things, he wouldn't give a single one back.

Made in the USA
Las Vegas, NV
26 November 2024